COURTING
CAN BE
KILLER

Also in the Amish Candy Shop Mystery series
by Amanda Flower

And in the Amish Matchmaker Mystery series

COURTING CAN BE KILLER

An Amish Matchmaker Mystery

Amanda Flower

KENSINGTON BOOKS
KENSINGTON PUBLISHING CORP.
www.kensingtonbooks.com

KENSINGTON BOOKS are published by

Kensington Publishing Corp.
119 West 40th Street
New York, NY 10018

All Kensington titles, imprints, and distributed lines are available at special quantity discounts for bulk purchases for sales promotion, premiums, fund-raising, educational, or institutional use.

Special book excerpts or customized printings can also be created to fit specific needs. For details, write or phone the office of the Kensington Sales Manager: Attn.: Sales Department. Kensington Publishing Corp., 119 West 40th Street, New York, NY 10018. Phone: 1-800-221-2647.

Kensington and the K logo Reg. U.S. Pat. & TM Off.

First Printing: December 2020
ISBN-13: 978-1-4967-2403-8
ISBN-10: 1-4967-2403-8

ISBN-13: 978-1-4967-2404-5 (eBook)
ISBN-10: 1-4967-2404-6 (eBook)

10 9 8 7 6 5 4 3 2 1

Printed in the United States of America

For Paul, Stephanie, Chloe, Isaiah,
Shiloh, Joelle, and Naomi

Acknowledgments

As always, thanks to my readers who want to return to the village of Harvest, Ohio, again and again. You have embraced Bailey of the Amish Candy Shop Mysteries. Thank you for embracing Millie from this series as well. I hope you enjoy as the characters cross over between the two series.

Special thanks, as always, to my agent, Nicole Resciniti, who always pushes me to be a better writer and bigger dreamer, and to my wonderful editor, Alicia Condon. You are both the very best. Thanks, too, to everyone at Kensington Publishing who make book writing a joy and are the easiest and kindest people to work with in the business. Also, thanks to Kimra Bell for being my second set of eyes.

Thanks, too, to Delia, Ellie, Noah, and Sofia for helping with the apple orchard research for this story.

Love and thanks to my family and especially to David, who listens to every plot a thousand times before the words ever hit the page.

And to my Heavenly Father, thank you for the gift of story.

The apple will not roll far away from its tree.
                                    —Amish Proverb

Chapter One

"This is the very best day of my life," my dear friend, Lois Henry, proclaimed as she wove up and down the aisles of the Harvest Village Flea Market. "Look at all this stuff! I should have brought more cash. Do you think some of these booths take plastic?"

It wasn't a question that I could answer since I was Amish and had never owned a credit card. If I bought anything on credit, it was store credit from an Amish merchant whom I knew well.

"I knew I should have gone to the ATM," she grumbled as she rooted through a patchwork purse that was big enough to carry a toddler. "I might have a few more bills at the bottom of this thing, but sorting through it is like digging to the center of the earth." Her cheeks flushed red under her heavy makeup from the exertion.

If the purse and makeup weren't clues enough, the spikey, purple-red hair and chunky, brightly colored costume jewelry would tell any passerby that Lois Henry was not Amish, nor had she ever been tempted to convert. In fact, the very thought of Lois living the Plain life was downright ludicrous.

My friend certainly stood out in the crowd of mostly Amish shoppers. I caught more than one Amish merchant give us the once-over as we walked by. I guessed that Lois and I made an odd pair. We'd been that way since we'd been girls. Lois was the flamboyant *Englischer*, and I was the sedate Amish woman. To be honest, although it might not look like it, I did get into my fair share of trouble too. I was blessed enough to have Lois, who was always willing to get into mischief with me.

Lois was either oblivious to the suspicious glances of a few of the Amish men who we passed in the market, or she just plain didn't care. I suspected the latter of the two. Lois had never cared what anyone thought of her. When we were children growing up on neighboring farms, I had been jealous of her exuberant way of going after whatever it was she wanted. When I was young, I associated her behavior with being *Englisch* because Lois and her parents were the only *Englischers* I knew. I have since learned that her *Englisch* upbringing had very little to do with it. Her devil-may-care attitude came from her and her alone. From her clothes to her words, Lois always expressed herself as she wanted to.

She yanked on my arm. "Holy smokes, Millie, do you see that? That chair is just like the one my mother had when I was growing up." She pointed at an orange, molded-plastic chair. "I have to see if I can snap it up!"

I glanced around the market. "I think you have a *gut* chance of succeeding. It doesn't appear that anyone else is looking at it."

"They may be just playing it close to the vest. I can't be the only one here who knows to act cool when negotiating a deal." Lois came up with a fistful of bills from the bottom of her purse. "I knew there was more in there. My granddaughter, Darcy, is always telling me to get more organized, but then I wouldn't find surprises like this twenty-dollar bill at the bottom of my bag."

"Act cool?" I asked.

She tried to smooth the crumpled bill the best she could. "Yes. When we talk to the vendor about the chair, we must act like we don't want it."

"But you do want it." I adjusted my grip on the shopping basket I had brought with me. As of yet, I hadn't added anything to it. Truth be told, I hadn't come to the flea market this day to shop. I was looking for someone.

She clicked her tongue. "Millie Fisher, you would be the world's worst gambler."

"Considering I am a sixty-seven-year-old Amish woman, I choose to take that as a compliment."

She shook her head. "Just know I won't be taking you on my next trip to the Rocksino in Cleveland. You would completely ruin my luck."

I patted the prayer cap on the top of my snow-white hair. "I thought you gave up gambling after you pushed your fourth husband into that hotel swimming pool."

"I took a break, yes, after that little incident." She finished smoothing the bill and tucked it into the pocket of her teal jacket. "However, in this life one should always be willing to take a chance and roll the dice." She grinned. "That sounds like one of the Amish proverbs you recite all the time, doesn't it?"

"It doesn't." I shook my head. "Not at all."

She winked at me, not the least bit offended by my remark. I wished I could be as easygoing as Lois, but on this special errand, that was impossible. I turned back to the vendor she had pointed out.

She grabbed my arm and spun me in the other direction. "Don't look at him. If you do, he will know we're interested in buying something from him."

I sighed and smoothed the sleeve of my plain green dress. "Do I have to remind you that *you* were pointing at him a moment ago?" Even shopping with Lois was an adventure. "Besides, why do you want that chair? It's orange," I said. "It doesn't go with a single item in your house."

She laughed. "Nothing in my house matches, and that's just how I like it."

That was the truth.

"Since I might have trouble acting cool, why don't you speak to the man about the chair, and I will keep looking for Ben," I said.

Finding Ben was the real reason we were at the Harvest Village Flea Market. I had been worried about the young man, and because I was the only one in the village—if not the state—who knew him well, I felt responsible to make sure he was all right.

"Good deal," Lois said. "By the time you find Ben, I will have that chair in my possession for half of what it's worth."

"Why don't we meet at the livestock judging area? I would like to know how the goats are getting on for my grandnephew Micah," I said.

Lois laughed. "Sounds like a plan, but I don't need to see the judging to know that Phillip and Peter are wreaking havoc for Micah and all the judges."

I grimaced but didn't correct her. Phillip and Peter were

challenging goats. In this case, Lois was probably right. She strolled over to the man with the chair, and I shook my head.

I knew she would come away with the chair. I only hoped that she didn't come away with a new husband too. Lois had a talent for collecting those as well.

With Lois occupied, I continued my search of the flea market for Ben Baughman. Ben was a nineteen-year-old Amish man who had recently moved to Holmes County from Michigan. I had known him since he was a child, because he came from the same community in which I had lived for ten years while taking care of my invalid sister. Ben had been a nearby neighbor in Michigan and a thoughtful one too. He was *gut* to both my sister and me, and he came over as often as he could to help me with the chores. He never let me pay him, and I was grateful for it. Taking care of my sister Harriett had been meaningful but hard work.

A few months ago, after my sister's death, I moved back to Holmes County, Ohio, where I'd grown up. To be honest, I didn't expect to see Ben again as I had no desire ever to return to my sister's community and I could see no reason why he would come to Ohio. However, a month ago, I received a letter from Ben. He said that he was planning to move to Holmes County so that he could find work in a larger Amish district. The Amish district where he lived was very small and most of the men worked with *Englischers*. Not that there is anything wrong with that, but Ben said he wanted a more authentic Amish life and felt he could find that in Holmes County, where the Amish population was so much larger.

I told him he was welcome to come, and I offered him

a room in my little house until he got on his feet. I don't think he was even there a month before he found a basement room for rent. He was determined to make a life of his own.

Behind me, I heard Lois's voice carry as she haggled with the antiques vendor over the chair. By the sound of the seller, he was already beginning to waffle on his price. I had expected nothing less.

I scanned the large barn for any sign of Ben. I was in the middle of a crush of shoppers and merchant booths that sold everything from produce to furniture to old toys and guns.

I wondered if I'd chosen the wrong day to be looking for him. Perhaps I'd come on a day Ben didn't have to work. He was a guard of sorts for the flea market. In the last few weeks, there had been a rash of robberies. Many of the vendors had been hit. When they threatened to leave to protect their goods and their families, the flea market owner had posted a job for an after-hours guard. I had seen the notice for the job on the community bulletin board at the Sunbeam Café, which Darcy Woodin, Lois's granddaughter, owned and operated. Lois worked there part-time, but her hours seemed to be irregular at best; she only worked at the café when she was bored or when Darcy was desperate for a second set of hands.

When I saw the posting, Ben had just moved to Ohio. I told him about it, and he applied and got the job right away. I thought I had done my duty, and my young friend was nicely settled. What I didn't know was that he was going to meet his match at the flea market and that it would lead to complications.

I spotted Ben beside the baked goods stand. It was the

end of September, so the stand was heavy on apple tarts, pumpkin pies, and sweet potato cookies. He wasn't alone. He was speaking with a woman in a flowered blouse, long skirt, and prayer cap. I knew right away that she was Mennonite from her almost plain dress and cap. She handed Ben an envelope. He nodded, folded it twice, and tucked it into the pocket of his navy work shirt.

The woman walked away, and Ben smiled as I approached him. His straw-colored hair stood on end despite the strict Amish bowl-cut that he adhered to. A dusting of freckles danced across his face. He might be nineteen, but when caught in the right light, he could pass for twelve. He certainly didn't look like someone old enough to be a night guard or to be falling in love and considering marriage.

He smiled wider, and I saw the gap between his two front teeth that also added to his youthful appearance. "Millie, it's so *gut* to see you. Do you need to do a little shopping here at the flea market? You will be hard-pressed not to find what you need here. It seems that everything is for sale."

I shook my head. "I'm not in the market for anything in particular right now, but I know that Lois will do enough shopping for both of us."

He laughed. "This doesn't surprise me. I'm on the way to my second job. I just . . ." His voice trailed off as he looked across the flea market.

"What job is this?"

"The lumberyard," he said. "Wait no. This one is stocking the Harvest Market. That's where I need to go next. Eventually, I will get it all straight. In a week it will be habit, knowing everywhere I need to go and when I need to be there."

I frowned. "How many jobs are you working, exactly?"

"Four." He paused when he saw the look on my face. "It was five, but I dropped one. Five was one too many."

"Four sounds like too many too," I said, concerned. "If you are forgetting where you need to be."

"It's worth it . . ." He trailed off and looked at the orchard stand. Now I knew why he was standing in this part of the flea market. He had the perfect view of the apple orchard stand and the lovely young woman selling the apples. Tess Lieb.

"How's Tess?" I asked.

His face broke into a smile that was made even more endearing by the gap in his teeth. "She's wonderful. Oh, Millie," he said to me quietly in Pennsylvania Dutch. "She's my match. I just wish her father could see that. I'm working so hard to prove to him that I'm the right fit."

Tess was an eighteen-year-old Amish woman who lived with her parents and younger siblings on their vast apple orchard just outside of the village. This time of year, her family's orchard stand did a brisk business, as both *Englisch* and Amish wanted to buy apples that were the best and crispest.

September was the height of business for the Lieb Apple Orchard. In the fall, the orchard was a hive of activity as the apple-picking season went into full swing. They sold apples to wholesalers, at the local markets, and even from the orchard itself with a pick-your-own grove of trees.

Tess and her siblings were spread out selling their

apples all over Holmes County; the family had a strong presence in all the markets, but Tess always seemed to be at the flea market, where Ben had first laid eyes on her.

Across the flea market, Tess handed an elderly man his quarter-bushel bag of apples. As she accepted his money, her eyes strayed in Ben's direction. When their eyes locked, she blushed. If not completely in love, she certainly was enamored with Ben's attentions. It was my job as a match-maker to recognize whether Ben and Tess were a perfect match, or whether it was just Ben's wishful thinking. Affection would make no difference to their matrimonial prospects if her family was against the match.

Tobias Lieb, Tess's father, stepped into the apple booth and glared at Ben before speaking harshly to Tess. She dropped her eyes and began bagging more apples. "The apple will not roll far away from its tree" was the Amish proverb that was on the top of my mind. That didn't bode well for Ben, I was afraid.

Ben looked away from Tess with a sigh. "As you can see, Millie, I have gotten nowhere with her father. I don't know how, but he seems to dislike me even more than he did weeks ago. I only want to prove to Tess's father that I am ready to settle down," he went on. "I know that I am young yet, but I can provide for the family I want to have. I will be twenty next week," he added, as if this gave weight to his argument.

"At twenty, you will still be a young man with your whole life in front of you. Give it time," I said, ready to share the wisdom I came to the flea market to impart in the first place. "Nothing lasts forever, not even your troubles," I said, reciting another Amish proverb.

He frowned at me. "Where's this coming from, Millie? I thought you would back me up."

I sighed. "I received a letter."

"A letter?" he asked. "Who from?"

I glanced at the apple booth and then back at Ben. "From Tobias." I swallowed. "And it was about you."

Chapter Two

Ben's face flushed red. "Why would Tobias Lieb send you a letter about me?"

I closed my eyes for a moment, realizing my mistake. I should have spoken to Ben in private, not out in the middle of the flea market. True, not all the shoppers paid attention to us, but I felt the prying eyes of a few on my back. One of those, I was afraid, just might be Tobias Lieb.

"Maybe we should go outside to talk about this," I said in a low voice.

Ben folded his arms. "I have half a mind to go over to Tobias right now and ask him what's going on."

I placed a hand on his arm. "Calm yourself, and please don't do that. It will only make things more difficult for you as far as Tess is concerned."

I noticed that the greengrocer in the next booth seemed to be *very* interested in our conversation. "Come, Ben, let's go outside."

"Fine," he said and stomped in the direction of the back exit.

I followed a few paces behind him and wondered how I could have bungled this so badly.

From the back of the flea market, we could see the secondary barns. The land we were on had once been a horse farm. I had never known the owners though. Sometime while I was in Michigan caring for my sister, it was transformed into the Harvest Village Flea Market.

I knew that my nine-year-old grandnephew Micah, as well as my two ornery Boer goats, Phillip and Peter, were being judged somewhere in one of those other two buildings. Months ago, Micah had asked if he could show the goats at the local competition, and I had agreed, even though I knew it would not be easy for him, or anyone, to handle Phillip and Peter. His mother, my beloved niece Edith, ran Edy's Greenhouse, the largest Amish greenhouse in the county. Because of all the valuable plants in the greenhouse, owning goats was not a good option on her land. So Micah was borrowing mine. He'd come to my farm every day for the last few weeks, trying to prepare the goats. Judging by the way the goats ignored his every command, I didn't have high hopes they would place. Even so, it was something Micah cared about, and I believed every child—every person, for that matter— needed a special interest.

"Please, Millie, tell me about his letter," Ben said. The frustration that had been on his face a little while ago was gone now. In its place was resignation. What had happened between the Liebs and this young man to cause such an expression?

"Tobias knows that I'm the closest person you have to family in Holmes County, and he wrote me to ask you to stop pursuing Tess."

He balled his hands into fists. "I suspected as much. It doesn't matter to him that Tess and I love each other. It doesn't matter to him that I would do anything for his daughter, absolutely anything. I am working all these jobs to prove myself to him, and her."

"I know this, but if her father doesn't approve—"

"You think I should give up on her?" He was hurt.

"I didn't say that. I said nothing like that. I think you should not be in such a terrible rush. It's very possible that her father is concerned that the two of you have developed such deep feelings for each other so quickly. You are only nineteen. She's eighteen. There is no reason to be in such a hurry. You don't want to make a match that estranges Tess from her family. In the long run, this will cause both of you pain. Patience is what you should hold onto now."

He shook his head. "*Nee*, Millie, that is where you are wrong. There are things that Tobias clearly didn't tell you."

"What things?" I asked. "Maybe if you told me what they were, I would have a better understanding of your position."

He shook his head. "I need to go to my next job." He gave me a small smile. "I do not blame you for your words, Millie. I know that you have told me this only with the hope that it will help me."

I studied his face. He was exhausted. I frowned. "I'm worried that you are stretching yourself too thin."

He shook his head. "I'm fine. I catch a nap here and there when I can."

"You're not sleeping at night?"

"I can't just now. I'm watching over the flea market. It's my job to make sure the market is secure overnight."

I frowned. "Have there been more robberies?"

He looked around as if he was afraid someone might overhear. "*Nee*, but a time or two I have scared off men who were set to cause trouble. I know if I hadn't been here, they would have taken whatever they wanted from the market."

I didn't like the sound of that.

"Who were they? Amish or *Englisch*?"

"They were *Englisch*. At least their dress was *Englisch*. I don't know who they were."

"Did you call the police?"

"Oh no, the owner of the flea market wouldn't like that. He hired me so that he wouldn't have to get the police involved. You know the Amish would rather take care of things their own way."

"The owner is Amish?"

"*Nee*, he's *Englisch,* but he wants to keep the Amish vendors calm, so they don't leave the flea market. Having the police poking around won't do that."

"Who's the owner?" I asked.

"Ford Waller."

"Are you working here tonight to guard the market?" I asked.

He nodded. "I will be here from nine at night until seven tomorrow morning, when the shop keepers come and set up for the day."

Ben walked me back into the flea market, and his gaze fell on Tess again. "Have you ever seen anyone so lovely?"

I smiled. "I have, but everyone thinks the object of their affection is the loveliest of all."

"They would be wrong. Tess is the only one." He grabbed my hand. "Millie, you have to convince Tobias that I am the right man for his daughter. You are the village match-maker. You should be able to do it."

"I can't change a father's mind as to what is best for

his child," I said quietly. "It may be that you will just have to wait until he believes Tess is ready."

He turned pale. "I can't wait. Time is too short for that."

I wanted to ask what he meant by that, but he released my hand. "I must be off, or I will be late. As it is, I will have to pedal fast on my bicycle to reach my next job on time." With that, he slipped through the back door again, leaving me wondering why a healthy young man would believe time was short.

Chapter Three

I debated going over to speak with Tess, but then I thought better of it. I could tell whether or not people were a *gut* match, but it was not my place to cause trouble between parents and their children. If Tobias didn't want Tess to marry now, or even be courted, Ben would have to be patient and wait. Sometimes it was the true test of a match when a couple had to wait for each other until the time was right.

I was scanning the flea market for Lois, when a quilt caught my eye. It was a log cabin quilt in purple, gray, and black cotton, and I knew it well. It was one of the quilts that my quilting circle, Double Stitch, had worked on the last few months. And now it was at the market, being sold by circle member Iris.

Iris Young was in her thirties with lovely auburn hair and delicate features. She was one of the kindest women in the district. I knew that her husband, Carter, thanked *Gott* every day for her. I had matched them nearly twenty years ago, an example of the kind of match that I wished for Ben.

Iris was also a talented quilter and had pieced the log

cabin quilt on her own. Double Stitch quilted it together as a group.

It wasn't the only quilt from Double Stitch in the booth. Iris had six of our quilts for sale. They were all beautifully displayed.

Iris was speaking to an *Englisch* woman about a four-square, toddler-bed quilt in cream and pink. "Oh, this would be just the thing for my granddaughter. She is moving from the crib to a toddler bed soon. My daughter is so nervous about the transition. This beautiful quilt might just be the thing that will make my granddaughter want to sleep in her new bed."

"It's a lovely gift," Iris said. "I had one just like it made for my niece."

The *Englisch* woman wrung her hands. "But toddlers are so messy. What if she spills something on it or has an accident? She hasn't been potty trained very long."

"It is very easy to wash," Iris said.

"But the colors will fade. The quilt won't be the same."

I spoke up. "These quilts are meant to be used. You won't see a quilt in an Amish home on display. It will be on a bed or even in the barn to warm the animals. We make the quilts with the hope they will warm you on a cold night or comfort you when you're ill. They are not only meant to be admired but to be used."

The woman nodded. "You're right. I'll take it." She wrote a check and handed it to Iris. Iris gave her the quilt and a handwritten receipt.

"Thank you so much, ladies. I will tell my daughter what you said if she says the quilt is too nice to use." She held the toddler quilt to her chest and merged with the rest of the flea market traffic.

"*Danki*, Millie. That woman was here for almost an hour debating about buying that quilt. It was almost to the point I was going to offer to just give it to her if it would cause her less anxiety. I hate to see a person so torn."

"You should never just give the quilts away," a stern voice said. "This is our livelihood, and the *Englisch* can afford to pay for them."

I tuned to see Ruth Yoder bustling toward us. Ruth was a broad, stern woman who also happened to be the bishop's wife. With that title, she tried to rule the district as much as possible. She was a member of Double Stitch and tried to rule the quilt circle too. In fact, I thought if Ruth had her way, she would be ruling the whole world, but it would be under the guise of supporting her husband, who, in fact, was only a figurehead.

"I wouldn't have given it away," Iris said, her voice shaking just a little. The younger women in the district found Ruth to be a tad domineering.

I didn't feel that way at all. I had known the bishop's wife since she was in pigtails, pushing other kids around the playground when they didn't listen to the elaborate rules she made up for our schoolyard games. I paid her no mind then, and I wasn't going to start now.

Ruth adjusted her shopping basket in her arms. I couldn't help but notice that it had apples in it. I took that to be bad news coming.

"Well, don't," Ruth said gruffly. All the while she spoke in Pennsylvania Dutch. She, of course, wouldn't want the *Englisch* shoppers to know what she really thought of them.

I folded my arms. "Leave Iris be. She was the one who

was kind enough to run our booth on this busy day at the market. You should be thanking her for that."

The booth was a new venture for Double Stitch. We had pooled our money together to rent the space. It wasn't cheap. To have a booth at the Harvest Village Flea Market took some doing. If we didn't sell well, we could be asked to leave too. Space was in demand, and the market set revenue goals for each booth. I knew Iris felt the pressure since the booth was her idea.

"How many quilts have you sold?" Ruth wanted to know.

"Just two," Iris said in a shaky voice. "One was a king-sized quilt, so it was the most expensive we had on display."

I could tell by her pursed lips that the king-sized quilt sale gave Ruth pause. The king-sized quilt went for quite a bit of money. Actually, it would be enough to pay for our booth for the next month.

"I'm glad to see that you have sold something," Ruth said. It was the closest to a compliment she could manage. "I had my reservations about Double Stitch having a booth at the flea market."

I cocked an eyebrow at her. "Even if none of the quilts sold," I said. "This is still *gut* exposure for our quilting circle. Maybe some custom quilts will come out of it. It's not as if we can put an advertisement on television."

Ruth narrowed her eyes.

"Don't mind her," I said to Iris. "She's not happy unless she's telling someone what they are doing wrong."

Ruth sniffed. "Speaking of someone doing something wrong, I came over here to talk to you, Millie."

I folded my arms. "For land's sake, what on earth did I do this time?"

"I was just at the Lieb Orchard booth, and Tobias Lieb told me you are encouraging Ben Baughman in chasing his daughter."

I stood up a little taller. "I most certainly am not."

"So you haven't been talking to Ben about Tess?" She tapped her foot.

"I have, but it is my job as matchmaker to counsel the young when they believe they have fallen in love."

"He says he loves her? How can he? He's not from our district!"

"I don't think love has anything to do with what district a man or woman is from. It's based on compatibility, and I believe they are a *gut* fit."

Ruth held up a hand. "Ahh, so you did tell him to pursue her even when her father was against it. I swear, Millie, you lost your head when you went to Michigan. What kind of Amish district did you even have there?"

I squinted at her. At times, Ruth gave me the smallest of headaches. I wouldn't tell her that, though. Knowing her, she would take pride in it. "I did not counsel him to go against her father's wishes. That's not something I would do. Of course, Tess cannot be courted without her father's approval. I counseled Ben to be patient. They are both young and have time."

"Oh," Ruth said, and shifted her feet.

I'd bask in my brief victory, but I knew she was only regrouping. She would find something else to say.

"Honestly, I can't believe I sold two," Iris said, returning the conversation to the quilts. "I never would have thought the booth would do so well. I know that most people coming to the flea market are looking for a bargain, so our pricey quilts might not be in the right place." She gave me a small smile, and I smiled back, grateful that she'd changed the subject away from Ben and Tess. If I could avoid speaking about my matchmaking with Ruth altogether, so much the better.

"Of course the booth is doing well," Ruth grumbled. "The quilts are beautifully made and reasonably priced."

Iris nodded.

"See," I said. "I knew this would lead to more business."

"I hope not too much business," Ruth said. "Our duty is to our families first, and we can't be taken away from them to make quilts. I know this is difficult for you to understand, Millie, as you have neither children nor a husband."

I opened and closed my mouth, ready to tell her what I really thought about her comment. Much to my chagrin, Lois walked up just as Ruth said that, and she wasn't held back by any Amish courtesy. "Millie takes care of everyone, Ruth. How dare you say that to her?" Lois stood a few feet away with her hands on her hips. "I think you owe Millie an apology."

Ruth scowled. "I should have known you would be here with Millie. It seems ever since the two of you reunited, you are always together. I didn't think that was healthy when you were girls and certainly not as mature women."

"Mature women?" Lois asked. "I never in my life have been a mature woman. You're going to have to apologize for that too."

Ruth just glared at her and turned back to Iris and me. "Now, both of you know that we have a Double Stitch meeting tomorrow morning?"

Iris nodded.

"*Ya,*" I said. "Darcy and Lois have been gracious enough to give us a space again to work in the Sunbeam Café."

Ruth frowned. She hated when we had meetings at the Sunbeam, mostly because Lois annoyed her. Clearly, the feeling was mutual. The difference was Lois seemed to bask in her annoyance because she knew she had an easier time driving Ruth batty than vice versa.

"We are looking forward to hosting you at the café," Lois said with a knowing smile. She was well aware that Ruth disliked meetings at the café. "Darcy has a delicious fall menu of baked goods and soups. If you like apples and pumpkins, the Sunbeam Café is the place to go."

Ruth sniffed. "I still believe it is better to host the meetings in an Amish home, but if this is what the group wants to do, I will go along."

"Kicking and screaming," Lois muttered under her breath.

Ruth, having overheard the comment, glared at Lois before saying her good-byes.

Lois and I left the quilt booth a moment after she did. We were only a few feet away when Lois said, "That woman really steams me. I would like to tell her what I really think."

I eyed Lois. "Since when haven't you told everyone what you really think?"

She cocked her head. "You have a point. I don't spare people my opinion. It's got me in hot water a time or two, but I think there is much more value in being honest than being polite."

I smiled. "It's possible that you can be both."

"Maybe," she said dubiously. "But not with women like Ruth Yoder."

"Well, I do appreciate the backup."

Lois laughed. "Backup? I got you sounding just like an Englisher."

I winked at her. "Don't tell Ruth that. She will bring it to the attention of her husband, and I'll be brought in front of the church."

"I would never tell her," she promised.

It was time to change the subject. Talk of Ruth always got Lois riled up. "What happened to the chair? Did you get it?"

She stared at me. "Did I get it? Is the pope Catholic?"

"I believe he is," I said.

"That's just an expression. Yes, I got the chair and for a steal too. I left it over by the merchant's booth. He was looking for a dolly for me to transfer it to my car." She clapped her hands. "Speaking of which, there it is."

A red-faced Amish teenager came up to us, pushing the dolly holding Lois's orange chair. It was no easy feat to maneuver the awkwardly shaped load through the crowd.

Lois hurried over to it. "Oh, have you ever seen a piece of furniture so unique?"

I studied the chair. I had not. It was nothing like the wooden Amish pieces in my home. The beauty of those pieces was found in their simplicity. The orange chair with its odd angles and bright color was anything but simple. I knew immediately why Lois liked it so much. If I had to describe her with a piece of furniture, it would be that chair.

"Do you need help getting it to your car?" the teenager asked.

"Oh," Lois said. "Aren't you a dear? Yes, I could use the help. The car is just at the entrance of the barn. I pulled it over there." She pointed.

The teenager nodded and without waiting to hear any more, he began walking to the main exit at the south end of the long barn.

Lois and I followed in the wake he made by wheeling the wobbling chair through the crowd.

Lois walked at a quick pace. "I really don't think the merchant knew what he had on his hands. As I promised, I played it cool."

That was a little harder to believe. "Congratulations." I smiled at her. "At least one of us had a successful visit to the flea market."

She cocked her head, and her bright pink, plastic earring hit her shoulder. "You didn't find Ben?"

"I found him, but talking to him just made me more worried about him. The young man is working extremely hard." I bit my lip to stop myself from saying anything about Tess.

"I thought all Amish supported hard work."

"We do," I said. "I am a strong believer in hard work, too, but he needs some time off. He is working four jobs."

Her penciled-on eyebrows went up. "Why so many?"

"To—"

"He's doing it to impress my father," a small voice said behind me.

Chapter Four

I turned around and found Tess Lieb standing there. She wore a pale green dress that was the same color as her eyes, and her blond hair was tied back at the nape of her neck in an Amish bun. On the top of her head, her prayer cap was secured in place with bobby pins.

"Tess," I said. "How long have you been standing there?"

She blushed, and her round cheeks reddened to look like the apples she sold in her market stall. I could see why Ben was so enamored with her. She really was a beautiful young woman, and there was a sweet, calm way about her. I wasn't surprised that Ben was attracted to her personality. From what my sister had told me, the household he'd grown up in was anything but calm.

At eighteen, Tess would have been out of school for four years now, if not more, but she still had the innocent look of a child. At the moment, some of that innocence was marred by concern.

"I haven't been here long," she said quickly. "I wasn't trying to eavesdrop, but I couldn't help but hear you speak of Ben. He's mentioned you often and said how much you helped him when he first moved to Holmes County. He sees you as a favorite aunt."

I smiled. It warmed my heart to hear that because I thought of Ben as a nephew as well.

She glanced at Lois. "Can I speak to you for a moment?" she asked me in a soft voice.

Lois took the hint. "I'll just go help that young man wrestle my new chair into the trunk of my car. I can't wait to put it in my living room. It's a real showstopper." Lois hurried out of the barn after the Amish teen with the dolly.

Tess glanced about as if she was searching the crowd of faces around us. I thought she might be looking for anyone else who could overhear our conversation and report back to her father. Usually in situations like this, I just switched over to speaking Pennsylvania Dutch, which most of the *Englischers* didn't understand, except for a few words. However, at the flea market over half of the shoppers and most of the vendors were Amish. That tactic wouldn't work here.

"Why don't we go outside to speak?" I suggested, just as I had when talking with Ben earlier.

"That is a *gut* idea, but I shouldn't be long. My *daed* is at the orchard booth, and he will be wondering what became of me."

I nodded, wove through the crush of people, and stepped outside. I let out a breath as soon as I was in the open air. The flea market was in what had once been a large horse barn. Though horse barns were some of the biggest buildings around, and this one had a high ceiling, with a few hundred people and several dozen booths in it, the place felt claustrophobic. It was so nice to be out in the open air.

Tess followed me out of the barn, and we walked to a large willow tree about twenty yards from the flea market. Whereas the market was a beehive of activity and excitement, the spot under the willow tree was quiet. A bench made of logs was situated under the tree, and I sat on it.

Tess hovered above me.

"*Kind*," I said. "I can't speak to you if you insist on pacing back and forth like that."

"I'm sorry, Millie. I'm very nervous, you see." She perched beside me on the bench. "I have never gone behind my *daed's* back like this before. I have always been an obedient daughter. I think that might be why *Daed* is having so much trouble with me now. He can't understand that this is what I really want. He believes that I am only flattered by Ben's flowery words and attentions. It's much more than that. I feel that he's the person I have been looking for all my life."

"And you have told your parents all of this?" I asked.

"I have. I think my *maam* understands, but she would never say anything to go against *Daed*."

"Are you sure that Ben is your match?" I patted her hand. "I can see the connection you share, but there's a large difference between having a connection with someone and spending the rest of your life with that person, raising children, and growing old together."

"Ben is my match, but my *daed* won't listen. I don't know what to do." She took a shuddering breath. "When I saw Ben talking to you, I felt for the first time that I had a little bit of hope. You are the village matchmaker. If anyone can convince my father he is wrong about Ben, it is you."

I wasn't so sure about that. It was my experience that

most Amish men don't like to be shown the errors of their ways by an older woman such as I.

"Did Ben ask you to talk to my *daed*?"

I nodded. "He did. Do you want me to talk to him now?"

"*Nee,* it's not a *gut* time. *Daed* is quite anxious about the apple crop this year. We don't have as many apples as in years past because of pests, so the apples we do have need to sell for top dollar. We make most of our money during this season, and the money we take in now will have to last for a good part of next year. But I had an idea that will give you a chance to speak to him where he will be more likely to listen."

"What's that?" I asked, thinking at the very least I should hear her out.

"You should come and pick apples at the orchard. That would be the best time to speak to him. I think that's my *daed's* favorite thing about growing apples. He loves to see friends and family gather together to pick apples."

I smiled. "I haven't done that in a long while, but I do remember enjoying it very much as a child."

"My *daed* doesn't approve of Ben as a suitor. He doesn't want me to think of marriage yet. He believes I'm too young and have more important things to do." She took a breath. "And I know that he needs my help at the orchard. I told him that just because I might marry, that doesn't mean I won't work at the orchard. He doesn't see it that way. Your speaking with him could change everything. I know that Ben thinks a lot of you. If you won't do it for me, do it for him."

Her green eyes bored into me. They were filled with

so much hope mingled with sadness that I had to look away.

After a long moment, I said, "I will try to speak to your *daed*, but I cannot change a man's mind when it is made up. It is possible that you and Ben will have to wait until your *daed* is ready to let you go." I squeezed her hand. "You are young still. The two of you have your whole lives to live."

She broke eye contact with me.

I frowned. I had been matching young couples for decades, and I thought I had heard every reason that a couple was in a hurry to marry. There was something more going on here, and if I was going to help Ben and Tess, I needed to know what it was.

I took a breath. "Before Ben left to go to his next job for the day, I told him the same thing. However, when I said that, he said he didn't have that much time to wait. What did he mean?"

She wouldn't meet my eyes. "I couldn't possibly know what he means."

I wanted to press her, but just then I heard a high voice cry, "Phillip! Come back!"

I looked up to see my black and white goat, Phillip, running toward me at full tilt. My grandnephew Micah was chasing the goat, but there was no way he was going to catch him.

Phillip's ears flapped in the wind and his tongue hung out of his grinning mouth.

Tess yelped and jumped onto the park bench.

I put my fingers in my mouth and whistled. The sound was high and shrill, but it did the trick. Phillip dug his front hooves into the grass, tearing at the lawn, and then leaped into the air before coming to a full stop.

Micah doubled over to catch his breath. "*Aenti* Millie!" His blond hair was plastered to his forehead.

I held up my hand. "Phillip, calm yourself down."

The black and white Boer goat stopped shimmying in place. I supposed I should be flattered that the goat was so overjoyed to see me.

"Micah, are you all right?" I asked.

The nine-year-old boy stood up straight and beamed at me. "That was so much fun, *Aenti*. Everyone at the flea market tried to catch Phillip, but no one could. He was so fast! He ran around and around. He must have known that you were here. He just wanted to find you."

I glanced at Phillip, who was still grinning as if he'd won some kind of prize. I liked to think that the goat had been looking for me, but more likely, he just wanted to cause trouble. I patted him between his horns. "How did the goats do?" I asked.

"*Aenti* Millie, Peter took second place!" Micah said happily. "The judge said that Phillip would have won the whole thing, but just when they were going to say it, he ran off. He got disqualified." He shook his head.

I put my hands on my hips. "Oh, Phillip. What on earth are we going to do with you?"

Micah giggled, and Phillip cocked his head. I turned around to introduce Tess to my grandnephew and my goat, but she was gone. I pressed my lips together. I hoped for the sake of her and Ben's future that the young couple would be patient with her father. If they refused, it could end very badly for everyone concerned.

How badly, in fact, I didn't know at the time.

Chapter Five

Lois and I returned to my farm with two goats in the backseat of her car and a giant orange chair in her trunk, precariously held in place with rope and prayer. Lois drove down the county roads with the goats leaning over the front seat of the car, as if it was the most normal thing in the world. In the side mirror, I watched as the trunk lid bounced up and down with every pothole we hit.

"I hope that chair doesn't fall out," I said as Lois turned into my driveway.

"Oh, Millie," she said. "You worry far too much. I had that Amish boy tie the chair down with so much rope, I will be lucky if I don't have to cut the chair out. I'm hoping that Uriah Schrock will be on the square. He can help me move it into the house."

I swallowed when she said Uriah's name. I had known Uriah my whole life. When we were young, he was sweet on me. At the time, I hardly noticed. I only had eyes for my love, Kip Fisher. Though Kip had been gone twenty-some years now, I had always believed he was the only man I would ever love. As a matchmaker, I firmly believed that every person had one match, but now,

I wondered. Uriah made no secret of the fact that he wanted to rekindle a friendship with me. I didn't discuss any of this with Lois. Since she was my childhood friend, she knew my history with the two men just as well as I did.

She shifted the car into park. "Should I tell you if Uriah asks about you?"

I gave her a look. "Thanks for the ride, and you know I don't want to talk about Uriah. I don't care if he mentions me or not."

"He's a very nice man."

I gave her another look.

"Fine, fine," she groaned. "Not everyone is in the market for a new husband."

My brow went up. "Are you? I thought you said you were done with men after your fourth marriage."

She sighed. "I never say never when it comes to love, Millie. And neither should you."

I shook my head and got out of the car. I opened the back door and the goats bounded out. "Bye, Lois," I said.

She winked at me before shifting the car into drive. The goats ran down the long gravel driveway after her car. When she turned onto the road, they stopped.

I whistled, and they ran back to me. I walked toward the house, my mind preoccupied with worries over Ben, and now Uriah. I tried to push both of them from my mind. I walked up the step to the front door and was just about to open the screen door when I saw a scrap of paper trapped there.

I frowned. I guessed that the note was from my closest neighbor, Raellen Raber, saying that she or her husband had borrowed tools from my barn. We shared as much as we could, including a shed phone that was kept on their farm half a mile away. Raellen was a harried mother of nine and a member of Double Stitch. It wouldn't be the first time I'd come home to an IOU note on my front door.

I didn't have any other close neighbors, so, to me, it seemed unlikely that anyone else would have left me a note. I opened the door just a crack and pulled the paper loose.

On the outside there was no writing. The piece of notebook paper was folded into fours. I unfolded it and knew right away that it wasn't from Raellen. Her writing was curvy and flamboyant, and this print was in a much tighter hand.

Dear Millie,

I am sorry if I pushed you at the flea market earlier today to speak to Tobias Lieb. I know that you are giving me the best advice you can. You don't know all the factors that are involved. You don't know that it would be best for everyone, including Tobias, if Tess and I married soon. We love each other, and I fear that our love will cause trouble for our families if it is stifled. Please understand that I don't want to put you in a bad place. I would never ask you to do this if I weren't desperate.

I know that Tobias is afraid I will take Tess to Michigan, but I will not do that. I can never go back to my home district or my home state. I know that you left the district long before I ran into trouble there. One day, I will tell you about it.

Just know that I can't go back. I don't want to go back. I wish I could make Tobias believe that.

I appreciate your speaking to him. If something happens . . . if you learn something about me that is surprising . . . know that I always saw you as a favorite aenti. Your kindness meant the world to me when I was a child.

If I am able someday to pay you back for that, I will. If I am not able, please know it's the truth and take heart in that in the days to come.

Your adopted nephew,
Ben Baughman

I stared at the letter for a long time, and a feeling of dread fell over me like a heavy quilt. What did it all mean? It seemed to me that Ben, and maybe even Tess, were in some kind of trouble. Was it trouble that had followed Ben from Michigan? After my sister died, I lost all contact with that district. They'd always viewed me as an interloper of sorts from Ohio. And my sister was too ill to smooth things over for me. I had gone to church, of course, but wasn't involved with the district much more than that. They hadn't wanted me to be. My sister's community in Michigan was small, made up of only twenty families. They had been leery of outsiders. Even when my sister married into the group, it took decades for them to accept her as a full member of the community. She had told me once it was because the founders of that community had left their Ohio district to make a new one. They thought their old district in Ohio was too lenient with its children and too easily wooed by the *Englisch* way of life. Since I was from Ohio, I was viewed with suspicion.

I shook the dark memories from my mind and wished that I could speak to Ben right then and there to make sure he was all right. It wasn't often that I wished we Amish were allowed telephones. I understood that the convenience of having them could become a crutch, making us too dependent on gadgets rather than relying on community. Even so, I wished that I could have called Ben to tell him not to do anything rash in order to impress Tobias Lieb.

I held the letter at my side and wondered if I should drive into the village and try to track Ben down and make him tell me what was going on.

I promised myself that I would go to the flea market the next day and have him explain the letter to me. Feeling better, I was about to fold up the page and tuck it into my apron pocket when it was ripped from my hand. Phillip grabbed it with his teeth and ran. He only went a few yards away, but it was far enough to keep me from saving the letter.

"Phillip!" I cried, but it was too late. With three chomps, the letter was down Phillip's gullet.

The goat grinned at me like a student who had won first prize in the school spelling bee. I put my hands on my hips. "Phillip, that was a very important letter."

The goat stopped bouncing and lowered his head. If I didn't know better, I would have claimed he understood every word I said. That was quite a reach—by Amish or *Englisch* standards.

"Oh, don't give me that sad face." I shook my finger at him. "You know I don't deal well when you or your brother are low."

He bowed his head a bit more. Ruth Yoder would have called me daft for having such a soft heart for farm animals, but since my move to Ohio, Phillip and Peter had become part of my family. I knew it might be hard for someone like Ruth, who had never lived alone a day in her life, to understand. But I found it was nice to come home to a creature who would greet me and be so very excited to see me each day.

Someone who doesn't understand the comfort of animals may not also know what it feels like to be truly lonely.

Because of this, I couldn't stay angry at Phillip for long. I looked at the brown and white goat, Peter. "Peter, what are you going to do with your brother?"

Peter ran over to the other goat and head-butted him. Phillip cheered up immediately, and the two danced around each other. I shook my head and let myself inside the house. When I opened the door, I was greeted by another animal. This was a young kitten named Peaches. Peaches had been born in the spring at my niece's greenhouse. From the moment I saw him, I knew that he was coming home with me. He meowed and wove around my ankles.

The goats, at least, had enough *gut* sense to know they weren't permitted in the house, but they stared at Peaches from the doorway. The kitten arched his back and hissed at them. He was still growing accustomed to the goats. He was a mellow kitten, and I think he would have liked the goats much better if they were a tad calmer.

Despite the goats' antics, I couldn't rid myself of worries over Ben. I told myself that I would clear everything up with him tomorrow. There was nothing more I could do that day. Tomorrow, all would be well.

I really wanted to believe that, but deep in my heart, I didn't.

Chapter Six

The next morning, I wanted to go straight to the flea market, but I didn't have the time. Peter had gotten tangled in a pricker bush early that morning, and I spent several hours removing burs from his coat while Phillip anxiously looked on. By the time I got all the burs removed and calmed both goats down, it was time for me to leave for the Double Stitch meeting in the village.

I debated skipping it, but then I was afraid I would have to answer Ruth's prying questions about where I had been. I already knew Ruth's opinion on Ben courting Tess and didn't want to hear any more about it.

I decided that I would find Ben later. Someone at the flea market would know where his second job was, even if it was only Tess.

This morning, I felt better about Ben's note. I told myself that it was just the romantic ramblings of a young man who was blinded by love. Everything seemed more tragic when a person was young and in love. Emotions were heightened. Feelings were tender. I knew that when I saw Ben again, he would be calm, and maybe then, when he was in a better state of mind, I could find out why he and Tess were in such a hurry to marry.

I parked my buggy in front of the Sunbeam Café. As usual, Lois had offered to come to my little farm and pick me up, but I'd told her it would be silly for her to do that when she lived within walking distance of the café. Also, I didn't want to tell her just yet about the note, so if I could leave the Double Stitch meeting and track down Ben myself, that would be the best. It wasn't that I didn't want to tell my friend—I told Lois almost everything—but I knew she would insist on going with me to find Ben. He wouldn't speak to me about what was going on with her around.

I stepped inside the café and found that I was the first member to arrive. Darcy, Lois's granddaughter, stood at the counter, chatting with a regular customer, Bryan Shell. Bryan was a writer and said he was working on a novel. He said that's why he was at the Sunbeam Café every day. He claimed it was the best place for him to write, but I think it was really because he was so enamored with the pretty café owner.

Darcy may have enjoyed his attentions, but as of yet, I hadn't seen her encouraging the relationship. She was still recovering from having her heart broken by another man. I knew it would take her some time to want to give love another try. But unlike Ben, Bryan seemed willing to wait.

I knew that things were different with the *Englisch* though. They didn't feel this great rush to get married as the Amish did. They didn't bat an eye at the idea of getting married after thirty. Or even after forty! If an Amish person waited that long to marry, it would be the talk of the district.

"Hi, Millie!" Darcy greeted me with a wide grin. "Grandma is in the back. She was just telling us about the chair she bought at the flea market yesterday. She's so thrilled with it and says it looks great in her home."

"Oh *gut*," I said with a smile. "I was hoping that the chair made it home in one piece. I had concerns . . ."

The back-kitchen door opened, and Lois came out carrying a tray of frothy drinks. "Of course, it made it home. Millie, you make it sound like I didn't have the situation well in hand just as I always do."

Darcy and I shared a glance, but neither of us made a comment. However, Lois never missed a thing and turned to the young writer for support. "Come on, Bryan. You're on my side in this, aren't you?"

He blinked behind his glasses as he slouched off to his seat by the window. Bryan was a tall man, but I had never seen him stretch to his full height. It was as if he had spent his entire life bent and folded at the waist. Perhaps he had started doing that because of a lack of confidence, and over time it just became the way he faced the world. It might be a fine way to approach the world as a writer, but it would not do if he ever wanted to be a spouse.

In fact, I believed his demeanor didn't bode well for his match with Darcy. Darcy might be in a weak spot now and enjoy his attentions, but she was a proactive woman who ran her own business. A time would come when a weak man would not be enough for her. I hoped that she would put him off and find someone who was more suited to her, or that Bryan had it in him to step up to be the man she needed him to be.

"Aww," Lois said when Bryan didn't voice his support.

"You all should cut me a break. I even made these drinks for Double Stitch."

The drinks in front of her looked far closer to straight cream and sugar than coffee. In fact, I wondered if there was coffee in them at all.

I wasn't the least bit surprised when Lois placed a frothy drink in front of me, even though she knew I would have preferred black coffee. It seemed to me that Lois took it as her mission to expose me to as many *Englisch* customs as I would allow. I stared at the drink. "Isn't the point of serving a customer at a café to give them what they would really want and ask for? The ladies would be fine with coffee. You don't have to go to all this trouble."

Lois shook her head. "You're not a customer, you're family, so that means I can order for you."

I eyed the drink as she picked it up and put it in my hand. "What is that?"

"Just taste it and let me know if you like it. Then I will tell you what it is."

"I think that's what every poisoner says to their victim before the victim drops dead."

"My, Millie, who knew you had such a dark imagination? That's not a very Amish thing to say. I think the fact that you solved a murder last spring might have gone to your head."

I made a face at her. "You're right. It wasn't very Amish. I know you wouldn't poison me. Well, I'm fairly certain that you wouldn't."

"Thank you. It does comfort me to know that you trust me in that way." She placed her elbows on the counter. "Now, out with it. What's up with you?"

I eyed her with the same wary look I had given my

drink. "I don't know if anything is, as you say, 'up,' but I do feel a bit of anxiety this morning. I didn't sleep well. I was kept up by some unsettling dreams." I hoped she would leave it at that.

"You're not one to have nightmares. At least, I can't remember you ever mentioning having one."

My brow wrinkled. "I know. I think that's why I'm so out of sorts over it." I pointed at my drink. "I'm sure this will set me to rights."

"Or give you a sugar high," Darcy said. "Just remember, I taught Grandma how to make the drink, but she likes to give it enhancements."

"My, my," Lois said. "Between the two of you, I'm starting to doubt my cooking skills."

"I didn't know you had cooking skills," Darcy teased.

Lois laughed. "It's true. My goal is to boil water without setting the pot on fire, but I think I'm improving."

Darcy gave her grandmother a hug. "You are. You are so much better than when you first started to help at the café. You make a mean pot of tea."

"You see, I finally got the knack of boiling water," Lois said and winked at me.

Darcy grabbed a mug and a pot of coffee and carried both over to Bryan's table, where he was already hunched over his computer.

Lois nodded at them. "What are the odds on those two, do you think?"

"Odds?" I asked and sipped from my drink. It was even sweeter than I'd imagined it would be.

"Oh, I know you don't like to speak in gambling terms," Lois said. "But do you think they will work together?"

I pressed my lips together.

Lois nodded. "Your silence is telling, and I feel the same way. I just don't want to say anything to Darcy yet. She is still reeling over her last boyfriend. I also don't want to tell her because I'm afraid my disapproval will spur her into liking him. You know how the young are when they think they are told not to love someone. They latch on like a catfish on a worm."

I did indeed, and that made me think again of Ben and Tess. It seemed to me that Ben and Tess were already invested in their romance. I still didn't understand why they felt they couldn't wait to marry. Even a year would make a world of difference to Tess's father. They might be even surer about their relationship in a year's time too.

She frowned. "You look upset. What's wrong?"

"I'm just worried about Ben. I think that's what brought the dreams on. When I spoke with him at the flea market yesterday, he looked so incredibly tired. For a man that young to look as if he could fall asleep at any second was startling. I'm worried that he is pushing himself too hard. I was the one who suggested he work at the flea market."

"You did, but you never told him to get four jobs and only sleep a few hours a day. That was all on him."

"Even so, I should have known better. Ben has always been the type to take a suggestion three steps past where you expected him to go."

She patted my hand. "Don't you worry. He will be fine, and the boy will find his balance just as we all have. It's part of growing up."

I cocked my head. "Since when have you been the one passing out sage advice?"

Lois grinned. "I guess all those Amish proverbs you

have been repeating over the years finally wore off on me." She chuckled at her own joke. "Drink that pumpkin latte. In my book, there's nothing that a little sugar can't ease. If that doesn't help," she added, "I will walk over to Swissmen Sweets and buy you a chocolate Jethro Bar."

"A Jethro Bar?" I asked.

"Oh yes, Juliet Brook's pig has become a celebrity since the release of *Bailey's Amish Sweets*. Because of that, the candy shop is now making white and milk chocolate pigs that look just like him. They are adorable. People are buying them like hotcakes."

Jethro the pig had been a bit of a celebrity in the village of Harvest even before his television debut. Juliet, who had recently married Reverend Brook, the pastor of the last white church on the village square, took the little pig everywhere she went. I'd heard her say that he was her comfort animal. A "comfort animal" in the Amish world was a completely foreign concept. Animals were livestock, beasts of burden or service. Yes, Amish kept dogs and cats, but even those "pets" were for practical purposes too. The dogs helped with farm work and the cats caught mice. Interestingly, both the *Englisch* and the Amish accepted Juliet and her pig everywhere they went in the village. Juliet was one of the sweetest women I knew, and everyone in the village loved her. Jethro, although cute and endearing, could be a bit of a handful, but he was tolerated in the village for Juliet's sake.

"I'm continually amazed at what *Englischers* will buy," I said.

"Not me. I knew when my second husband bought a

singing bass for our living room wall that there were no more rules when it came to good taste."

I was going to ask her more about this bass when the front door of the café opened and Raellen walked inside. Raellen always looked a little bit overworked and harried, but that could be put down to the fact that she was the mother of nine children ranging in ages from one to fifteen.

"Oh, Millie, thank goodness I have found you. I went to your little farm as soon as I heard the news, but you weren't there. Your goats chased me right out of the yard! You would have thought they hadn't seen a human at the farm in years by the way they acted." She took a breath. "When I saw that you weren't at the house, I knew to come here because of the meeting. I told the older children to watch the little ones. I had to get to you as quick as I could. I didn't want you to hear it from someone else first."

Raellen might be sweet, but she was a terrible gossip, and it wasn't unusual for her to want to be the first one to share news, but this was the first time that she had tracked me down especially for it.

"Is it my niece?" I asked. "Is Edith all right?"

My niece Edith had had a rough go last spring when she'd almost married the wrong man. Ever since then, I kept an eye on her and helped out at the greenhouse once a week. Now that it was the end of September, the greenhouse was all but closed for the season, and Edith was starting to plan for the next year. She didn't need my help there as she did in the spring and summer. I'd seen her at church the Sunday before, and both she and her children looked well. There had been no signs that there was trouble brewing.

"It's not about Edith." She paused. "Is there something I should know about Edith?"

"Don't be a nosy parker about Edith, Raellen," Lois cautioned. "And spit out what you came here to say."

Without preamble she said, "The Harvest Flea Market is on fire!"

"What?" Lois and I both cried.

The *Englischers* who were quietly reading and eating in the café stared at us.

Raellen leaned across the counter. "It's true. My husband got a call on the shed phone to go help with the fire."

"Shouldn't they have real firemen taking care of that?" Lois asked.

"They do, but it was taking so long for the fire department's water trucks to get there, the men got a bucket chain going from the well. All the men in the district were called up."

"Oh dear, was much of the flea market lost?" Lois asked.

Raellen shrugged. "I haven't heard. My husband has been gone for nearly two hours. I will be sure to find out all the details from him when he gets home."

That, I didn't doubt. There was nothing Raellen liked more than gathering new information.

"That's just awful," I said. "Lois and I were there only yesterday. Was anyone hurt?"

Raellen took a breath. "That's what I came here to tell you. I wanted you to hear it from a friend."

"What?" My heart began to race as I waited for her to get to the point.

"A young man died in the fire."

I gripped the edge of the counter. "Oh, Lord in Heaven. Please don't tell me it's—"

"It's Ben Baughman," Raellen practically shouted to the room.

It was the name I had expected to hear.

Chapter Seven

"Ben?" I repeated.

"I'm so sorry, Millie," Raellen said. "I knew you would be so upset to hear the news, but I also knew it would be better coming from me, a friend, than from someone else."

Lois pressed her lips together, and I was surprised that she didn't say anything. Raellen was a kind neighbor, but that didn't excuse the fact that she had just announced Ben's death to the entire café. She may have wanted to tell me because she was my friend and cared about me. I didn't doubt that, but I also knew her well enough to know that she wanted to be the person to tell me because she loved the reaction she received when she gossiped.

"*Danki* for telling me, Raellen. I . . . I think that I will have to skip the Double Stitch meeting today. I was the closest person that Ben had as family here in Ohio. I should go to the flea market." I pushed my pumpkin drink away and stood on shaky legs. "Bessie is out front."

"Oh no!" Lois crowed. "You are not taking your buggy to a fire scene. That's a terrible idea."

I frowned at her. "Lois, I have to go."

"I know that," she said with her hands on her hips. "That's why I'm going to drive you."

"Oh," I said in a small voice. My head was still spinning over what I had heard. Ben was dead, and there was a little voice in the back of my head that told me it was my fault. Would he have still been alive if I had acted on that note instead of waiting?

"Yes, you should go, Grandma. Bryan can help me in the café if I need an extra set of hands." Darcy shooed her toward the door.

Upon hearing his name, Bryan jumped out of his seat, toppling his chair over behind him. His face turned beet red as he picked it up and tucked it back under the table. "Ye . . . yes, I would be happy to help Darcy out."

Lois eyed him. "Don't be knocking anything else over, okay?"

He nodded and his Adam's apple bobbed up and down. Lois shook her head as if she didn't know what she was going to do with him. I had a feeling that Bryan was bewildered by the same issue.

A few minutes later, we were in Lois's car driving to the flea market. Lois, for once, seemed to sense that I needed silence and didn't speak. Her car smelled faintly of goat.

As we drew close to the flea market, we began to slow down. There were dozens of cars and buggies parked along the side of the county road. It seemed to me that we weren't the only ones who wanted to come see what was happening.

I held onto a kernel of hope in the back of my mind. Maybe Raellen was wrong. It wouldn't be the first time she'd spread untrue gossip. It was possible that Ben was not the person found in the burning flea market. Wouldn't it take time to identify someone who'd died in a fire? How could anyone be so sure this soon?

Lois squeezed her car between a buggy and a giant SUV. "I think this is as close as I'm going to get."

"We can walk," I said, and unbuckled my seatbelt. "If we were unsure, we certainly know which way to go now." I pointed to the giant plume of smoke on the horizon.

Lois whistled. "It must be one heck of a fire to cause that much smoke. It will be a wonder if there is anything left of the flea market at all."

I had a feeling she was right. I winced when I thought about all the Amish and *Englisch* vendors whose liveli-hoods were based on sales from the flea market. Part of renting space in the market building meant that they could leave their wares there overnight. A lot of money must have been lost, and, at least for the Amish merchants, there would be no insurance to cover what the fire had stolen. Double Stitch's quilts would be counted among those lost items. But in comparison to the loss of Ben's life, that meant nothing.

I pressed my hands together in silent prayer. I was still hoping and praying that Raellen had got it wrong. Perhaps there was just a rumor that Ben had been trapped in the fire. Everyone in the district knew that he was working as the night guard. Maybe they just thought he'd died.

As we walked up to the flea market, Amish women stood with their children on the side of the road crying. I recognized most of them as families who had had booths in the market building. This fire represented a great financial loss to them.

Please let that be the only loss, I prayed.

Lois seemed to sense my tension, and she grabbed my hand and squeezed it. Hand in hand, we walked the rest of the way to the drive leading up to the entrance of the flea market.

A young officer stood at the bottom of the driveway behind a wooden barricade. He waved his arms. "I'm sorry. I'm very sorry. I understand you all want to know what happened to your booths, but this is still an active fire scene until the fire chief says it's clear. You cannot enter." He was firm, but his voice wavered just a little.

The timidity of the officer didn't surprise me. It was young sheriff's deputy Luke Little. Deputy Little was the youngest member of the sheriff's department, and he always seemed a little uncertain when Deputy Aiden Brody wasn't around. Deputy Aiden was second in command in the department, outranked only by Sheriff Marshall. The sheriff wasn't well liked in the Amish community because, if he had his way, he would blame the Amish for everything that went wrong in the county. He would do it, too, if Deputy Aiden didn't step in time and time again.

Lois, still holding my hand, bustled up to the barricade. She dragged me behind her. "Hey, Deputy Little, over here." She waved at him.

His eyes went wide, but instead of ignoring Lois, he walked over to us. She touched the deputy on the shoulder, causing him to lean in, and then she said something in his ear. When she was finished speaking, Deputy Little straightened up as if there was a pole stuck under his shirt. He moved the barricade just enough for Lois and me to slip through. When we had passed, he put the barricade back.

"That's not fair," one of the men in the crowd shouted.

"Why are you letting them inside and not us?" another

asked. "They don't even have a booth at the market. They shouldn't be allowed in there when we're not."

I looked over my shoulder as the group of angry Amish merchants shouted at Deputy Little.

"Come on." Lois tugged on my hand when I came to a stop. "Let's go before he changes his mind and makes us leave."

I stumbled after her, but after a few steps I was in sync with her stride again. "What did you say to Deputy Little?"

"I told him that you're Ben Baughman's aunt and next of kin."

I stopped in the middle of the gravel driveway. "But I'm not his *aenti*."

She tugged on my hand. "You're the closest thing to it. You've said that to me countless times as you helped him out over the last few months."

I didn't move.

"Millie," she said. "Sure, it was a little fib, but I made it, not you. I will own up to it if it comes to that and be sure to tell Deputy Little or Aiden Brody that I was just dragging you along behind me." She sighed. "Which I'm not doing that well since you're not moving at the moment."

"I didn't stop because of your fib, even though I wish that you hadn't resorted to lying." I swallowed. "It's that." I pointed.

Lois turned around, and I knew she was seeing what I had seen. The long horse barn that had been converted into the Harvest Village Flea Market smoldered at the top of the hill. Billows of black smoke poured out the back of the red building. I didn't see any flames, and if it had not been for the smoke, it would have been hard to tell that the building was on fire. The portion of the barn that faced the driveway still looked the same as it had the day before, except for the dozens of firemen, sheriff's deputies, and emergency workers walking around it. Lining the driveway were fire trucks from as far away as Canton.

"Holy smokes!" Lois said.

Considering the scene, it seemed like a most appropriate outburst.

I scanned the police officers and firefighters for someone I knew—not that I was acquainted with many of them, even after my involvement in that terrible business last spring— and then I saw Deputy Aiden standing to the left of the building speaking to an *Englisch* man in jeans and a green flannel shirt.

I pointed him out to Lois. "There's Deputy Aiden. He's the one we should talk to."

"Then, let's go. We'd better have a chat with him before someone else kicks us out." Lois hiked her large purse over her shoulder.

As we walked up to the two men, we got a few strange looks from firemen, but they seemed to be too tired to ask us who we were or why we were there. I knew that wouldn't last much longer.

"I'm ruined," the man in denim said. "Do you hear me? This fire has ruined me! I will lose everything. You have to let me in there to see what I can salvage. Maybe I can save part of the barn before it's a complete loss."

"Believe me, Mr. Waller, the fire crews are doing everything they can to save as much of the building as possible, but you cannot go in there until the fire inspector declares the building safe. There is too great a chance of you being hurt, or an officer or fire officer being injured trying to get you out." He took a breath. "And I know that many of the merchants feel the same way you do. They want to know what's become of their booths. Please know that I'm sympathetic."

"Who cares about the merchants!" Waller snapped. "They can make their little trinkets again. I'm the one who won't be able to come back from this. I'm the one who's lost the building."

Deputy Aiden's right cheek twitched, but he didn't say anything in reply.

Waller shook his finger at Deputy Aiden. "You let me in there today, or I will have your job."

Deputy Aiden straightened up. "Sir, I will remind you that you are speaking to an officer of the law. Even though you might be too upset to see it, we are keeping you from going into the barn for your own safety. If you go into that building before it's declared safe, you will be arrested. That is not an idle threat. Am I clear, sir?"

Waller opened and closed his mouth as if he was surprised someone would speak to him in such a way. Then without another word, he spun around and walked straight into Lois and me. He pushed Lois in my direction, and I caught her before she could fall. Lois shook her fist at him. "Watch where you're going and respect your elders while you're at it!"

Waller didn't so much as glance in her direction.

Deputy Aiden rubbed the side of his face. "What are the two of you doing here?"

"We are here about Ben Baughman," Lois said.

The color drained from the deputy's handsome face.

Chapter Eight

"You know Ben?" Deputy Aiden asked.

"Very well," I said. "He was like another nephew to me. We heard . . ." I swallowed. "We heard that he was caught in the fire."

Deputy Aiden's thick hair peeked out from under his sheriff's department baseball cap, and his brown eyes were tired. I wondered what time he had awakened to rush to the fire.

Deputy Aiden frowned. "You said he was *like* a nephew to you, so he's no real relation?"

"He's relation enough," Lois said. "He moved to Holmes County from the village in Michigan where Millie lived. He even stayed with her until he got on his feet."

Deputy Aiden didn't comment further on our relationship. "How did you two even get this close to the barn?" he asked. I knew that he was avoiding answering my question. I supposed he felt he couldn't tell me because Ben and I weren't "real" family.

"Deputy Little let us through the line," Lois answered.

"I told him about Millie's connection to Ben. He let us right in."

Deputy Aiden scowled, and from the look on his face, the younger deputy was going to get a talking-to about protocol around active fire scenes.

"It wasn't Deputy Little's fault," I said. "We may have suggested that I was his actual *aenti.*"

He raised his brow. "You lied?"

"Millie would never lie," Lois exclaimed. "I may have exaggerated."

Deputy Aiden shook his head.

"Please," I said. "Ben *is* a nephew to me. He helped me take care of my ailing sister in Michigan. I consider him my kin." I took a breath. "Please tell me what has happened."

"I'm sorry, Millie," the kind deputy murmured.

That's all he had to say to confirm the rumor, and I faltered as the wind was knocked out of me. Ben was so young and had his whole life in front of him. A life with so much to look forward to. He'd told me the day before that he would be twenty the next week. It was a terrible loss, and the type that made me wonder where *Gott* was in all of this. I closed my eyes and said a silent prayer for peace. It was all that I could ask for because I was afraid there would be no understanding why Ben was taken from this earth so soon.

Lois linked her arm through mine. "If you can't stand, I will hold you up," she whispered. "Just like you have held me up countless times."

I couldn't look at the smoldering flea market. Instead, I turned in the opposite direction, pulling Lois along with me. Across the road from where the flea market stood was a pasture. Dozens of beef cows dotted the hillside, quietly chewing on the grass. They had no idea what was happening on the other side of the street. It made me wonder how many people were going about their own days, happily or unhappily, unaware of the suffering around them. Not knowing was a gift of sorts. It would be too much to absorb all the suffering in the world. However, when it was your personal suffering, you could only marvel at the fact that the world did not stop and take notice of what you had lost.

Ben had been a *gut*, hardworking young man. He just wanted to make his way in the world. He had always been cheerful, even when life was difficult for him. I could not imagine why *Gott* would take a life like Ben's from this world so soon. The world needed earnest young men like him. It all seemed like such a terrible waste. I knew it wasn't my place to question *Gotte's* ways, but even so, there were so many questions in my heart.

"Millie?" Deputy Aiden asked in a gentle voice as he joined us looking at the pasture. "Are you all right? Do you want Lois to take you home?"

It was a good question. I would have loved to go home to my cat and goats, but I knew I couldn't now. I owed it to Ben to find out what had happened.

"Millie, do you need to sit down?" Deputy Aiden asked.

I shook my head and straightened my spine. Even with my determination to appear strong, I was grateful to Lois for not letting go of my arm. "*Nee*, can you tell us what happened?"

"You're not his next of kin," Deputy Aiden said.

I couldn't lie to him. "I'm not, but I am the closest thing he has to it in Holmes County. He has family in Michigan."

Ben's letter came to mind, and specifically the line in it where Ben had hinted that he had had some sort of falling out with his district.

"If you aren't real family, Millie, I can't tell you what happened. I'm sorry." He said this as if he really was sorry.

Lois let go of me and put her hands on her hips. "Sure, you can. We are your best source for learning more about Ben. Isn't that what you want?"

Deputy Aiden gave her a look. "You're right, but if my sheriff found out I spoke with you, I could be in real trouble."

"We would never tell Sheriff Marshall," Lois said. "Not to put too fine a point on it, but I detest that man and make it my goal to avoid him."

"Lois," I said.

She shrugged. "I know what I think, and I say what I think. He's not kind to the Amish, and my best friend just happens to be Amish. I can dislike him if I want to." She stomped her foot as if she needed to drive her point home.

I shook my head and turned my attention back to Deputy Aiden. "How did you know that it was Ben you found?" I pressed my lips together. "I suppose in a fire that it can be hard to tell."

He sighed. "Ben was easily identifiable. I know I shouldn't be telling you this, but yes, I do need information about him in order to investigate the case. He didn't have any burn marks on him. He died from smoke inhalation."

I let out a breath. I don't know why, but that made me feel better. Ben was still gone, but I shivered to think of him, or anyone, being burned alive. Just the thought of it made my stomach turn over.

Deputy Aiden smiled at me kindly, as if he knew what I was thinking.

"Where was he in the building?" Lois asked. "From the looks of it, the back of the building was what caught on fire."

Deputy Aiden nodded. "It was, and the back is almost a complete loss. I didn't tell Waller this, but I would be surprised if the entire building isn't condemned and has to come down. As for Ben, he was in a small office by the front door. We are lucky the fire didn't burn that part of the building too. It came very close, and there is certainly smoke damage. The fire spread fast. There is a lot of dry timber and hay in these old barns, and they go up like kindling."

"Did he have a means to escape?" Lois asked. "Was he trapped in that room?" She shivered. "I can't imagine how awful that would be."

"That's one of the issues we are struggling with. Ben could have gotten out if he wanted to. There was a window in the room. He could have smashed it and easily climbed out to escape the fire, but from what we can tell, not a single thing in the office was moved. The door was never opened, the window never even cracked."

My brow wrinkled. That didn't make any sense at all. Something must have been in the way to stop Ben from making his escape. He wouldn't have just sat there and waited for the fire to reach him. I couldn't believe that. "Where was Ben in the room?" I asked.

He frowned as if he were debating whether or not to tell me this next bit. "He was lying on the floor. His head was on a pillow, and he was under a blanket. It appears he was asleep."

"Asleep?" Lois shouted. "In the middle of a raging fire?"

Deputy Aiden nodded. "That's what it looks like."

"How could he sleep through that? A fire that large must have made a terrible noise." I folded my arms around myself.

"That's what I would like to find out." Deputy Aiden squinted as the sun came out from behind a cloud. "From all evidence, he was sleeping when the fire struck, and it appears that he never woke up or had a chance to escape."

"Could he have been dead before the fire?" Lois asked.

Deputy Aiden removed sunglasses from the breast pocket of his uniform and slipped them over his eyes. "It's possible. The coroner will have to make that determination. I saw the body, and as far as I could tell, there was no injury on him. It could have been something internal that killed him."

"Like poison?" Lois asked.

Deputy Aiden eyed her. "Poisoning is not as common as the mysteries in books and on television shows would have you believe. Now, I did my part in telling you what happened. It's your turn. Tell me more about Ben. It seems to me the people we have interviewed know very little about him. I can't tell if they honestly don't know, or if they simply don't want to speak to me about him because they are Amish and I'm a cop."

"How were you able to identify the body?" Lois asked. "If no one admits to knowing him."

I cringed at her question, but it was something that had to be asked.

"Ford Waller, the man that you saw me speaking to a few minutes ago, is the owner of the flea market. He identified the deceased as his night guard, Ben Baughman. Other than knowing who Ben was, he wasn't much help in telling me about him. He said that Ben told him he was renting a room from an Amish family and didn't have relatives in the area. That's all he knew."

"He's renting from the Keims," I said. "The family with the Christmas tree farm."

Deputy Aiden's brow went up. "I know it well. Emily Keim works for Bailey."

I nodded and realized that I should have remembered that. Bailey King was the owner of the popular Amish candy shop in Harvest, Swissmen Sweets. She owned and operated it with her Amish grandmother, Clara King. Bailey was Deputy Aiden's girlfriend. They had been together for a long while now, and everyone in the village wondered if they would ever get married, but no one more than Deputy Aiden's mother, Juliet Brook. The Juliet Brook of the comfort pig. Even amidst the sorrow nearly consuming me, there was a small spark of joy about this town and this community. Ben had seemed happy here, too, certainly more so than he'd been in Michigan. My word, I could not believe he was really gone! My eyes welled up, and it felt like a buggy was parked on my chest.

"So it's Emily and her husband I should be speaking to," Deputy Aiden mused aloud, oblivious to my thoughts.

"Doesn't it seem strange to you that an Amish flea market should need a night guard?" Lois said. "Ben died because that was his job, but I don't think in all the time I've lived in Amish Country that this town ever needed such a precaution."

"It is unusual," Deputy Aiden admitted. "I'll admit that. I don't know of any other business in the county—Amish business, I mean—that has a guard like this."

I held the corner of my apron the way I did when I was a child. Realizing what I was doing, I dropped the apron and stood a bit straighter. "Ben said it was because things were being stolen from the flea market at night. After he was hired, he chased off would be robbers on two occasions."

"This was never reported to the sheriff's department. Had it been, I would have known about it."

I shrugged. Deputy Aiden and I both knew the reason for that. The Amish who rented space at the flea market would have been made uncomfortable had the police been on the grounds.

"Who broke into the flea market? When were they here? What do you know about this?" Aiden's tone sharpened.

"I—I don't know much. I don't even think Ben knew," I added. "He just said that he thought they were young men. I asked him if they were *Englisch* or Amish, and he couldn't say anything other than they were wearing *Englisch* clothing. I don't think he even saw any of their faces. They realized there was a guard at the flea market, and they left."

"How could he have been sure they were intent on robbing the flea market?"

I shrugged. "I know that's not a great deal of help."

"Okay," Deputy Aiden said. "What did they want to steal, or what did they steal last time, assuming that it was the same group of young men?"

I frowned. "Ben didn't say that either. I didn't think to

ask, but I wasn't at the flea market to learn about his work. I just wanted to check on him and see how he was getting on before he went to his next job."

"What job was that?"

"Stocking shelves at the market. He worked so many places. He was always busy."

The deputy rocked back on his heels. "How many places was he working?"

"Four," I said.

"Why so many? I know the Amish take pride in hard work, but that seems a lot even for the Amish."

"He was just starting out here and wanted to earn money. He was living alone for the first time in a new place. There were many expenses, and he didn't know that many people. I would have helped him, of course, but he didn't want to take charity. I could barely convince him to stay at my home for a few weeks before he found a more permanent place to live."

Deputy Aiden nodded as if he were considering my explanation.

"Deputy?" I began. "If Ben died from smoke inhalation in the fire, was it an accidental death?"

"Or murder?" Lois blurted out.

Deputy Aiden looked at us both in turn. "Would either of you know a reason someone would want to hurt Ben?"

Out of the corner of my eye, I saw Lois on the verge of speaking. Since I was afraid she might say something about Tess, I shook my head. I didn't want to bring Tess into this just yet. The poor girl would be distraught as it was when she heard about Ben, if she hadn't already. It would be no help to her to have the police arrive on her doorstep asking questions about her relationship with Ben.

A man in coveralls waved at Deputy Aiden.

He nodded at the man and turned to us. "Ladies, thank you for your help. Now that I know where Ben has been living, we have a good place to start. I have to go, and . . ." He looked at us both. "I would ask you to leave the area. This is a crime scene until otherwise stated and a dangerous one at that." He walked away.

Chapter Nine

"We aren't going anywhere yet, are we?" Lois asked.

I smiled at her. My heart still hurt over the loss of Ben, and it would for a while yet, I knew, but it was *gut* to have Lois by my side. In my many years on this good earth, I'd watched so many friends and relatives and neighbors, both young and old, enter this world and leave it. Even as my heart broke, I reminded myself of the limitations of this world, and the joyous kingdom that awaited us—all of us—in *Gotte's* kingdom. Not for the first time, I was grateful for my faith. Loss, especially the loss of one so young, was never easy to accept. But if I kept my thoughts focused and open, then the peace of our faith would come to me. Faith was the blessing that saw us through the most difficult of days.

"What should we do now?" Lois asked. "Leave like he said? Maybe we should check on Double Stitch's booth?"

I nodded dumbly. I was so confused and overwhelmed by Ben's death, I wasn't up for making decisions just then.

Lois wrinkled her nose. "I doubt there is anything left, so maybe trying to find out is a waste of time. The quilting circle's booth was at the back of the building where the fire started. Even if every quilt wasn't burned up, they would be water-logged and full of smoke. I think you should just write them off as goners."

I nodded, knowing she was right. I hoped Ruth Yoder didn't make too much of a fuss over it, and I hoped that she wouldn't come down too hard on Iris Young about the loss either. Having the booth had been Iris's idea, and I knew Ruth had a tendency to blame people with new ideas. This was especially true when something went wrong. What could be more wrong than losing all our quilts in a fire? Losing a person, I realized, like Ben. My heart twisted in my chest.

Lois patted my shoulder. "Don't you worry, Millie. We will get to the bottom of this."

I blinked at her. "The bottom of what?" I asked.

She put her hands on her hips. "Ben's death, because Ben was important to you."

Lois had told me once that she couldn't be Amish because what she wore told people who she was. Told? Perhaps shouted was a more apt term. Wearing a bright yellow blouse with a black belt cinching her waist over bright purple leggings, she stood out in the crowd of uniformed officers and Amish spectators. In her spiky purple-red hair, she had added a black and purple headband. Yes, her statement was certainly true.

"Both of us know the Amish aren't going to talk to Deputy Aiden about Ben," she said. "In fact, they might be more hesitant than usual to talk about him because he was new. They won't feel the need to find justice for him, but we do."

As much as I wanted to say she was wrong about that, that my people did care about Ben, there was truth to her words. One of the primary desires of the Amish was to be left alone by the *Englisch* world. Since Ben wasn't from Holmes County, many would not want to get involved because they didn't want to talk to the police. Their distrust of law enforcement would keep them from helping the sheriff's department find out how a stranger might have died. "All right. Then we need to find out the identities of these young men who Ben scared off."

"Right," she said. "We need suspects. Amish Marple and her lovely sidekick are on the case."

"I wish you wouldn't call me that," I said.

"Amish Marple is the perfect name for you. It's here to stay. We still haven't picked a code name for me. I need something with an edge, like Viper."

"Viper?" I asked.

"Okay, maybe not that particular name, but in that direction."

I sighed. "We should find out who was breaking into the flea market and what was taken. That might lead us to how the fire began. We know the quilts weren't among the stolen items because this was Double Stitch's first week with a booth."

"That's a start," Lois agreed.

"I just don't know what they would do with the stolen items. People in Harvest and Holmes County would recognize them right away if they were Amish made. They might even know the craftsman who made the pieces. It seems to me that it would be difficult to do anything with the stolen goods."

"Not really," Lois said. "There are dozens of ways to unload stolen goods. I might have learned a little bit about that from my second husband. You know that I kicked him to the curb when I found out he was fencing. I'm too pretty to go to prison for aiding and abetting."

When she spoke about fencing, I knew she didn't mean the kind with pastures. Or the kind with swords.

"People steal things and resell them online all the time," Lois said. "If they steal from the Amish, they have the added comfort that the Amish would most likely not report the theft, and they certainly wouldn't run across their stolen goods on the Internet. I've actually worked that into my novel."

"You are still working on your book?" I asked. Lois had decided months ago that she was going to write a novel about the Amish, but she hadn't mentioned it recently.

"I've already written three chapters, and they are wonderful."

I eyed her. "I don't know much about writing, but I can't imagine that an author says that about the first draft of her book."

"What I lack in talent, I make up for in confidence." Lois grinned.

I smiled. It was one of those times that I envied Lois's willingness to plunge ahead into any new venture.

Her chatter had distracted me from Ben's death for a moment, but it came rushing back. I swallowed as I thought about the note he had left on my door. If I had done something about it yesterday, would he still be alive?

Lois linked her arm through mine again and pulled me in for a half hug. "Come on, let's go see what we can find out. Detection is a good form of distraction, and that's what you need right now." Lois let go of my arm, and I followed her around behind the flea market. We stayed well out of the way of the scene, keeping over twenty feet back.

This side of the barn where the fire had started was in shambles. Smoke rose from the smoldering pieces of blackened wood.

Lois and I edged close to the two smaller barns where the animal judging had been held the day before. A horse stuck his head out of one of the stalls, and I realized how lucky he and the other animals were. Had the wind been different, it could have blown embers from the fire over to these smaller outbuildings, putting the animals in jeopardy. I petted the horse's nose, hoping to comfort him.

I shook my head. "It looks like the worst part of the fire was right near the location of Iris's booth. Poor Iris is going to be so upset. So will all the women." I patted the horse one more time. "But quilts can be remade. Lives cannot."

"What do we do now?" Lois asked.

"I need to tell Deputy Aiden about the note that Ben left me, and then I need to find Tess Lieb." I wrung my hands. "She must know about the fire by now, but does she know about Ben?"

"Note?" Lois asked.

"Oh, I didn't tell you. Everything happened so fast after Raellen came into the café." I quickly told her about the note I'd found on my front door the day before.

"It has to be related," Lois said.

"I think so too, which is why I feel horrible that I didn't act on it last night."

"You couldn't have known," Lois said.

Maybe not, but it was hard not to blame myself.

"Do you think that the barn was burned to kill Ben?" Lois asked. "Who would want to get rid of him?"

One name came to mind. Tobias Lieb. This thought made me want to speak to Tess even more.

"There are no spectators on this crime scene. You need to leave," a firm woman's voice said.

The woman standing in front of us was tall and narrow. Her hair was tied back into a bun on the back of her head, not dissimilar from the way Amish women wore their hair, but she wasn't Amish. She wore a gray uniform with red piping around the sleeves.

She pointed at us. "How did you get back here? You need to leave, and if I find out you took any pictures, I will take your phones." Her voice was raspy.

"Sorry," Lois said, and held up her hands. "I didn't take any photos, and Millie doesn't have a phone. Who are you?"

"I'm Captain Chandra Slate, the arson investigator on this case. From here on out, I'm in charge."

"I thought Deputy Aiden Brody was in charge," I said.

She narrowed her eyes at me. "He is not. Until this is determined not to be an arson case, it's mine."

I swallowed. Arson? It was the first time that anyone had said the word. Deputy Aiden had been so careful not to tell us whether or not the fire had been deliberately set. But Captain Slate just came right out and said it.

"How did the two of you get back here anyway?" she wanted to know.

I wasn't going to mention Deputy Little this time, and I hoped that Lois would know enough to do the same. Deputy Aiden would give the younger deputy the benefit of the doubt. I doubted that Captain Slate would be as forgiving.

Lois smiled. "We just wandered back here to check on the animals to make sure they were all right." She patted the horse's nose, which was still poking out of the stall window. "They seem fine."

Captain Slate nodded.

Out of the corner of my eye, I saw Deputy Aiden make his way toward us, and he wasn't smiling.

"Lois, Millie," Deputy Aiden said as he walked up to us. "I thought I asked you to leave the grounds."

Captain Slate turned to him. "You know who these women are?"

He frowned at her. "Yes, they live in the village."

"We can't have civilians this close to the fire. The flames are out now, but the scene is not completely secure."

"I know, Chandra, and I asked them to leave." He glanced at Lois and me. "I'm sure that this was just a case of their being sidetracked."

"Oh, we were," Lois said. "By the animals. We worried about the animals and whether they were being taken care of. You know Millie's goats could have been here during the fire. Thankfully, we took them home yesterday. Knowing them, they would have tried to break out of their stalls if they were scared."

"Goats?" Captain Slate asked. "I have an investigation to continue. I can't waste my time talking about goats. Deputy Brody, since you know these women, I will hold you responsible for getting them out of here." With that, she marched back in the direction of the blackened flea market.

Deputy Aiden sighed. "What's going on? I asked you two to leave the grounds and trusted that you would."

"We were on our way out," Lois said.

He frowned as if he didn't believe her. I doubted that I would have under the circumstances either.

"Deputy Aiden," I said. "There's something else I need to tell you before we go."

Deputy Aiden turned around with his eyebrows raised. "What's that?"

"Yesterday evening, Ben left a note on my front door. It was there when I got home. I can't help wondering if he knew that something bad was going to happen. The tone of the note was . . . well . . . best described as melancholy."

"That is concerning," Deputy Aiden said. "Why didn't you tell me about it when we spoke earlier?"

"I think I was still in shock over his death."

"What time did he leave the note?" Deputy Aiden asked.

"I don't know, but it had to be sometime between when I saw him at the flea market and when Lois dropped me off at home. That's at least a six-hour window of time between nine in the morning and three in the afternoon. However, my best guess is he would have left it on the way to his second job. When he got to the job, he would not have been able to leave work and come over to my house to leave the note."

"Did the handwriting look like his? Are you sure it was from him?"

"I—I don't know for sure. I can't remember ever receiving a note from him before."

He nodded. "Where's the note? Do you have it with you?

I need to read it, and I will have to take it in as evidence in the crime."

"Crime?" Lois asked. "Captain Slate said the fire could be arson. Is that true?"

He frowned. "She shouldn't have told you that. We can't know for sure until the investigation of the scene is complete. But we have to be open to all possibilities. If it's arson, Ben's death was murder." He shook his head. "It's hard to believe we could have another murder in the village so soon."

I nodded. Over the last few years in Holmes County, murder was on the rise in the Amish community. Many times it involved the *Englisch* world too. It seemed that as our two worlds became more and more intertwined, it was likely that crime would continue to rise. The Amish might want to remain separate from modern life, but that was getting harder to accomplish as the *Englisch* world encroached on our lives.

Centuries ago, we were all riding in horses and buggies and living close to where we were born. That was no longer the case. The Amish continued those practices, but the *Englisch* decidedly did not. Now, it was not uncommon to see an Amish teenager or man with a cell phone. It was something that they needed for business in order to compete in this rapidly changing world.

"If it is an arson case, and Ben is involved," Deputy Aiden said, "that note could be important in helping us find out who was behind the fire."

I made a face. "That's the thing . . . I don't have the note any longer."

His eyes narrowed. "Why not?"

I winced. "My goat ate it."

Chapter Ten

Deputy Aiden stared at me for a long moment. "Your *goat* ate it?"

"Deputy Aiden," Lois said, coming to my defense. "You have to know that goats will eat anything, and Phillip and Peter are two of the orneriest goats that this county has ever seen. I'm surprised they haven't chewed through the walls of Millie's little house yet."

He removed his departmental baseball cap and scratched the back of his head. "I should come to expect answers like this after being a sheriff's deputy in Holmes County for so long, but they still take me by surprise."

"It was Phillip," I said. "Peter wasn't involved. Phillip is the more rambunctious of the two goats. Also, in his defense, he didn't know the paper was important."

"Of course, he didn't," Deputy Aiden said. "He's a goat. Can you tell me what the letter said?"

Lois held up her hand. "Not yet, Millie." She turned to Deputy Aiden. "Before she does that, tell us how the fire started."

He scowled at her, and just when I thought he wasn't going to answer, he said, "It looks like a lantern fire."

I looked at Deputy Aiden. "Accidental?"

He sighed. "Could be, but we are treating it as arson until proven otherwise. In a tinderbox like the flea market, the flames took over quickly." He folded his arms. "Now, tell me what was in that letter."

I told him the best I could, but I was careful not to mention Tess. Again, I wanted to speak to Tess before the police did. I knew once Deputy Aiden or another officer started asking her questions, she would clam up. Part of me felt a twinge of guilt at this deliberate omission, and I vowed to be more forthright with Deputy Aiden just as soon as I had a chance to talk with Tess.

"What happened in Michigan for him to say that he left the state on bad terms?" Aiden asked.

"I don't know," I answered. "I left months before he did. I know he had very strict parents, and he was an only child in his family."

"That's unusual for the Amish," Lois said.

I nodded. "It could be that his parents could only have one. I don't know." I shifted my feet. "When I moved to that community to care for my sister Harriet, they didn't exactly welcome me with open arms. Because of that, I don't know the backstory of many people in that district. Ben was only eight when I moved there. His family lived next to my sister, and he helped me with the chores around her property. He accepted nothing in return for his kindness. Although he wouldn't take money, I was able to pay him with my cookies and pies."

"That's the kind of payment plan I would like to be on," Lois said.

"Was that all?" Aiden asked. "There was nothing else

in the letter that told you what may have happened in Michigan?"

I shook my head, relieved that he hadn't phrased his question, "there was nothing *else* in the letter." It was true that there had been no more about Michigan, and the way he'd stated the question saved me from mentioning Tess just yet.

"All right," he said with a nod and waved to Deputy Little, who stood a few feet away.

Deputy Little stepped over to us.

"Now," Deputy Aiden said. "I do need you to go home. You can't be here. You might compromise the investigation, and Captain Slate is already angry that you were on the scene in the first place. I trust you to leave, but just to make sure that you do . . ."

Deputy Little puffed up his chest and held out his arm in a grand sweep, encouraging us on our way. As we walked away from Deputy Aiden with Deputy Little, Lois whispered to me, "I think Deputy Aiden caught on that we are troublemakers."

"What was your first clue?" I asked.

We reached Lois's car, and Deputy Little stood there as we climbed in and buckled our seatbelts. Lois rolled down her window. "Little, you don't have to stand guard over us. We're leaving."

He shook his head. "I'm not making that mistake again. I need to make sure you both go."

Lois started to roll up the window, and he waved for her to stop. She lowered the window again. "What did we do this time?"

His Adam's apple bobbed up and down. "Are you going into Harvest?"

Lois cocked her head. "Sure are."

He reached into his pocket and withdrew a boxed deck of cards. It said "Rook" on the box. "I was going to give this to Charlotte Weaver at Swissmen Sweets today." He swallowed. "She mentioned that she likes to play Rook with her friends but misplaced her deck. I—I happened to be in a store where there was a set and picked it up for her. I'm going to be busy with this for a while and don't know when I'll see her. Can you give it to her?"

Lois took the deck. "Sure thing." With that she rolled up the window and pulled her car out onto the road.

She handed the deck to me. "That's a deck of trouble right there," Lois said.

I stared down at the deck. I couldn't agree more. Charlotte was the Amish cousin of Bailey King. She was not baptized in the church yet, but she was still Amish. I didn't know exactly what this deck of cards could mean for her, but I had my guesses.

We rode in silence as Lois drove us back to the Sunbeam Café. As we entered the center of the village, the square and the downtown area came into view. The square was a large plot of grass in the middle of four interconnecting streets. Main Street was one of those crossroads. Main Street was lined with small Amish shops, including a gift shop, cheese shop, pretzel shop, and Swissmen Sweets, the candy shop that Deputy Aiden's girlfriend ran. Large trees peppered the square's green, and right in the middle of the square sat a large white gazebo. It was a landmark in the village, and a place that many locals used when giving directions. On Church Street, which was on the opposite side of the square, there was the big white church with the purple front door, the local playground, and the

Sunbeam Café. Lois parked a few doors down from the café.

Much to my surprise, all the members of the Double Stitch were there. I could see them through the front window. They were bent over their quilting, and their mouths moved rapidly as they chattered, no doubt about the fire.

I tucked the Rook deck into the pocket of my apron. I would give it to Charlotte later. I certainly needed to talk to her about it. Months ago, she had asked me to match her with an Amish man, but now I wondered if that was what she really wanted.

Lois led the way inside the café.

"There they are," Raellen cried. "We were starting to become worried about you."

"Are the quilts lost?" Iris asked with tears in her eyes.

"I'm sorry, Iris," I said.

A tear spilled over her cheek. "It's my fault. It was my idea to sell our quilts at the flea market." She took a breath. "And now all of our hard work is lost."

"Iris, there was no way for you to know," said Leah Bontrager, another member of our group. Leah was just a little bit younger than I was and had a gift shop nearby. She and her husband ran the shop and had a large family with five children and eleven grandchildren. "Quilts can be replaced," she added. "It's the loss of life that cannot be undone."

Iris grabbed a napkin from the table to stifle a cry. "I know. I know. How can I be so horrible when Raellen has told us that Ben Baughman died in the fire?" She looked up at me with watery eyes. "Is it true, Millie?"

I settled into the empty chair at the table. "*Ya*, I am afraid that it's true."

"My word," Ruth Yoder cried. "I had thought for sure this would be another time that Raellen spouted off a rumor without checking the facts."

"I would never do that," Raellen cried, and threw up her hands. She almost knocked over Leah's coffee in the process.

The rest of us shared a look.

"I wouldn't!" Raellen insisted.

"Well, it is the truth," Lois said as she leaned on the counter. "And now Millie and I mean to do something about it."

Ruth's head whipped around in my direction. "What is this, Millie Fisher? I hope I am wrong in thinking that you and Lois plan to find out what happened to Ben."

Before I could answer, Lois piped up again. "You're not wrong. You are one hundred percent right. We are going to get to the bottom of who killed Ben."

"Shh, Lois," I said and glanced around the rest of the café. Bryan was at the window writing or making a big show of pretending to write, and there was a middle-aged *Englisch* couple in the back corner. Thankfully, we were in the café between the breakfast and lunch rush, so there weren't many people that might overhear Lois's outburst. Even so, I would rather not telegraph our plans to the entire county.

"No one can hear me," Lois said.

Bryan shifted in his hard, wooden chair. I knew he could.

I pressed my lips together.

Raellen leaned forward over the quilting in her lap.

"Who killed Ben? Does this mean that the fire wasn't an accident?"

"It most certainly was not," Lois said.

I rubbed my forehead. Lois knew that Raellen would shout the news all over the county the first chance she got.

"Lois, at least have a seat," I pleaded.

"Fine, fine," she said as she grabbed a ladder-back chair from a neighboring table.

Ruth shook her finger at me. "I told you, Millie, that Ben Baughman was up to something. Look at all those who have suffered."

"We don't know that the fire was started in order to kill Ben." The knot in my stomach turned as I said it. I wished that I still had the letter Ben had left me. I thought I remembered it well, but there could have been a line I might have forgotten or a hidden meaning that I might have picked up in a second reading.

There was no hope of getting it now that Phillip had eaten the letter. I loved my goats so much, but at times they certainly tried my very last nerve.

"You will have to find a way to prove it then, because as of right now, everyone in the district is thinking the same thing—that Ben is responsible," Ruth said.

I stared at her. "But he's dead. He can't be responsible."

"It's what people in the village are saying." She shrugged.

A knot twisted deep in my stomach. This was even worse than I'd expected it to be. But I understood why people in the village would wish that Ben was responsible for the fire. Because he was an outsider. If you can blame an outsider, you can make the problem go away. He made the perfect scapegoat.

I swallowed. "What are they saying, exactly?"

"That the fire was Ben's fault, and some are even saying that he was the one who started it."

"That's ridiculous. Why would he start the fire and then fall asleep?" Lois asked.

I folded my hands in my lap. "How can this already be the talk of the village? His body hasn't even left the flea market yet." I felt ill as I said this and was relieved that I hadn't seen Ben in death. That would have been too much to bear.

Now, I felt even more urgency to find out who'd set the flea market on fire. I might not have been able to help Ben as much as I wanted to when he was alive, but the very least I could do was to keep his reputation safe in death. As the saying went, "The best way to escape from your problem is to solve it."

Chapter Eleven

I could barely sit through the rest of the Double Stitch meeting. As soon as it was over, I was out the door. Lois followed me onto the sidewalk. "Millie, are you okay?"

I looked at my friend. "*Nee*, but I will be. I need time to think. There has to be a way we can stop this rumor about Ben from spreading."

"Solving the crime," she suggested.

I nodded. "That might be the only answer."

Darcy poked her head out the door. "Grandma, can you stay and help in the kitchen?"

"Darcy, honey, Millie needs me," Lois protested. "Put Bryan back to work. He doesn't look like he's writing much anyway."

"While you were gone, he dropped two trays. Honestly, I don't know why he is so nervous all the time." Darcy shook her head.

Lois and I shared a look. We knew why. It was because he was half in love with the curly-haired café owner.

"He needs to get some backbone," Lois said. "Or make more trips to the kitchen if he can't carry as much. Millie needs me."

"*Nee, nee*, go help your granddaughter," I said. "I promise I won't chase down any killer without you. I'm going to take this card deck to Charlotte and go home."

"You had better not." Lois put her hands on her hips in mock annoyance. "I can pick you up after the lunch shift and we can get sleuthing. I have a hankering to do some apple picking."

I smiled. "I do too," I said, knowing that she meant for us to go to the Lieb Orchard and track down Tess. That's what I meant to do too. "No matter how sour the apple, you have to bite into it, now and again."

"That's a good saying, Millie," Lois said as she went back inside the café.

After checking on Bessie, who had been tied to the hitching post on the street in front of the café for a long while now, I made my way across to the square. Although autumn typically brought much cooler weather to this region, the sun shone bright overhead and the air had a subtle warmth to it. As I went, I kept my eyes peeled for the square's temporary groundskeeper, Uriah Schrock. Part of me wanted to run into him, and another part of me did not.

Since I'd moved back to Holmes County, Uriah, who had been a classmate of mine over forty years ago, had made no secret of the fact he wanted to be friends again. Like anyone, I could use all the friends I could get, but I knew that when we were young Uriah had a crush on me. I didn't know if that was still the case, but I had my suspicions.

It felt like a betrayal of Kip in some way to be having such fond feelings for another man. I knew in my heart that Kip would not have wanted me to be alone for the rest of my life, but I had made peace with my widowhood over a decade ago. Since my husband's death, I had poured myself into helping others find their perfect match. I had that in Kip. I never expected to have it again. It seemed selfish to want such love more than once in this life.

But I couldn't deny that there was something about Uriah that made me smile, and that I found his attention flattering. It was no matter. He was only in Holmes County for a short time. He'd moved to Shipshewana when we were young, and there he'd met his wife. It was a *gut* match, he told me, even though I never met her. His children still lived in Indiana. He would return to them just as soon as he accomplished what he'd come back to the county to do. As of yet, he had not told me what that was. It was not the Amish way to pry into another person's business.

I made it across the square with no sign of Uriah. I let out a sigh of relief—or was it one of disappointment, or, most likely, a mix of the two? In the wake of Ben's passing, I knew Uriah, having lived as long as I had, would've been a source of comfort.

I waited for a bus full of tourists to load up and leave Swissmen Sweets before I crossed Main Street to the shop. I stepped inside the building and was greeted by a large white rabbit, a small orange cat, and a polka-dotted potbellied pig. Puff, Nutmeg, and Jethro, respectively.

"Oh my," Charlotte Weaver cried as I walked through the door. "It's you, Millie. Thank heavens. I thought it was that bus of tourists coming back inside." Both she and Emily stood behind the counter, looking absolutely exhausted.

"Busy morning?" I asked.

"The busiest," Charlotte said. A long strand of her bright red hair sprang out of the Amish bun at the nape of her neck.

Emily, on the other hand, although clearly tired, wasn't frazzled. Her blond hair was perfectly in place and her delicate features glowed.

I pointed to the animals at my feet. "I see you have the whole crew here. Where's Bailey and Clara?" I nodded at Jethro. "And what about Juliet Brook? Shouldn't he—Jethro—be with her?"

Jethro snuffled my feet and proceeded to sit on my right shoe. Puff seemed to think that was a grand idea and sat on my left shoe. Nutmeg turned his tail up at the three of us and pranced under one of the tables in the front of the shop, looking for customers. At the moment, there was no one at those tables, but I knew the shop must have been full to bursting when the bus was here.

Charlotte sighed dramatically. "Bailey is in New York filming for her television show, and Clara is visiting a friend. It's only Emily and I in the shop today. Usually on a fall weekday that's not a problem."

"We didn't know the bus was coming," Emily agreed.

"And Jethro is here because Juliet had some type of preacher's wife luncheon in Millersburg and they said that she couldn't bring her pig. Can you imagine that? Preacher's wife luncheons must be very stuffy." Charlotte shook her head.

"I had better go in the kitchen and make some more candies. The tourists completely wiped us out of fudge. It was nice to see you, Millie." Emily smiled as she went through the swinging door that led to the shop's kitchen.

I frowned, sorry to see her go. I wanted to talk to Emily about Ben. He had rented a room on her husband's Christmas tree farm, after all. I could talk to her before I left, and maybe it would be better if I was alone with Charlotte when I gave her the deck of cards. I wasn't sure how she was going to react to them.

"Ever since Bailey's show has been on television, we have been getting more and more busloads of tourists. They were mighty disappointed when it was just Emily and me here and no Bailey. Even so, they bought all the fudge and all the Jethro Bars."

"Jethro Bars?" I asked and glanced down at the pig on my foot.

"*Ya*," she said enthusiastically. "They are solid white chocolate bars with dark chocolate dots on them. Bailey made the mold, and they look just like Jethro. We can't keep them in the shop."

"Oh yes, Lois mentioned them to me," I said.

"Although most of them sell through the online store that Bailey set up. Yesterday, I mailed three dozen Jethro bars all the way to Alaska. Can you imagine? Someone living in Alaska knows who we are!"

"That is hard to imagine," I agreed as I carefully freed my feet from the clutches of the pig and rabbit.

Jethro grunted his disdain. It seemed my black walking shoe made a very nice pillow indeed.

"Charlotte, I have something for you. A friend asked me to give it to you."

Her green eyes went wide. "For me? No one ever has anything for me!"

I put my hand into my apron pocket and took out the

Rook deck. I held it over the domed glass counter to her. She stared at it.

"Would you like to take it?"

She wiped her hands on a tea towel and then took the deck of cards from me. "Are you sure these are for me?"

I nodded. "Do you know who they are from?"

"If they are for me, I do. Deputy Little and I were chatting about games the other day, and I mentioned that I had misplaced my Rook deck." After one more look, she tucked the deck into the pocket of her apron. "I might be in trouble, Millie."

"Are you in trouble or at a crossroads? Having to make a decision about what your life will be is not a trouble. It's part of life. Do you think you have put that decision off too long?"

She sighed. "I know I have. When I first left my community and my parents, I thought I would leave the Amish altogether. My experience growing up Amish was harsh and restrictive, but when I came to live with Cousin Clara, I saw that it could be different. Her district welcomed me. They let me travel to New York with Bailey for her show. They let me play the organ at Juliet's church. I thought maybe that's where I would always want to be. Then . . ."

"Then, you caught Deputy Little's eye."

She nodded. "He's such a kind man, but he's *Englisch* and a police officer to boot. I could never be Amish and be married to him." She dropped her head. "I don't know what to do."

"You asked me once if I would find an Amish match for you. Do you still want that?"

"I don't know, Millie. I think I have met my match. It's just not who I expected it to be."

"They rarely are," I said and smiled at her.

"I need to decide if I am brave enough to grab onto this chance at happiness." She lowered her voice and peered over her shoulder at the closed kitchen door. "I don't know if I am."

"Prayer and conversations with those who will not judge will help. Also, I am a big fan of a pro and con list."

She looked at me oddly. Ah, it seemed that Lois and all her *Englisch* words were rubbing off on me. "List all the *gut* things about making this choice and then list all the bad things," I explained. "I believe it is always better to go into a new way of life, knowing—as much as possible—what to expect. If for you, the *gut* outweighs the bad, you will know the choice you should make."

She patted the pocket where she'd tucked the deck of cards. "*Danki,* Millie. I have never had anyone put it to me like that. When I left my district, I just ran away without weighing the pros and cons. It was the right thing to do for me, but I wonder if it would have been easier if I'd thought of all the consequences that might have come from that choice."

I nodded. "Well, I am happy to be the one to deliver the cards."

"I am glad it was you too." She paused. "If you see Deputy Little soon, can you tell him *danki* for me?" She smiled. "I mean, can you tell him that I said thank you?"

"I will." I paused. "Would it be all right if I came around the counter and spoke with Emily in the kitchen?"

Her mouth made a little O shape. "It's about Ben Baughman, isn't it? A neighbor popped in just before the bus arrived and told us about the fire. I should have asked you about it straight off. My only excuse was the tourists. I'm so very sorry about Ben. Emily prayed it wasn't true. I think she is still holding onto that hope."

I frowned. "I hate to be the one to tell her, but maybe it's better coming from me. Deputy Aiden knows that Ben rented a room from the Keims."

She nodded. "Go on back."

Chapter Twelve

I stepped into the kitchen.

Emily didn't look up from the caramel she was stirring on a burner. "Charlotte, can you grab the sea salt for me?"

"Charlotte is still out front, but if you tell me where it is, I can fetch it."

She jumped. "Oh, Millie, I didn't expect it to be you, but, *ya,* the sea salt is in a large plastic container on the shelf there." She pointed at the wall. "You can't miss it."

I pulled it from the shelf and set the container on the counter next to her.

"*Danki.* I don't need it just yet, but I always like to have it handy when making salted caramel fudge. The salt has to go on top before everything hardens up."

I nodded. "Understood."

She continued to stir. "Are you here about Ben?" she asked.

"I'm afraid I am."

"I'm so sorry, Millie. I know that Ben was a *gut* friend of yours. He was a very nice young man."

"Was he a *gut* tenant?" I asked.

"*Ya*, but truthfully, Millie, I never saw him. He rented

a small room in the basement of my husband's *grossmaami's* house. I think in the few months that he lived there, I saw him no more than three times, and he was always just leaving. My husband tells me that he was working four jobs."

I nodded. "And one of them was the overnight guard at the flea market."

"That must be why I never saw him. I would already be here at the candy shop when he got home from that job, if he came home at all before going to the next one."

"Did he have any friends? Did anyone come to visit?"

She looked down at her caramel. "It's about ready. It doesn't take long to make. Bailey taught me to make caramel, and now it's one of my favorite things to do in the shop."

"Emily, did anyone visit him?"

She looked up at me as she took the pot off the burner and placed it on a trivet. She continued to stir it. "Not while he was there, but one day, someone came looking for him."

"Who was it?" I asked.

"It was a young *Englisch* man. He didn't give me his name, nor did I ask for it. I had the feeling he was looking for trouble. He wanted to know if Ben was there, and I said *nee*. He left right after that. I was glad. I was working in the garden at the time, and there was no one else on the farm but my grandmother-in-law. I went back in the house after that and didn't work on the garden again until my husband came home."

"Were you afraid of the young man?"

"I don't know if afraid is the right word, but he made me nervous. I felt he was watching my every move."

"What did he look like?"

She poured the cooling caramel over the top of a tray of chocolate fudge. She made a swirling pattern with it, and the caramel settled into a lovely design. She then sprinkled the salt I had brought her on top of it.

"He was *Englisch*," she said as she began a new pan of caramel. "It was on a hot day, and he wore a T-shirt with the sleeves rolled up. He had a tattoo on his arm."

"What was the tattoo of?" I asked.

"It was an apple. A bright red apple."

I blinked at her. I didn't know much about *Englischer* tattoos, but to me a red apple on a young man's arm seemed an odd choice.

I thanked Emily and left the kitchen. Charlotte was with a customer at the front of the store when I went out, and so I waved good-bye to her. I took a moment to say good-bye to the animals too. Jethro snuffled at the edge of my apron as if he hoped there would be some treats in my pocket. "None today, little pig," I said as I left.

Outside of Swissmen Sweets, I put my hands on my hips. I had at least another hour before Lois would be free to go to the apple orchard. I wondered if there could be some sort of connection between the man with the apple tattoo and the Liebs' orchard. Could he just be a fan of apples with no connection at all? It seemed unlikely.

In any case, I needed to get Bessie home if Lois was going to drive me around the county for the rest of this investigation. I was sure she would insist on it. I was certain that she was dying to escape the café so that she could return to sleuthing. She took being the sidekick to Amish Marple very seriously indeed. She was right; it was time that we came up with a *gut* code name for her.

I walked back across the square. Again, there was no

sign of Uriah. When I was in front of the Sunbeam Café, I spotted Lois through the window filling up people's mugs of coffee. The place was packed. It was a very *gut* thing that Darcy had asked her grandmother to help out. It appeared that Bryan had been conscripted into service too.

I walked to the hitching post, untethered Bessie, and climbed into the buggy. "Bessie girl, let's go home."

She turned around without so much as a flick of my reins.

The ride home was uneventful. It was a beautiful day in late September. The sky was bright blue, and the sun was high, but there was a coolness in the air now that reminded me that winter was well on its way. High at the tops of the trees, the leaves were beginning to change, and some had already fallen to the ground.

It would be October in a few days. My first year back in Holmes County had gone by so quickly. I had been apprehensive about moving back to Ohio, but now, months later, I knew it was the right decision. I was among friends. I had my large network of nieces and nephews close by, and I had found Lois again. The last of those might be the most impactful change.

I turned the buggy onto my long, gravel driveway and frowned. Typically, if I had been away for any length of time, the goats came running. They were nowhere to be seen. I drove Bessie back to the barn. She had had a long day already, so before going in search of Phillip and Peter, I put her in her stall with fresh water and feed.

After I latched Bessie's stall closed, I walked around the barn. There still was no sign of the goats. Now, I was worried.

"Phillip! Peter!" I called as I walked toward my little ranch house.

Much to my relief, Peter, the brown and white goat, came galloping around the house.

"Where have you been?"

He jumped in place and twirled around twice, then ran back around the house.

I wrinkled my nose and followed him. The goats were up to something. I just needed to find out what it was.

As soon as I came around the back of the ranch, I saw why the goats hadn't come running. They already had company. Tess Lieb sat on the bench beside my rock garden. This late in the season, the garden was a mixture of withered vines that needed to be pulled out and colorful mums that I'd tucked in between the rocks. I had a small fountain in one corner of the garden because the sound of running water soothed me. It seemed to soothe Tess Lieb too.

"I hope it was all right that I sat back here and waited for you," she said. "I didn't want anyone to see me from the road."

"But how did you get here?"

"My wagon and horse are on the other side of the barn. I made sure to hide them too."

I raised my brow. If I had just walked around the side of the barn, I would have seen the wagon and horse.

She licked her lips. "I was making an apple delivery and decided to stop to see if you were home. Then, your buggy came up the driveway. I am so glad that you returned home before I had to leave. I am spending too much time away from the orchard as it is. My *daed* will soon notice that it's taken far longer than it should to deliver my load of apples to the grocer in Harvest. Even so, I had to stop and see you. You are the only one who can understand."

"Understand what?" I asked.

"What I've lost." Tears were in her eyes, and I knew that she spoke of Ben. Obviously, she'd already heard of his death.

"I'm so very sorry, Tess."

She nodded and smiled at Phillip and Peter. "Your goats have been entertaining me while I waited. They are very fine goats. They have kept me from thinking too much. Although I can't seem to stop."

Phillip bounced in place and Peter shook his head back and forth when they heard her praise. If I didn't know better, I would say they understood what she said. Ruth Yoder's voice popped into my head: "Animals can't understand humans!" Ruth Yoder never had goats like mine.

"You shouldn't expect yourself to be able to do that. It only just happened."

Her face fell. "You mean Ben."

I sat next to her on the bench. "I am sorry."

A tear rolled down her face. "I thought he was the man I was going to marry, but now . . . that's not going to happen. I can't believe he's gone. I don't know what to do. I don't have any choices now."

"Choices about what?" I asked.

She pressed her lips together and didn't answer.

I patted her hand. "Ben cared for you very much."

She swallowed. "I know he did. I cared about him too.

I wanted to stay here, and he was going to make that possible."

"What do you mean?"

"My *daed* didn't dislike Ben just because he was an outsider. That didn't help, but my *daed* didn't want anyone to court me."

I blinked. This was surprising news. Tess was at an age that she would be thinking of her future and marriage. Why would her father want to keep her from doing that?

"It's because of a promise he made to his sister," she said with a sigh. "My *daed* wants to send me to Wyoming. My *aenti* married a man out there, and now they have triplets, only a few months old. She doesn't have any family there and asked my *daed* if he could spare me. I am the oldest unmarried daughter in the family and would be the most help to her."

"He would send you even if you don't want to go?"

"He would. My *aenti's* husband came to Holmes County once, met my *aenti,* and the two fell in love. My *daed* was furious when she left. She was always his favorite sister. They had a terrible fight when she moved away. I believe he's trying to make amends for that now by sending me out there. It's not fair that I have to be the one to make up for his mistakes."

"Did you and Ben hope to marry and go there together?"

She removed a piece of cloth from her pocket and twisted it in her lap. "*Nee*, that would never have done. There wouldn't have been enough work there for Ben, and as hard as it's been for him to blend into the Amish community here, it would have been even more difficult there. The community is very small. There are only seven families. And my *aenti* can be demanding. She would not want me to move there as a married woman because it would distract me from caring for her children."

"Did you tell your *daed* that you don't want to go?" I asked.

"Many times, but it makes no difference. He made up his mind months ago, and now I have to leave in October."

"That's next week."

"I know," she whispered.

"Ben was the reason you wanted to stay in Harvest?"

"In part. Also, my *aenti*, she can be harsh and difficult. I know if I go to Wyoming, I will be miserable. She was hard on me when she was here and lived in our house. It will be worse living in her home and taking care of her babies." She took a breath. "And I think she only wants me to go there so she will have someone to order around. The babies are too young now. I do feel for them when they get older. She is a difficult person to get along with. She is much like my father in that way."

"Doesn't your father know that she's harsh?" I asked.

"He does, but that's not what's important to him. He says that it is our duty to take care of family, even if the person made a poor decision. He still believes that his sister made a big mistake by marrying and moving so far away from everyone and everything she knows." She took a breath. "But it was her choice. Not mine. I shouldn't have to suffer for it." She stood up. "I won't go!" There was sternness in her voice that hadn't been there before. "If he tries to make me go, I will run away. I will become *Englisch* if I must. Just because Ben is dead—" Her voice caught. "Just because he's gone, that does not mean my father wins this argument."

There was a question that I needed to ask her, and I didn't see any gentle way to put it. "Your *daed* thinks Ben was the one keeping you here." I took a breath. "Would he have killed Ben so that you would go?"

Tess opened and closed her mouth as she seemed to consider my question. "He . . . he would never do that. My *daed* is a *gut* man. He's strict, but *gut*. He would never kill anyone. I . . . there would be no reason for him to do that." She shook her head. "I've been away from the orchard for far too long. I must go."

"Why did you come here, Tess?" I stood up from the bench too. "What's your real reason?"

She stared at me with her big brown eyes. "I—I wanted to talk to someone about Ben, someone who would miss him too. No one I know cares that he's gone. Perhaps my family is even relieved. They never gave him a chance, and that wasn't fair." She took a breath. "I know you must be thinking what my father thought—that I fell in love with Ben in order to avoid going to Wyoming. That's not true. What is true is that he would not want me to go. Because it's not what I want. He told me so many times that just because we are Amish, that doesn't mean we can't make our own lives or have our own ideas. No one ever told me that before. I'm going to do both of those things in his honor."

"As you should," I said.

Chapter Thirteen

An hour after Tess left, Lois's car rolled up the driveway. I was sitting in the backyard sipping a cup of coffee when the goats took off for the front of the house.

I stood up and watched them career around the side of the building. "So you will run and greet Lois, but not me. I see how you two are," I muttered, setting my empty mug on the small table in the garden, and walking at a much slower pace around the side of the house.

Lois waved the goats away. "Calm down, you two. You saw me yesterday. No hoof marks on my sweater!"

The goats backed off, but jumped in place as if Lois was in on whatever game they were playing.

"Millie, I don't agree with Ruth Yoder often, but those goats are too much to handle. I think they got it in their heads that they are puppies by the way they romp about," Lois said.

"Puppies are more sedate than these two. Puppies sleep. These two go all day."

"It's a wonder you get any rest."

"They don't go in the house. Even if I wanted to let

them inside, Peaches would chase them out. He's a very territorial kitten."

Lois laughed. "Oh, my word, I thought I was never going to escape the café. It seemed like every person who came in wanted to talk about the flea market fire. It's a very hot topic all over the village. Are you ready to go to the orchard and get to the bottom of it?"

"I don't think we should go to the orchard today. It would be better to wait for tomorrow."

"Wait, why? You were all for it earlier."

I told her about Tess's visit. "I don't want to make more trouble for Tess today. It's likely that her father reprimanded her for coming home late from the market. I don't want him to think that her detour was in any way related to me. That will only put her in more hot water."

Lois frowned. "I was really looking forward to doing some sleuthing this afternoon."

"We can still do that. It would be helpful to find out where Ben went after he left the flea market yesterday morning."

"You said he went to work."

"*Ya,* but at some point he stopped here to tuck that note in my door too. When was that?"

"How are we going to find out?" she asked. "I doubt his employers are going to be running forward about his comings and goings when there are so many rumors about him and the fire flying around."

"Emily's husband, Daniel Keim, is our best hope." Briefly, I told her about my conversation with Emily. "Emily might not know the other places where Ben worked, but I think if Ben told anyone, it would be Daniel. They are about the same age."

"Don't you think Deputy Aiden has already checked that?" Lois asked.

"I'm sure he has, but he would have no reason to tell us what he learned. He doesn't want us to have anything to do with the investigation."

Lois shook her head in mock sadness. "He doesn't know us very well, now, does he?"

"I think he's starting to get an idea of who we are." I smiled.

"Between us and Bailey poking our noses into his police investigations, he has his hands full."

He did indeed.

"And we can pick apples tomorrow morning?" Lois asked hopefully.

I nodded. "You bet."

She laughed. "You're starting to talk like me, Millie!"

After telling the goats to behave themselves, Lois and I climbed into her car.

"You don't have to tell me how to get to the Keim Christmas Tree Farm. I got my tree there last year and know exactly where to find it."

I nodded and settled back in the seat.

Before I knew it, Lois turned down the bumpy driveway that led to the Keims' farm. Thad Keim and his son Daniel ran the place, and Thad's ailing grandmother lived in the *daadihaus* on the extensive property. The Keims had one of the biggest stretches of land in the county. They had to. Growing trees takes up a lot of space.

As we bumped down the driveway, the large house, *daadihaus*, and barn came into view. According to Emily, Ben's room had been in the *daadihaus,* where Grandma Leah, Thad's grandmother, lived. I had heard that she was feeling poorly of late. I hoped that we wouldn't have to disturb her in order to see Ben's living space.

Behind the buildings, there were fir and pine trees as far as the eye could see. Some were ready for Christmas decorations, and others were just saplings.

"Do you think that Daniel is out in the Christmas trees?" Lois asked. "There are so many rows. I don't know how we would find him."

I was about to answer when a tall young man came out from around the side of the house. He had an Amish beard that indicated he was married, but the beard wasn't very long. He and Emily would have only been married for a year in January.

"I guess we don't have to go looking," I said.

Daniel walked up to our car, wiping his hands on an oily cloth. "*Gude nammidaag,* Ladies." He looked at his hands. "I was just in the barn trying to fix an old tractor motor," he said as if he needed to explain his dirty hands.

"I remember when Kip was running our farm," I said. "It seems to me that he spent just as much time mowing as fixing the mower."

Daniel nodded. "That sounds about right." He paused. "We don't get that many visitors out here before the holiday season. Are you trying to get a jump on your tree hunt?"

"Always," Lois said. "It will be October next week. You can never stake out your tree too soon."

Daniel nodded. "I believe the same."

I glanced at my friend. "Lois might be in the market for a tree, but I would like to speak to you about Ben Baughman."

The jovial expression fell from his face. "Ben. That's

a terrible shame. I never would have pegged him for someone one who'd cause so much commotion. If I had, we wouldn't have let him live here." He shook his head. "And to think he was renting the basement room under my great-grandmother's house this whole time."

"Whoa, whoa, whoa!" Lois said, holding up her hands in the universal stop sign. "Do you think that Ben started the flea market fire?"

Daniel's face turned a deep red. "I . . . I . . . that's what I was told."

"Told by who?" I asked.

"Well, by Tobias Leib. He's a tree man, too, and his orchard is just a little ways from here. He stopped to tell me that the flea market was closed and about the fire. He mentioned that Ben killed himself in the fire."

"That's a terrible lie," Lois said. "Ben didn't start that fire to kill himself."

Daniel swallowed hard. "It's just what I was told. Tobias usually knows what's going on in the county, so I took his word for it. I was so very sorry to hear it. I liked Ben. He was always a *gut* tenant. He paid his rent on time and was willing to chip in around the farm when he could. To be honest, he wasn't here all that often."

I frowned as I listened to Daniel's story. What could Tobias hope to gain by spreading such a horrible rumor? Even if the police denied Tobias's words, I knew some Amish would continue to believe his account simply because they'd heard it from a reputable Amish man. Was his aim to upset his already grieving daughter? If that was it, I couldn't imagine anything more cruel.

"It would be a great help, Daniel, if you would tell people that isn't true, Ben didn't set the fire," I said.

"Oh," Daniel said uncertainly. "I've never known Tobias to be misinformed."

"This time he may be blinded by his family situation."

Daniel pressed his lips together. "Because of Tess?"

I nodded.

"I see," Daniel said. "I won't repeat it again."

I wasn't surprised by Daniel's change of heart. He knew what it was like to be a young couple in love and without approval. Emily's family had not wanted them to marry. They had gone ahead anyway, but it had been at a cost. Emily's brother and sister had cut her off and hardly spoke to her now. It was heartbreaking to see division in families like that. I wished I could say that the Amish were immune to such conflict, but we were not.

"*Danki*," I said. "Lois and I are trying to find out where Ben went yesterday. We thought you might know the places where he worked."

Ben rubbed the oily cloth over the back of his hand, but it had no effect. His hand was as black as ever. "Ben worked at several places. There was the flea market, of course. He also stocked shelves at the grocer in Harvest. And I think he worked a couple construction jobs, but I don't know where or with whom. Like I said, I rarely saw him because he worked so much, and, when I did, I didn't question him about his movements. As long as he was respectful of my family and farm and paid his rent, I wasn't interested in much else from him."

Lois and I shared a look.

"Have the police been here?" Lois asked.

"The police? Why would they come here?"

"They might want to see the place where Ben lived to look for clues, just like us," she answered.

He wrinkled his nose. "*Nee*, and I hope they don't come. My father would not like it."

His comment reminded me that I had heard rumors that Daniel had run into some trouble with the law last year. It was before I moved to Harvest, so I didn't know all the particulars.

"Can we have a look at Ben's room?" I asked.

Daniel studied me. "*Ya*." He paused. "I know it seems crass, but I don't know what to do with his things. He doesn't have any family in the area that I can call."

"I'm the closest person to family he had nearby. I can take a look and make suggestions, but I would hold onto everything for a little while yet. Lois is right. I would not be surprised if the police come here and ask to look around."

He scowled at this comment.

I didn't mention that I was the one who'd told Deputy Aiden that Ben lived at the Christmas Tree Farm. Daniel didn't need to know that tiny fact.

"I'll show you where he was staying." Daniel turned and walked toward the *daadihaus*.

Lois and I followed him. She leaned close to me. "What do you think Tobias's game is, spreading a rumor like that?"

I shook my head. "I don't know. Now that Ben's dead, there doesn't seem much point in his continuing to punish Ben or trying to ruin his reputation."

There was a white door on the side of the house. Daniel pointed at it. "This leads down to the room he was renting. The room has its own entrance, so the tenant doesn't bother my great-grandmother with his comings and goings. It's not locked. I don't think Ben ever locked it," Daniel said. "You are welcome to go down and look."

Lois went first, and I followed behind her. When I reached the bottom floor, I could hardly see. The only light in the space was provided by two small basement windows, but they were half obscured by large bushes outside the house.

"Wait, I got it." Lois rooted around in her massive purse and came up with a large flashlight. When she turned it on, it was almost like daylight in the basement.

"How on earth does that fit in there?"

"Oh, I can fit anything in my bag. It's almost like a magician's hat."

I wrinkled my brow, not sure what she meant by that. Then I looked around the room. It was sparse, worse than sparse actually. The only furniture in the room was a single bed, which was neatly made. An upside-down milk crate served as a bedside table. There were pegs on the wall to hang clothes and other items to keep them off the concrete floor, but that was it.

"He didn't have anything," Lois said.

I glanced at her. I had been thinking the same thing. Ben had few possessions. Of course, in the pursuit of a simple life, the Amish didn't have as many things as the *Englisch*, but I had expected to find a few books. Maybe even a trinket from his life back in Michigan. There was nothing. The only personal items in the room were a pair of boots and an extra set of clothes that hung from the pegs.

Daniel stepped into the room. "Ben was the first person to inquire about the room, and Emily wanted to do more to make it homey for him. She offered him a rug and a side table. He turned all of them down. He asked us not to go to any fuss since he would be working so much. He said this was just a place to sleep."

I frowned.

"And I noticed, too, he didn't have many things." He paused as if considering what he was about to say next. "He was almost like an Amish runaway. You know, when they leave the faith with just the clothes on their back, but Ben was Amish, so it couldn't be that."

"Did Ben have so little when he lived with you, Millie?" Lois asked.

I frowned. "I suppose I didn't pay attention to what he carried with him. He came late at night, and I showed him the guest room. He only stayed a few weeks, and I never went into his room during that time."

Now, I wished I had paid better attention to Ben while he was in my house. Something strange must have been going on with him.

In the corner of the room, a door creaked open. I saw the cane first, and then Grandma Leah stepped through the door. I had been so overwhelmed by the sparseness of Ben's room, I hadn't noticed the tiny door that was an entrance to the basement bedroom from the house.

"Grandma Leah!" Daniel hurried over to his great-grandmother, who I guessed was over one hundred years old. "You shouldn't be out of bed. You know *Daed* wanted you to rest today, since you are insisting on going to church on Sunday."

Her white hair was in a loose bun at the nape of her neck, as if she'd twisted it into the knot as an afterthought. Her plain dress hung on her slight frame. I hadn't seen her in many weeks, and it broke my heart to see how frail she had become. Even so, there was snap and sparkle in her eyes. She pointed her cane at her great-grandson. "I'm not dead yet. Don't you try to rush me off to my grave."

Daniel ducked his head.

"It's nice to see you again, Millie Fisher," Grandma Leah said. "And this must be Lois Henry. Ruth Yoder made sure to tell me that the two of you were getting in trouble again just like the old days. She's concerned."

"Ruth must have had a slow news week when she told you that," Lois said.

"Maybe so," Grandma Leah said with a nod. "Not like this week." She shook her head. "I feel awful about Ben. He was a *gut* boy, but a troubled one. He told me so much about his life in Michigan. He had a hard go of it, and it just doesn't seem right that this was how it ended for him. He had so much hope that things were about to turn around."

Part of me felt envy well up. I knew Ben, and I'd known him in Michigan. Why did he go to Grandma Leah and not to me? I could have been a sympathetic ear.

"He was head over heels for the Lieb girl," Grandma Leah said. "It was the real thing. Didn't you see, Millie?" she asked as she pointed her cane at me.

I nodded. I had believed it was the real thing too—at least on Ben's side. Now that I knew Tess had hoped to use marrying Ben to keep her father from forcing her to move to Wyoming, I was not as sure of her feelings for him. They might have been confused, at least partly, a means to an end.

"Did Ben tell you what happened in Michigan that made him come here?" I asked.

She looked at me. "I thought you knew."

I shook my head.

"Ben was kicked out of his home. His father remarried, and the new wife chased him out."

I stared at her. "What? How? I've never heard of something like that in the Amish community."

Grandma Leah leaned on her cane. "You would have if you'd lived as long as I have. Ben said his new stepmother turned his father against him and chased him away. She said it was time he moved out on his own and they needed the space for her four small children. Ben came to Holmes County because he was too embarrassed to stay in his community in Michigan once that happened. He came here for one reason."

Lois and I leaned forward. "What reason was that?" I asked.

Grandma Leah looked me straight in the eye. "You. He came here because of you."

Chapter Fourteen

I stared at her. "Me?"

Grandma Leah leaned on her cane. "Of course, you. He told me how kind you were to him when you were in Michigan and how you told him stories about Harvest. When he had no place to go, Harvest sounded like the perfect location for him to start over." Tears gathered in her wrinkled eyes. "I wish he had really gotten that chance. He was a *gut* man and had his whole life in front of him."

"Did Ben tell you all the places he was working?" Lois asked.

"I know he worked for the grocer in Harvest and the flea market. He also worked at Miller's Lumberyard. He worked very long days."

Lois and I shared a look. Now, at least we had three of the four places where Ben had worked figured out.

Grandma Leah put a hand to her back. "This old body can't keep up with me. I think I will go sit down."

Daniel was at his great-grandmother's side. "Let me help you upstairs, Grandma Leah."

She eyed him. "Usually I don't like being coddled, but

this time I will allow it. Walking down those steps took more out of me than I would care to admit."

Daniel's face creased with concern.

"We can show ourselves out the back door," Lois said. "Thank you both for your time."

Daniel nodded and helped his grandmother to the door that led into the house. Lois and I listened as they slowly made their way up the creaky steps.

"If I live to be one hundred, I want to be just like Grandma Leah," Lois said.

I smiled at her. "Amish and living in a *daadihaus* on your grandson's Christmas tree farm?"

"No," she said slowly. "But full of spunk."

"I have no doubt you will be just that." I knelt and peeked under Ben's bed.

"What are you doing?" Lois asked.

"Looking for clues. Isn't that what Amish Marples are supposed to do?"

She handed me her flashlight. "You bet," she said, going over to the clothes on the wall and checking the pockets.

I shone the flashlight under the bed but didn't see anything more than some extra-large dust bunnies. They were dust bunnies that would rival Puff the rabbit in size, and she was no tiny bunny. I peered under the mattress too. Still nothing. My knees creaked when I stood up. "Nothing."

"You might have found nothing, but I have something right here." Lois pulled a note from the pocket of the trousers on the wall. "It's a letter."

"*Gut* work. Let's take it into the light."

"Right," Lois said. "I don't want Grandma Leah to

come down here and chase us out with her cane. I bet she can pack a wallop with that."

As I emerged from the basement, I blinked against the bright sunlight.

"Ugh." Lois held her hand in front of her eyes. "Now I know what it must feel like to be a vampire."

I shook my head. "Can I see the letter?"

She handed it to me. It was a simple piece of lined notebook paper in a plain white envelope. Both the envelope and the paper had been folded many times, so the paper's fibers were soft at the creases.

"Dear Ben, Your new mother and I believe it is best if you leave the community. We plan to have children of our own, and your presence here will only be a distraction. It's time you made your own way. Enclosed is fifty dollars. Take care, son. Your father."

Lois cleared her throat. "That's one of the most depressing letters I have ever heard. How could his father just kick him out like that? It's so cruel."

The money wasn't in the envelope. I imagined Ben had spent that long ago on his food or rent. I frowned. Poor Ben. It was a cruel way to leave home. I knew of parents who had asked their children to leave before, but in all those cases it had been the best decision for both the family and the child. I wasn't sure that was true in this case.

Lois and I walked back to her car just as a sheriff's department SUV turned into the Keims' driveway. Deputy Aiden was driving with Deputy Little in the passenger seat.

"Uh oh," Lois said. "We are about to get a talking-to."

I knew she was right.

As the two young deputies climbed out of the vehicle, neither one of them was smiling. Deputy Aiden walked toward us with Deputy Little a few steps behind him, as usual. "Millie, Lois, what are the two of you doing here?"

"It's never too early to be looking at Christmas trees," Lois said.

Deputy Aiden folded his arms. "Oh really. You're here about the Christmas trees? You're not here because this was where Ben Baughman lived?"

"You know that's the case, deputy." I saw no reason to lie about it. "We were just in his room and found this." I handed him the letter.

He raised his brow. "Another mysterious letter?"

"I thought I would give you this one before the goats got to it."

He nodded. "Thank you for that." He opened the letter, read it, and refolded it. "So Ben was asked to leave Michigan?"

"Could that have something to do with his death?" Lois asked.

"Is there anyone else from Michigan here in Holmes County?" the deputy asked.

I shook my head. "Not that I know of."

"Bag this, Little." Deputy Aiden held the letter out to the younger officer. Deputy Little clumsily took it from his hand and put it in a plastic bag.

"Why are you here?" Deputy Aiden asked.

"Because there are rumors flying around the county that Ben was the one who started that fire. Lois and I want to find out what really happened so we can stop those rumors."

He sighed. "I know about the rumors, but they are

wrong," Deputy Aiden said. "The lantern was thrown from outside the building. It's impossible that Ben would stand outside the flea market, throw the lantern, and then go inside and fall asleep while the fire took off. Self-preservation would have kicked in."

"But it's not completely impossible," Lois said, "if he was suicidal."

Deputy Aiden frowned. "There are other ways to kill yourself that are much quicker and less painful. Do either of you have a reason to believe he wanted to end his life?"

"*Nee*. He had a lot to live for and was working hard for his future with . . ."

He narrowed his eyes. "With who?"

"With his work. He enjoyed work," Lois jumped in. "You would have to, working as many jobs as he did."

He frowned as if he didn't quite believe her. "If the two of you are keeping a secret from me, I will find it out."

Lois laughed. "We would never do that."

I rubbed my forehead. Lois was laying it on a little too thick. I was certain that Deputy Aiden knew it too. He was a very smart man.

"I believe when we get the official report back from the coroner, it will prove that Ben could not have killed himself," Deputy Aiden said.

"I'm glad you don't think he did, and, in my heart, I know you are right, but it doesn't change the fact that a large portion of the Amish community believes Ben set the fire."

"Unfortunately, even if the coroner clears Ben, I'm not sure the rumors will go away. People choose to believe what they want," Deputy Aiden said. "It's something I learned a long time ago in law enforcement. You can have all the evidence in the world, but if public opinion differs from the facts, there's not much you can do to change their minds."

"Maybe in some cases," I said. "But I have to believe that if the real culprit is caught, then the community will no longer vilify Ben."

Deputy Aiden nodded. "I plan to find the person responsible for the fire. The way Ben was killed was brutal. Even though we don't know if the culprit intended to kill him or not, his death isn't any less horrible. He deserves justice. The question is whether the arsonist aimed to kill Ben or just destroy the building."

Deputy Aiden looked as if he wanted to lecture us even more, but he was interrupted when two shiny black buggies turned into the Keims' long driveway. The first buggy was a two-seat courting buggy with two wheels on each side of it. A middle-aged Amish man in black trousers and a blue work shirt jumped out of the courting buggy. Just as soon as his feet hit the grass, he reached back into the buggy and pulled out a notebook and a pen.

Behind us, I heard the front screen door of the Keims' house bang closed, but I didn't turn around to see who was there. I was far more curious about what was happening right in front of me.

The man in the blue work shirt smiled. "Hello, I'm making a buggy delivery today. Is there a Ben Baughman here?"

I gasped, and Lois grabbed my arm as if she thought I might need support.

Chapter Fifteen

Deputy Aiden took a step forward. "That buggy is Ben's?"

The Amish visitor eyed Deputy Aiden, clearly uncomfortable talking to him. The sheriff's deputy appeared very intimidating in his navy uniform, with a holster hung at his hip too.

The man gripped his suspenders. "*Ya*, he bought it from my shop, and we just finished it this morning. I thought I would surprise him by delivering it early. He wasn't expecting it for another week."

"What's your name?" I asked.

He turned to me and appeared to be relieved to be addressing someone who wasn't wearing a badge. "Frederick Kline. I own Kline's Buggies in Sugarcreek." He looked around. "Do I have the right place? This is the address Ben gave me."

"You have the right place," Deputy Aiden said. "When did Ben order the buggy?"

Frederick Kline turned his attention back to the deputy. "He put the order in just about four months ago. He's been paying me in installments every other week for all that time."

A teenager hopped out of the other much-larger buggy and watched us.

"Who's that with you?" Deputy Aiden asked.

Frederick glanced over his shoulder. "That's my son John." He frowned. "If I'm in the right place, can I leave the buggy here? I must return to my shop. We have a lot of buggies that are in for service as everyone is getting ready for winter."

"It's clear he doesn't know Ben is dead," Lois whispered to me or thought she whispered. But she'd spoken loudly enough to get Frederick's attention because his head swiveled in our direction.

"Dead? Ben Baughman is dead? Is that why you are all staring at me like you have seen a ghost?"

Deputy Aiden scowled at Lois, but she only shrugged in reply. The deputy rubbed his forehead as if Lois's telling Frederick that Ben was dead had caused him an instant headache.

"Ben was killed in an accident yesterday," Deputy Aiden said.

"What accident?" Frederick asked. "Was he hit by a drunk driver? That seems to be happening more and more. I know because I have to try to fix the buggies that are hit."

I shivered at that.

"No," Deputy Aiden said. "He died at the Harvest Village Flea Market."

He covered his mouth. "In the fire? Everyone in Holmes County is talking about it. Ben was in that? How awful. That is just terrible. He was a *gut* young man. Never late on the payment for his courting buggy. It's a terrible shame. I had even asked him to come and work for me, so I could teach him the craft of buggy making. He told me that he already had more work than he could handle."

"You had better take the buggy back to the shop then," Deputy Aiden said.

"I can't do that. It's paid for," Frederick said. "So I don't feel *gut* about keeping it. He must have family who would want it. It's a top-of-the-line buggy. Some of my best work, in fact. Ben wanted a buggy to impress."

To impress Tess's father, I realized. I didn't know how it was possible, but I felt even worse about Ben's death after learning about the buggy. He wasn't ready to die. He had been preparing for the next stage of his life, and he had wanted that stage to include beautiful Tess Lieb. The courting buggy proved to me that he would go to great lengths to win both Tess and her father over.

"Paid for? That must have cost him a fortune. How much does an Amish courting buggy cost?" Lois asked.

Frederick looked as if he didn't want to answer, but Deputy Aiden spoke up. "I would say anywhere from five to eight thousand dollars new. Is that right, Frederick?"

The buggy maker nodded. "That sounds about right."

"This is why Ben lived like a pauper in the basement of Grandma Leah's house," Lois whispered to me. "He was spending all his money on this buggy."

I gave a slight nod and was relieved that this time Lois had whispered quietly enough so that no one else overheard what she said.

"When was the last time you saw Ben?" Deputy Aiden asked.

Frederick rocked back on his heels. "That would have

been when he came in with his last payment, which was a month ago. I told him that the buggy wouldn't be done for another four to six weeks yet, and he could give me the last payment then, but he said that he wanted to take care of it while he was at the shop." He took a breath. "It was a brief visit. He said he had to get to work."

"Work where?" Deputy Aiden asked.

Frederick shook his head. "He didn't say. I'm so sorry about Ben, but I have to get back to my shop. I'm behind on orders and repairs as it is." He waved his son over, and the young Amish teenager started to untether the horse from Ben's buggy.

"How was Ben going to drive the buggy without a horse? He didn't buy a horse, too, did he?" I asked.

"Not as far as I know," Frederick said. "Ben said that he had a friend who had an old mare that he knew she would let him borrow."

The moment he said that, I knew the old mare was Bessie, and that made the friend me. Oh Ben, I would have happily lent you Bessie for your courting buggy, and now, I'll never get the chance.

The screen door to the *daadihaus* opened, and Daniel came out. He walked up to us just as Frederick's son released the horse from the buggy and walked it back to the other horse. Daniel put his hands on his hips. "What's going on here?"

Deputy Aiden gave him a brief summary of the conversation.

"I can't take the buggy," Daniel said. "If it's Ben's, it should go to his family."

"Ben doesn't have any family in Ohio," I said.

"Then, it should go to you, Millie," Daniel said. "You are the closest thing to family that Ben had around here."

"What am I going to do with a courting buggy?"

"I'm not taking it back to my shop," Frederick said. His tone held finality.

"Then take it to Millie's farm. I don't want it here. It would be wrong to keep it," Daniel said, then turned to me. "You should take the buggy, Millie. You can at least hold onto it until we hear from Ben's family. They might want it or want to sell it."

I nodded. The buggy rightfully belonged to Ben's father. I certainly had enough room to store it in my barn until he made a decision about it. I looked to Deputy Aiden for his approval.

"I have no objection to this," the deputy said.

Frederick waved his son back toward the courting buggy and gestured that the teen should bring the horse with him. "We can deliver it to your farm as long as it's not too far from here."

"It's not far at all," I said and recited the directions.

"All right," Frederick said and looked to his son. "Hook the horse back up to the buggy. We have to deliver it to another place."

John didn't question his father but just did what he was told.

"*Danki* for doing this," I said to Frederick. "It's very kind of you to deliver the buggy to my farm. I know that wasn't part of your plan today."

"*Nee*, it wasn't, but it's no trouble. Ben was a good egg. I hate to hear what happened to him, but I'm glad that his buggy will reach his family. That does give me some comfort."

The teen finished hooking up the horse, and he went back to the second buggy. Frederick climbed into the courting buggy. He looked down at me. "I'll just park the buggy beside the barn if that's all right."

"That's just fine," I said.

"Be careful of the goats when you're there," Lois called.

Frederick's brow wrinkled, but he didn't say anything to that.

I gave Lois a look.

"What?" she asked. "The man deserves to be warned."

Frederick turned the horse around in the yard. The two buggies headed down the county road in the direction of my farm.

"Daniel, we need to talk to you about Ben before we leave," Deputy Aiden said.

"I thought that was why you were here," Daniel said with a frown. He turned and started walking toward the house.

Lois tugged on my arm. "I think that's our cue."

Deputy Aiden stepped in front of us. "Before you go, I want you both to remember one very important thing."

"What's that?" Lois asked. Her hand was still on my arm.

"Arsonists are a different breed. Fire is very difficult to control, and an arsonist likes that he doesn't know what will happen when the flame is lit. That's not the type of person to trifle with. I'd much rather you not get involved, but since I know telling you not to interfere is a waste of my breath, I will say be careful. Very careful."

I shivered as the two deputies walked away in the direction of the house.

Chapter Sixteen

"Where to now?" Lois asked as we turned onto the street.

"Let's start with the grocery market," I said. "The owner is much more likely to talk to us about Ben than anyone at Miller's Lumberyard is."

"Are we not going to Miller's Lumberyard at all?"

I shook my head. "We will go. I just need a plan before we do."

"If anyone can come up with one, it's you, Millie."

"Millie? I'm surprised you didn't call me Amish Marple."

"Well, I don't want to overuse it and wear it out. It's such a great name. It needs lasting power."

I sighed.

A few minutes later, she turned her car into the gravel parking lot beside Harvest Market. It was the middle of a weekday, and there were a number of buggies and horses on the hitching posts as well as a few cars in the lot. Lois parked beside a minivan. The inside of the store was always much more crowded than the parking lot would lead you to believe. Many villagers walked or rode bicycles to pick up their groceries.

In Harvest, this was the place to shop. It was the kind of store where there was one kind of ketchup or pickle, and things were sold in bulk. If you wanted any more options or smaller portions, it was up to you to find a ride to a larger town or the county seat of Millersburg. There were many *Englisch* living in Harvest, but it was primarily an Amish village. The Amish were content with fewer choices and liked to purchase bulk sizes for the sake of economy.

"I wonder if I should text Darcy to see if she needs anything for the café while we are here," Lois said. "Her apple pie has been a real crowd pleaser. I wonder if we're low on cinnamon."

I didn't have time to answer her because I was nearly knocked over by a woman in Mennonite dress storming out of the store. She had a canvas bag on her arm, which she swung in her haste to get away from the building. She hit me in the hip with it. "Oh." She stopped. "I'm so sorry. I wasn't watching where I was going." She glared back at the store. "It's no wonder. Are you all right?"

I rubbed the spot where she had hit me. There might be a bruise there later. My body wasn't as resilient as it had once been. "I'll be fine." I cocked my head. "Didn't I see you at the flea market yesterday?"

"Probably, yes. It's where I work."

"You have a booth there?" Lois asked. "What is it you sell? I hope your stock wasn't lost in the fire."

"No, I work for the owner. I'm the office manager of the flea market. As you can imagine, right now everything and everyone is up in arms over the fire. But we will rebuild."

"On the same spot?" Lois asked.

"Yes, I think so. I'm glad you're not hurt. I must be on my way." She shuffled by me.

Lois watched her go. "Who was that?"

I frowned. "I don't know, but I saw her talking to Ben when we were at the flea market. If she works for the market, that could be the reason." I shook my head. "Let's see if Ben was here recently."

We went into the market and were hit with a blast of air conditioning. I shivered in my dress. It was beginning to become cooler outside as winter approached. I thought the market could safely turn off the air conditioning now.

"This is like an icebox," Lois said. "I would have loved this place when I was having hot flashes a few years ago." She looked around. "Who should we ask about Ben?"

There was an Amish teenager in the snack-food aisle. "He'll do." I walked over to him. "Excuse me."

The young man looked up from the crackers that he was lining up on a shelf. With a slightly put-out expression on his face, he asked, "Can I help you find something?"

"I hope so. I wanted to know if Ben Baughman was here yesterday. I heard that he works here."

He turned pale. "Ben?"

I nodded.

"Umm, I think you need to talk to my manager. Wait here." He dropped the box of crackers he was holding on the floor and hurried off.

Lois picked up the box and put it on the shelf. "I'm sorry for whoever buys these. The ones on the bottom are surely crushed."

A moment later, the stock boy came back, followed by a heavy-set Amish man. He was bald except for some tufts of hair above his ears. I recognized him right away as Ansel Beachy. He wasn't a member of my district, but every spring my niece Edith sold some of her plants through this market. I had made several deliveries of flowers last spring to help her out when she was going through a particularly difficult time.

"These are the ladies who are asking about Ben," the young man said breathlessly.

"Millie, it's *gut* to see you," Ansel said. "I have been expecting you to come asking after Ben." He shook his head. "It's a terrible, terrible shame." He turned back to the young man. "I can take it from here, Eli. Return to your work."

The young man grabbed his cart and pushed it out of the aisle as if his shoes were on fire.

Ansel shook his head. "Eli is only nervous about it because the police were here about an hour ago asking the same questions. It really put the boy on edge. He's not used to speaking with sheriff's deputies."

"And you are?" Lois asked.

It was a fair question.

"More than he is, I would guess, but I suppose that comes with age. Also, I'm the only grocer in the village. Everyone comes here at one time or another. Sometimes deputies stop by to ask me who I've seen and when. They were *gut* to me when I had vandalism in the store, so I do my best to help out." He looked around. "Why don't we talk outside? I don't want to scare any of my Amish customers off, and nothing makes the Amish more uneasy than speaking about the police."

Lois and I followed Ansel out the front door of the market. To the left, there were two picnic tables under an overhang. They served as a shaded place for the Amish to wait for their rides or wait out bad weather before climbing onto their bicycles and pedaling home. I had used the benches a time or two in bad weather.

He sat on one side and the wooden seat groaned under his weight. Lois and I sat on the other.

Ansel was a known talker. Although not a gossip like Raellen, he liked to talk to folks. It could be about something important or it could be about nothing at all. If there were ears to listen, Ansel would make up words to fill them.

Because of that, I thought I would just cut to the chase. "Why did you think I would come and ask you about Ben?"

"Well, because you were his reference when he applied for the job, of course. When he told me that he knew you, I hired him on the spot. You have always been such a *gut* judge of character, I didn't need anything more. I'm glad I hired him too. He was a *gut* worker. I'm heartbroken over what has happened. Such a terrible accident. It just doesn't seem like the Ben I knew at all."

My heart sank. "So you have heard the rumor too?"

"The rumor that he was the one who started the fire? *Ya*, I have. It's difficult for me to believe, but if that's what people are saying . . ."

"Just because you have heard it from more than one person, that doesn't make it true," Lois said hotly.

"I suppose," he murmured. "The sheriff's deputies coming here a little while ago to ask after Ben didn't help. My whole staff, not just Eli—who is, I will admit, a jumpy young man—were all in a lather over it. Some were angry, too, because they have families who have booths in the flea market. It's common knowledge that everything in the building was lost."

"I think the police came to find out if Ben worked here yesterday. That's what I am asking too," I said.

"He did. He worked a four-hour stocking shift. I knew he wanted more hours, but the most I could give him was fifteen hours a week."

"When was he here?"

"It would have been nine-thirty in the morning to two in the afternoon."

"Do you know where he went after that?" I asked.

"Can't say. I know he has another job, other than the flea market, I mean."

"At Miller's Lumberyard," I said.

He raised his brow. "He worked there too? I thought his other job was at Tinker Mick's."

"Tinker Mick's?" Lois asked. "What's an Amish man doing working there?"

I glanced at her. "What's wrong with an Amish man working there?"

She shrugged. "Nothing is wrong with it, but it's pretty un-Amish to be rewiring things and fixing motors."

"Oh, a lot of young Amish men know how to fix a motor and wire things. I think we all played at that when we were on *rumspringa*. Besides, more and more districts are allowing the use of tractors and lawnmowers instead of horse drawn or push power. I think the old-timers would be loath to admit it, but times are changing in Holmes County. Amish culture can't be lost, but sometimes we have to be flexible to hold on. More and more young folks will leave if we aren't. I really believe that."

"And here I was thinking that Daniel's working on the motor today was an Amish anomaly," Lois said. "Does familiarity with technology lead to people leaving the faith?"

"The vast majority of Amish who are born Amish stay that way," I said.

Ansel eyed me. "Is that because they believe in the faith or because they don't want to be cut off from their family and the only life that they've ever known? I don't necessarily believe using threats is the best way to keep a community together. I can tell by the look on your face you don't agree, and that's fair," he said. "I'm a new-order Amish, so of course, I'm a bit more progressive. I believe that we should adopt some *Englisch* ways in order to succeed in this world, but that doesn't mean we will put our community at risk. I'm not suggesting we drive cars, for goodness sake!"

"That would be crazy," Lois said.

He looked over his shoulder. "I should get back. I'm sure my workers are whispering about where I might have gone." He stood up.

I held up my hand. "Ansel, one last question before you go."

He nodded as he edged toward the market's door.

"Did Ben ever say that anyone was upset with him?"

He stopped moving and studied me for a moment. "You mean enough to kill him?"

"*Ya*," I said.

He shook his head. "*Nee.* The only person I knew who was upset with him was Tobias Lieb. He even came to the market once and made a scene. I had to ask Tobias to leave. He hasn't been back to my market since. I still sell his apples, but his daughter brings them."

That's what Tess had been doing when she came to my home earlier that day.

"And what did they argue about?" Lois asked, even though I think we both already knew.

"Tess, Tobias's daughter. Ben was sweet on her, and Tobias told him that he wasn't allowed to court her. Ben was devastated."

Poor Ben.

"When was this?"

"Three weeks or, maybe a month ago."

I frowned. Ben had known for almost a month that Tobias didn't approve of him courting Tess, but he'd still tried. He either really did love her or he didn't back down from a challenge.

"*Danki* for your time, Ansel. We will let you get back to work," I said.

He nodded and went back inside the market.

Lois and I sat in silence at the picnic table for a while longer.

"It's getting late," Lois said. "I should go back to the café for the dinner rush. I can take you home first though. I have enough time for that."

I shook my head. "*Nee*. If it's all the same to you, I'd like to help you and Darcy in the diner. I—I don't want to be alone with my thoughts just yet. I need to keep busy. If I go home, I will quilt, and there's nothing to keep thoughts at bay while quilting. Although I do have much to do on the quilt I'm making for an *Englisch* customer."

"Not a problem," Lois said. "Darcy would love the extra set of hands, and I would too."

"*Danki.*"

"*Wilikumm*," she said with a smile.

Chapter Seventeen

The next morning, I was more determined than ever to get to the root of what had happened to Ben, and I was finally ready to face Tobias at the apple orchard. I was up at five, and with Bessie's help, moved Ben's courting buggy into my barn, where it would be protected from the elements. I had been too tired the night before to move the buggy. The goats bounced around the shiny black vehicle and tried to climb inside it. They loved to explore anything new. I shook my finger at them.

"This is not my buggy, which means that you have to be extra careful around it. No goats in the buggy." Peter and Phillip shared a look, which I didn't think boded well for keeping the buggy in pristine condition for Ben's father. That reminded me that I needed to speak with Ben's father to see what arrangements must be made for Ben's funeral. I hated even to think about it, but I couldn't put the task off forever.

By six in the morning, I'd walked the half mile to Raellen Raber's farm. I needed to jump on this investigation, and to do it, I needed Lois's help. She was right when she had said months ago that I needed a sidekick with a car.

Phillip and Peter galloped behind me. They loved a field trip. I had tried to put them in their pen before I left, but it had been to no avail. The goats bobbed and weaved, following my every move. They thought that when I went on a walk, it meant they could go on a walk too.

The Rabers raised sheep, and the bright white wooly creatures dotted the pasture as we walked toward the small outbuilding that held the shed phone. The goats danced at the view of the sheep, and I could tell they were itching to run with the flock.

I shook my finger at them. "*Nee, nee.* The last time I let you run with the sheep, you got me in trouble with Roman Raber, Raellen's husband. He said you got the flock riled up and they wouldn't calm down for days." I shook my finger again. "So there will be none of that romping about with the sheep. And if you run off after them, I will lock you in the barn the next time I take a walk. I hate to do it, but there are lessons to be learned."

After that dressing-down, the rambunctious goats, although still bouncing in place, stayed by my side.

The wood of the old shed that held the phone was gray and weathered. From what Raellen said, it was the oldest building on the farm. The original house had been torn down to build a much bigger one that could hold the Rabers' large family, and the same went for the large barn needed for their impressive flock of sheep.

I lifted the wooden latch and stepped into the shed. There were no windows, so the only light came through the door. I left it open so that I could see—much to the delight of Phillip and Peter.

I called Lois's cell number, which I had committed to memory. The phone rang and rang, and then finally went to voicemail. I left a message for Lois and hoped that she would hear it before I showed up on her doorstep. I was most anxious to clear Ben's name.

I stood in the booth and debated calling Ben's father as well. It was early morning, but Linus Baughman, Ben's father, was a farmer. He would be up by now. I reached into the pocket of my cloak and pulled out my small address book, flipped to the page for the Baughman shed phone in Michigan, and dialed. As I expected it to, the call went to the answering machine.

After the machine beeped, I cleared my throat. "Linus, this is Millie Fisher in Ohio. I'm calling because of Ben. I think you must have heard the news by now." I stopped myself from announcing the news in case he had not heard it. I could not imagine learning that your child was dead over an answering machine. I took a breath. "I have some of Ben's things that should be yours, and I wanted to talk to you about arrangements. Umm. Please call me as soon as you can." I rattled off the number to the Rabers' shed phone.

I stepped out of the phone shed, closed the door behind me, and relatched it.

"You're using the telephone quite early this morning," a deep, male voice said to me.

I turned around to see Roman Raber standing a few feet away. He was dressed for a day of farm work in old trousers, a worn work shirt, and work boots that were splattered with mud and I didn't even want to guess what else. His blond beard was combed and at the perfect length. When it came to the rules of the district, Roman followed them just as carefully as Ruth Yoder did.

"*Gude mariye*, Roman. I just was calling a friend."

He nodded. "I heard about Ben Baughman."

I imagined he had. He was Raellen's husband after all. I doubt there was any village rumor that his wife had not repeated to him once—or a dozen—times.

"It is a great shame that the flea market was lost. A lot of members of the community depend on that place for their livelihood."

I nodded. "It is very sad."

He frowned. "Ben Baughman started that fire," Roman said. "He's the only one who would have done it."

I blinked at him. "Why on earth would you say that? You didn't even know Ben."

"I knew him well enough. He's the type of young man who comes into a community and makes trouble."

I frowned. "Ben wasn't like that at all."

He folded his arms. "You might want to ask yourself how well *you* knew him."

I wanted to ask him what he meant by that. I had known Ben well, better than almost anyone else in Harvest. He had been a hard-working young man, who wanted to join the community and marry Tess. What more did Roman know about him? I was about to ask that question when I heard one of the goats baa with glee. Peter ran full tilt into the field of sheep.

The sheep panicked and scattered in all directions.

Phillip, who typically was the bigger troublemaker of the two, took off after his brother to join in on the fun.

"Get those goats away from my sheep!" Roman shouted.

I groaned. I knew that I should have tried harder to lock

the goats in their pen. I had been in such a hurry to reach the shed phone, that I hadn't argued with them when they followed me. I put my fingers in my mouth and gave an ear-splitting whistle, just as my late husband, Kip, had taught me to do. When we had a farm, he would always whistle like that to call the cattle into the barn at night. I'd learned that the trick worked just as well on goats.

Phillip and Peter froze in mid-romp. They knew if I gave that whistle, I meant business. I whistled again, and they came running. They skidded to a stop just in front of me with their tongues hanging out of their mouths.

"Get those goats off my property," Roman said through clenched teeth.

"I'm sorry, Roman. I won't bring the goats here again," I said. I shot Phillip and Peter a look. Peter had the good sense to duck his head. He knew this time he was the bigger culprit.

The sheep were still in a tizzy over the goat invasion. They baaed and ran around the field in a giant circle.

"It's going to take me all morning to calm them down."

"I really am sorry," I said again.

He glared at me. "Sometimes sorry is not enough. You have caused a lot of turmoil in my marriage."

I blinked at him. Raellen had never said anything like that to me.

"You're lucky that I let Raellen be in the quilting circle with you," he said. "I don't like the idea of her being this close to a police investigation. Her place is here at home with her children."

I curled my hands into fists.

"The quilting circle was a fine little hobby until *you*

moved to Harvest. Now, it's become a source of strife between myself and my wife."

"I haven't involved Raellen in the investigation."

"But since she is your *friend*, she is," he said. He glared at me. "Police work is not the business of an Amish woman."

"I do not claim to do the work of the sheriff's deputies," I said, standing up a little straighter.

"Would Deputy Aiden Brody agree with you? Does he want your help?"

I didn't say anything.

"I think your silence is answer enough." He walked by me. "Now, I must calm my sheep."

I watched Roman walk away. I sighed and looked down at the goats. "You two are not making life any easier for me, are you? Roman was already annoyed with me. Now, you have been banished from the Raber farm forever."

The goats hung their heads.

I sighed. "I know you will miss your sheep friends."

The sheep continued to baa and run in a circle in the pasture. I wasn't sure they would miss the goats.

I debated whether to say hello to Raellen but decided against it. Our friendship was already on thin ice as far as her husband was concerned. I didn't want to cause any more trouble for her.

As the goats and I walked home, the sun rose over the rolling hills of Holmes County. The pink and orange sunrise faded into a bright yellowish haze. It would be hot, as many days at the end of September were. It was as if the summer was making its very last stand.

I looked at the goats. "The two of you have had enough

adventure for one day. You're not coming with me to the village."

They jumped in place and then ran around me. It was no wonder they got the sheep riled up. They would not stand still.

"*Nee*, your antics are not going to change my mind. Also, Peter, I never expected you to be the instigator. I think you have been following in your brother's hoof-steps a little too much here."

The brown-and-white goat hung his head but recovered quickly and gave me a goaty smile.

"What am I going to do with the two of you?" I asked.

They didn't have any answer for that question.

"Now, off to the barn with both of you."

They must have sensed I meant business this time because the pair of them bolted for the barn. I followed at a much slower pace. It was time to get Bessie and set out for the village. After my conversation with Roman, my need to clear Ben's name was greater than ever before.

Chapter Eighteen

I knocked on the front door of Lois's rental house. It was a little, yellow ranch home three blocks from her granddaughter's café. When the weather was nice, she walked. As she said, she had to keep herself in shape in case she ever ran into husband number five.

There was no answer, so I rang the doorbell. I could hear its loud clang from outside the house. The clanging was quickly followed by muttering. "Who would be at my door at this time of day?"

I peeked at the pocket watch Kip had given me. It was a quarter to eight. Not the crack of dawn . . . at least not by Amish standards.

Lois flung the front door open a moment later. She was dressed but had a towel around her neck. In her left hand, she held a giant can of hair spray and a pink comb. "Millie, what are you doing here so early in the morning? Is everything all right? Did something else burn down?"

Her questions came in such rapid-fire succession, I had to think of which one to answer first. "Everything is okay. Nothing burned down. I'm just anxious about Ben's reputation and want to get back on the case."

"Well, if it's that, you should have called, and I would have been ready. I can't go anywhere until I have my hair done. Witnesses aren't going to want to talk to us with my hair looking like such a fright."

Her hair was . . . interesting. Her short red and purple locks stood out from her head as if they were matted with glue. I guessed it wasn't glue but the entire bottle of hairspray that she held in her hand.

"I called you from the shed phone on the Raber farm, and you didn't answer."

"Of course, I didn't answer. I turn the ringer off when I sleep. Who wants to be disturbed by a telemarketer when you are trying to catch come Z's?" She stepped back. "Come on inside."

I went into Lois's house. I had been in it many times over the last few months, and it was as crammed as ever. I had never seen so many pieces of furniture and knick-knacks in one place. Every flat surface had some sort of trinket on it. Nothing matched. In one corner, I spotted the orange chair that she had purchased at the flea market. There were two pillows on it. One was embroidered with a Halloween witch, and the other was covered in brown faux fur. You could barely see the chair itself.

"Let me go finish my hair, and then we can talk. I can tame it in five minutes."

I stared at her head. I wasn't so sure of that, but Lois was certainly the expert in *Englisch* hairstyles, not me. She squeezed herself between an upright piano and a nine-foot-long sofa and disappeared down the hallway. I stood in the middle of the room. There were places to sit, but there were almost too many choices. Did I sit on the sofa, a trunk, one of the armchairs? Or one of the stools tucked into one corner of the room? I opted to stand, for fear I would make the wrong choice. I didn't want to sit on one of her antiques or "finds" as she called them.

True to her word, Lois was back five minutes later, and her hair was in place. It was still red and spikey, but it didn't look like it was capable of stabbing me in the eye any longer.

"Why didn't you sit down?" Lois asked.

I shrugged. "I didn't know where to sit."

"The sofa is fine. It's a reproduction, not a real mid-century sofa. If I found a real one, it would be thousands of dollars. As much as I would love the real thing, I don't have that kind of cash. This reproduction does very well."

I sat on the end of the sofa closest to me.

"Now, what's got you running over here in such a state?" Lois asked.

"The rumors that Ben was responsible for the fire are worse than ever in the Amish community. Just trying to call you to say that I wanted to go to the orchard this morning, I ran into Roman Raber, and he said that Ben was responsible too."

She wrinkled her nose. "Of course he would think that. Raellen is his wife. Now, I know she's a nice woman and your friend, Millie, but her gossiping is going to get her in a whole mess of trouble someday. I don't doubt it for a minute."

I didn't doubt it either, and an Amish saying came to my mind. "Many things have been opened by mistake, but none as frequently as the mouth." I only hoped that Raellen would change her ways before that happened.

Lois perched on the arm of the sofa at the opposite end. "Millie, maybe we should look at this a different way."

I frowned. "What do you mean?"

"I don't want to play devil's advocate, but could it be possible that Ben did start that fire?"

I stared at her. "How can you even ask me that?"

"Well, he might have been depressed. He was in love with a woman who was inaccessible and whose father was about to ship her off to Wyoming."

"He wasn't that depressed."

She frowned. "We can't really know the demons a person is fighting."

"You're suggesting that he burned down the barn to kill himself."

She dropped her head. "Like I said, I didn't want to say it. I just think we shouldn't completely close the door on that possibility."

I pressed my lips together. In the Amish faith, suicide is a terrible sin. Many in the community would lose respect for Ben if this was proven true, and I hated even to think how it would make Tess feel. She was already struggling with his death and her impending move to Wyoming.

Lois stood up. "I should have kept my mouth shut. I can tell by the look on your face that you're startled over what I said."

I shook my head. "*Nee.* I don't want us to have the kind of friendship where we can't each say what we think. I don't believe that Ben would do this, but you're right, we must keep an open mind. When we close off our minds to possibilities, that's when we miss something."

She nodded. "Also, I'm not saying I believe this. I'm only saying it's possible."

I stood up. "We have to clear this up, not just for Ben's reputation but because I will never feel settled if I don't know the truth about what happened to him. He didn't deserve this."

"Then, I say we go pick some apples."

I nodded. "Let's."

Thirty minutes later, Lois drove her car into the bumpy, pebble-covered parking lot at Liebs Apple Orchard. Liebs was called an apple orchard, and it was true that apples were their main fruit, but they were also known for summer berries and for pears. However, what everyone was there for on this particular fall day was apples. The scent of ripened apples hung in the air. Despite my anxiety to get to the reason for Ben's death, my mind wandered to thoughts about apple cobbler, crisp, and pie. There were so many things that you could bake with apples. My mouth watered just thinking over the possibilities.

There were at least a dozen cars in the gravel parking lot. Families loaded children into wagons as they made their way into the orchard to pick their own apples. It was something that I had loved to do as a child with my siblings and with Lois growing up.

Lois must have been thinking of the same thing because she said, "Remember when your oldest brother was making fun of you and I threw an apple at him, knocking him off his ladder?"

I chuckled. "I do. You always came to my defense, Lois."

"As you did mine."

I smiled at her and, not for the first time, thought the best part of moving back to Ohio was rekindling this dear friendship. Now, if I could just find out what had happened to Ben. According to Grandma Leah, I was the reason that Ben had moved to Ohio. That only compounded my guilt over his death.

At the far end of the parking lot, there was an open-air building that held huge crates of apples of every kind, size, and tartness. I expected Tess to be there, but as we got closer, I didn't see her. I assumed the teens and older children selling the apples were her siblings and perhaps even cousins. When it came to Amish farming, the entire family was involved.

"Oh! Do you see they have baked apples for sale?" Lois asked. "My mother made an amazing baked apple. It was always my favorite fall treat."

"Lois, we are here to find Tess."

"Oh, right." She walked away from the table of baked apples. I had to admit that they smelled lovely, sweet and full of cinnamon and allspice.

I went up to a young Amish girl who stood on a stool as she stacked apples in a crate to keep them from rolling off the pile onto the dirty concrete floor. She smiled at me and asked in Pennsylvania Dutch, "Can I help you?"

"I hope so. I was looking for Tess Lieb. Is she here at the orchard today?"

The girl turned pale, and with an apple still in her hand, she hopped off the stool. "She's not in the shop today."

"But is she at the orchard?" I asked.

The girl's eyes filled with tears. "She's my sister, and she is moving. She's packing in the house."

"Moving to where?" I asked, even though I knew that it must be Wyoming.

"She has to go because *Daed* said that she has to go. We must obey our parents. It's in the Bible."

"Where can I find her?"

"She's packing," the girl said.

"I know that she's packing, but where is she?" I asked.

The girl looked around as if to make sure there was no one nearby whom she didn't want to overhear. "She's supposed to be packing, but she's not. She's in the orchard. She made me promise not to tell *Daed*."

"Where in the orchard?" I asked.

"By the Cortland apples. Those have already been picked. There won't be any pickers there."

"*Danki*," I said. "What is your name?"

She swallowed. "Melanie."

"*Danki,* Melanie. You have been a great help."

I pulled Lois away from the baked apples and out of the building.

"I'm getting one of those apples before I leave," she grumped.

"That's fine, but first come with me. I know where Tess is hiding."

Chapter Nineteen

"She's hiding?" Lois asked. "From what?"

"From her father, I would guess."

Lois nodded. "Because he wants to buy her a pair of cowgirl boots and ship her off to Wyoming."

"The Amish don't wear cowgirl boots," I said.

"They don't wear them here, but you can't know what they do in different districts. Didn't you tell me every district is different?"

I sighed. "You made your point. Let's just go find Tess before she goes back out to the big house to pack. I doubt we will be able to reach her there."

She nodded. "Her father wouldn't like that at all."

Lois and I walked to the pasture, where families, both Amish and *Englisch*, walked ahead of us.

The families turned off when they found the row where they wanted to pick.

There was a wooden sign on a post at the end of each row. I could see the logic of that; signs were necessary to tell people where they could and could not pick. Different kinds of apples came in at different times, so they couldn't be picked at the same time. The Cortlands, where Tess was supposed to be, were past their prime. When the last family with a wagon turned off, I kept walking.

"Where are we going?" Lois asked. "I thought that she was in the orchard."

"She is," I said, walking at a determined pace but taking care on the uneven ground. "Her sister said she was hiding in the Cortlands, which are out of season."

Lois caught up with me. "All right. I'm game as long as I leave here with a basket of apples."

I promised her that she would, and we walked by the rows of trees. The trees themselves weren't more than six feet tall. They were cultivated to grow shorter for easy picking. I saw evidence of where high branches had been cut away to encourage more growth lower to the ground.

The Cortland trees were five rows away from where people were currently picking. It made sense to me that Tess would want to be that far from all the commotion and from her father.

Lois and I walked down the row, and I put a finger to my lips about halfway down. Then I pointed. Tess had tucked herself up under one of the green-leafed apple trees. There were just a few withered apples still clinging to the branches above her head.

Tess looked so small crying under the tree. Her knees were pulled up against her chest, and her blue skirt was tucked in around her legs. She bent her head toward her knees, so we couldn't see her face. All the same, I knew it was Tess.

Lois leaned in. "With her blond hair, blue dress, and white apron, she looks like Alice from *Alice in Wonderland* sitting under that tree. Only the Amish prayer cap mars the effect." She looked around. "If a white rabbit shows up, I'm out of here. I don't want to fall down some rabbit hole and meet the Queen of Hearts. She will definitely say 'Off with her head!' to me."

I stared at her. "Lois, truly, I don't know what you are talking about half of the time."

"You know, Millie, I think that's really what makes this friendship work so well."

I shook my head. "What should we do? She looks so upset. I hate to disturb her."

"We came here for information, and we have to get it. Also, if she's upset about Ben, then who better than you to talk about him with? I don't think she will get much compassion about his death from her family, do you?"

I shook my head. I inched forward. "Tess?"

She didn't look up. She didn't even give any sign that she had heard me.

I took two more steps. "Tess, it's me, Millie."

The girl's head jerked up, and she smacked it against the trunk of the apple tree. She winced, and tears spilled over her cheeks. I didn't know if those tears were from her crying or from hitting her head.

"Wow," Lois said. "You really hit that hard. You had better look for a bump."

She blinked at Lois. "A bump?"

"On the back of your head from hitting the tree." Lois rubbed the back of her own head as if she was sore in the same place.

"I don't have one. My bun hit the tree the hardest. I was startled, that's all."

"Good to know that the Amish buns can also be used as a defense mechanism," Lois said. "I can't say I will give it a try. Short hair for me all the way."

Poor Tess appeared to be more confused than ever, and I couldn't say I blamed her. Lois was a great sidekick, but she did have a tendency to get the conversation off track at times. I didn't know how long Tess would be willing to speak to us, so I needed to find out what I could about Ben while I had her attention.

"How did you find me?" Tess asked.

"Melanie told us where you were," I said.

She scowled. "She shouldn't have done that. I told her not to tell our *daed*."

"Apparently," Lois said. "She didn't apply your warning to random strangers too."

"What are you doing, sitting out here by yourself?" I asked.

She stood up and brushed leaves and dirt off her skirt. "I just needed to get away for a little bit. I—I had to think. My father plans to have an *Englisch* driver take me to the train station in Alliance tomorrow." She closed her eyes for a moment as she thought about it. "I'm supposed to get on a train that is bound for Wyoming. My *aenti* will be waiting for me at the station in Wyoming."

"You're leaving tomorrow?" I asked. "That's soon."

"It was always supposed to be tomorrow. I just never expected to go, because I had Ben. He would have kept me from going, but now Ben is gone." She buried her face in her hands and began to cry again.

Lois walked over to her and wrapped her hand around her shoulder. Much to my surprise, Tess leaned into her. I was sure that the girl was just looking for the support she clearly wasn't getting from her family.

"Shh," Lois said. "Now, pull yourself together. You're not going to find a way out of this mess by crying over it.

I know everything seems awful now, but there is always a way out, you'll see."

Tess looked up at Lois. "How do you know? You're not Amish. There is not always a way out if you're Amish, especially if you're an Amish woman still living with your parents."

Lois squeezed her shoulder again and then let go. "Sure there is. Sugar, no one can make you do anything you don't want to. If you don't want to go to Wyoming, don't go. Put your foot down."

She blinked at Lois. "I—I don't know if I'm strong enough to do that."

I was certain no one had ever said such a thing to Tess before.

"You look plenty strong to me," Lois said. "Besides, I'm not even sure that you can leave."

"Why?" Tess asked.

"The police might not let you go. You are in the middle of a murder investigation. Right smack dab in the center of it."

I hadn't thought of it before, but I realized that Lois was probably right.

"I'm not in the middle of a murder investigation. I don't know anything about it."

"But you are," Lois said. "Ben was killed, and you were his girlfriend or whatever it is the Amish call each other when they're dating. That makes you a person of interest, if not a suspect. The cops are going to want you to stay around for a while yet."

Tess opened and closed her mouth. "*Nee.*" She turned to me. "Millie, tell her that she must be wrong. The sheriff's deputies will never think I could hurt Ben, or anyone."

I smiled at her with sympathy. "They might not see you as the most likely suspect, Tess, but I do think Lois is right. They aren't going to want you to leave the state when the investigation is going on."

"But do they even know of me?" Tess asked.

Lois and I shared a look. That was a *gut* question. I hadn't told Deputy Aiden about Tess. I hadn't because I had wanted to protect her. Now I wondered if that was a mistake. If Aiden did know, that might stop her *daed* from shipping her off to his younger sister's home on the other side of the country.

"Did you tell the police about me?" she asked.

I couldn't lie. "I didn't, but it's possible that someone else did. It wasn't a secret that Ben was courting you or wanted to court you. He spoke about it often. He loved you very much."

"I didn't kill Ben." She closed her eyes and then opened them again. "I know he loved me. I wouldn't do that. I couldn't do that. The police will know that, won't they?"

"But did you love Ben back?" Lois asked.

I frowned. Lois had asked the question I had been wanting to ask but couldn't seem to work up the nerve to pose. I suppose I was afraid of the answer. If Ben had loved Tess and died for that love but she didn't love him back, it would be a terrible waste.

Tess took a deep breath. "I loved him . . . or I think that I could have. It's so hard to know if it's love or not. I've read so many books from the library. My *daed* doesn't know that I go there to get books. He wouldn't like it."

"But the Amish are allowed to read, aren't they?" Lois asked, aghast.

I gave her a look. "*Ya*, we are allowed to read. Many Amish districts allow members to use the library, and the library book mobile visits Amish schools."

Tess nodded. "We are allowed to read, but it's what we read that is different from *Englischers*. My *daed* wouldn't like the kind of books that I chose. I read these sweeping romantic books about when a hero meets his love, and they know from the moment they see each other that they were meant to be."

"That's censorship if he says you can't read something," Lois said hotly

"Lois, it is the Amish way," I said. "The man of the house can make such rules."

She harrumphed. "I would never survive as an Amish person."

"That has been well established," I said. Then I turned back to Tess. "Was it like that for you and Ben? Love at first sight?"

She looked at me with tears in her eyes. "I—I don't know. I wanted it to be, but if it actually was, I think I would be sadder about his death and less sad about going to Wyoming. You must think I'm a horrible person for saying that. You must really think that, because I know how close you were to Ben. He respected you so much."

"It's not horrible for you to say that," I said. "You didn't know each other very long, and you didn't have time to fully decide how you felt about him."

She nodded. "*Ya*, that's it, but I knew that I would love him one day. I could grow to love him. I did want to marry him, and it wasn't just to escape my fate. He wasn't my only suitor."

"Wait, you have another suitor?" Lois asked. She looked at me and mouthed "suspect."

I rolled my eyes. I wished that my friend was capable of being a little less obvious.

"It wasn't a serious one. He's the teacher at the schoolhouse. He asked my father if he could court me as well. *Daed* said *nee*. You see, he wasn't just against Ben courting me, he was against anyone courting me because of the promise that he made to his sister."

"What's the teacher's name?" I asked.

"Isaiah Keim. He's a nice man, but he's not Ben. I never felt about him like I did about Ben." She looked as if she might start crying again.

"Keim. Is he related to Daniel Keim?" I asked.

She nodded. "They are cousins, I think."

"Everyone is cousins in Holmes County," Lois said.

"I will miss that about this place. Everyone is family. I don't know anyone in Wyoming. I just will not go." There was a new note of determination in her voice. "I'm sad that I must go to Wyoming or leave my family and leave my faith. It's a terrible decision to have to make, but my *daed* does not understand how much I want to stay in Ohio. This is my home. Why must I go? He never even asked for a volunteer in the district. There could have been another young woman who would have enjoyed the adventure. I'm not the adventurous sort. I never have been."

"I would say leaving the Amish community is very adventurous," Lois said.

"But I would be here in Harvest where I want to be." She straightened her shoulders. "It's been helpful to talk to you both. I know what I need to do, and now, I need to get back to the apple shack. My *daed* will be looking for me, and Melanie clearly can't keep a secret." She walked down the row of apple trees with her head held high.

Lois picked one of the withered apples from the tree. "Do you think Tess is doing the right thing by leaving the Amish?"

"I don't know. It's not for me to decide. Every Amish person must make that choice for themselves." I paused. "I do think she's making the choice in a reactionary way. I just wonder if there is not a compromise that she can come to with her father, or if there is not another district in the area where she could find a job instead of leaving our faith. I don't know that she's suited for the *Englisch* life."

"I don't know if I'm suited for the English life," Lois said. "But goodness knows I'd be a terrible Amish person."

She got no argument from me on that point.

When she saw a worm in her apple, Lois yelped and threw it into the brush. "Apple picking is not for the faint of heart."

"What's worse than finding a worm in your apple?" I asked.

"What?"

"Finding half a worm," I said.

She wrinkled her nose. "Is that one of those Amish proverbs you quote all the time?"

"*Nee*, but it should be."

There was a rustling in the tree to our left. I glanced in that direction, expecting to see a squirrel scampering among the branches. Instead, I saw a person hurry by. I gasped.

Lois turned to me "What? What was it?"

"There's someone there!" But when I pointed at the place where the person had been, they were gone.

Chapter Twenty

"Are you trying to scare me?" Lois asked. "First the apple, and now you are seeing people in the trees?"

I put a hand on my chest as if to hold my beating heart in place. "I saw someone there."

Lois marched over to the tree in question and shook the branches. "There's not anyone there now." As she shook the tree, leaves fell on her head. "Ack, I can't let them get into my hair." She brushed the leaves away.

Watching Lois flail about in the apple tree calmed me down. "Maybe it was just a child who wandered off during apple picking."

"Did it look like a child?" Lois said.

I shook my head. "I can't say for certain that I saw someone at all now. It was just an impression."

Lois cocked her head. "If it were October and if you weren't Amish, I would say that you have Halloween on your mind."

"Let's go back. I remember you said something about wanting a baked apple."

Lois clapped her hands. "Yes, I can already taste it."

As we left the Cortland row, I looked back and a light

breeze moved through the trees, sending leaves into the grass. Maybe I had imagined the whole thing.

When we were back in the apple shack, as Tess had called it, Lois peered at the plastic containers of baked apples. "I have to pick the perfect one or two. I'll get one for Darcy, and then maybe I can convince her to add them to the menu at the Sunbeam Café. We need to get some apples as well. I think half a bushel would work. Darcy needs them for all her fall recipes."

The shack was full of apples. "What kind does she want?"

"Granny Smiths," Lois said without looking up from scrutinizing a baked apple. "She likes to bake with tart ones so that she can control the amount of sweetness."

I walked over to the Granny Smith apples and found a half-bushel basket beneath the table. I wouldn't be able to carry the basket, at least not very far. I hoped one of the Lieb children would transfer the apples to Lois's car.

I began piling the apples into the basket. I took care to pick the very best ones I could find for Darcy. I suspected I would have all the apples picked before Lois made up her mind about the baked apples. It was surprising when I took time to consider it, but Lois could be very particular at times.

"What are you doing here?" a man asked me.

I straightened up from bending over the apple basket, pressing a hand into the back of my spine to set it right. When I was upright, I found Tobias Lieb standing on the other side of the Granny Smith apple pile, glaring at me.

"Hello, Tobias. Lois and I are here to buy apples for her granddaughter's café. You know the Sunbeam, don't you?"

He frowned. "That's not the only reason you are here.

You have put the thought into my eldest daughter's head to disobey me. I know that you have been doing this for some time. I wouldn't be the least bit surprised if you were the one who sent Ben after my daughter."

I glanced around and saw that people in the apple shack were staring at us now. Tobias spoke in Pennsylvania Dutch, so at least the *Englischers* couldn't understand what he was saying. They could, however, pick up on his angry tone.

"I didn't send Ben after anyone."

Lois stomped over to us with a baked apple in each hand. "What's going on here?"

"Tell your *Englisch* friend to stay out of this," Tobias said in our language.

"Hey, speak English. It's rude not to." Lois shook one of the baked apples at him for emphasis.

He glared at her before saying to me in Pennsylvania Dutch, "Stay away from my family." He marched off.

Lois scowled at his back. "That man needs an attitude adjustment. What did he say to you?"

I sighed. "He blamed me for Tess's behavior. I think he knows now that she doesn't plan to get on that train to Wyoming."

Lois frowned. "If she doesn't, she can't stay here. Her father would be a nightmare to live with."

That was true.

"Do you still want the apples and baked apples?" I asked.

"Of course, I do," Lois said. "I won't let some grumpy Amish man put me off my dessert."

I smiled and said, "Be kind to unkind people. They probably need kindness the most."

Lois snorted. "That's not one of your proverbs I can get behind, Millie."

I shook my head.

We made our purchases, and an Amish teenager carried the half-bushel basket to Lois's car. He wouldn't look at us or speak to us the whole time. I suspected that he was one of the Lieb children and had been ordered not to. As quick as he could, he set the half bushel of apples into Lois's trunk and scurried away.

Lois watched him go. "I would say we're on some kind of bad apple list. Get it? Bad apple."

I sighed. "I got it."

"Cheer up, Millie. We learned something knew. We now know that Ben had competition for Tess. Isaiah Keim sounds like the perfect suspect to me."

We climbed in the car and buckled our seatbelts. "He does, but I can't stop feeling upset over the situation Tess is in. I wish I could help her more."

"Don't you worry, Millie. You will find a way to help her. You always do."

I wished that I had her confidence on the matter.

"Where to next?" Lois asked. "The schoolhouse to talk to Isaiah Keim?"

I shook my head. "He will have students there right now, and we shouldn't discuss this in front of his pupils."

She nodded. "Mixing children with murder investigations is typically frowned upon."

"Let's go back to the flea market."

She glanced at me. "You want to snoop around?"

"Don't you?" I arched my brow.

"Of course! I'm always game for snooping. I have my

lock picks." She patted her giant purse, which was on the console between us.

I knew that she had more than just lock picks in that bag.

The apple orchard was far out in Holmes County, so it took Lois a half hour to make our way back to the flea market. Unlike the day before, there was no one on the street. The only creatures we saw were the cows that continued to graze in the pasture across the road from the sad remains of the Harvest Flea Market.

"It almost looks worse the second day," Lois said as we climbed up the low hill that led from the road to the flea market. The very center of the building had caved in. The day before it had looked as if the front side could be salvaged, but that was not the case.

"The entire building has collapsed," I said. "That front room, or what's left of it, was where Ben was."

Lois increased her pace as we made our way up the incline. Being the shorter of the two, I had to double my pace to catch up with her. Large yellow cones had been placed on either side of where the main entrance to the flea market had once been. I could see the charred remains of the old barn door. A line of police tape ran from one end to the other.

"We'd have to cross this police line to look for clues."

"Not a great idea," I said.

"A terrible idea, actually," a voice said.

I turned around to find a Mennonite woman standing about twenty feet from us, holding an expensive-looking camera. It was the same woman I had seen with Ben the morning before the fire and the same woman who had bumped into me at Harvest Market. I thought that seeing her three times in relation to Ben was no longer a coincidence.

"Can I ask what you are doing here?" the Mennonite woman said.

"Can we ask what *you* are doing here?" Lois shot back.

"I'm working." She held up the camera.

"We are working too," Lois said. "Unofficially."

"Do you work for the fire department?" I asked.

"No," the Mennonite woman said. "I work for Waller Properties, which owns this property. Neither of you do." She looked us up and down. "Nor do you look like you work for the sheriff's department." She folded her arms. "Let me guess, you are some of the Amish who had a booth in the flea market. We made calls yesterday, so you should have heard that everything was lost and there is nothing we can do about it. If you did not get rental insurance for your booth, Waller Properties is not liable for what you might have lost in the fire."

"We lost some quilts," Lois said before I could speak. "Our booth was Double Stitch. It's a quilting booth. The best quilting circle in the village actually. I'm sure that you have heard of it. By the way, I'm Lois Henry, and this is my friend Millie Fisher."

"I'm Flora Kimble, and I manage all of the booths at the flea market, so yes, I have heard of Double Stitch. However, I don't remember the name Lois or Millie on the application."

"It would have been under Iris Young," I said. "She is another woman in our circle."

Flora nodded. "That sounds right. Now, I am sorry that you lost quilts, but many businesses lost more than that. Also, Waller Properties will suffer from losing this building and the lack of business. Even so, we plan to reopen on Saturday for a limited period of time."

I looked around. "How on earth would you be able to reopen on Saturday? That's only five days away."

She frowned. "Clearly, we won't be using the building, but Mr. Waller has rented a large tent. Vendors can sell from there or outside the tent on the grounds. You should have gotten all of this information when I called your contact person earlier this morning. I thought I remembered speaking to a woman by the name of Iris."

"Oh," I said. "I haven't spoken to Iris since the call. I'm sure she will tell everyone at the quilting meeting this evening."

"If that was all—"

"It wasn't," I said quickly. "I was wondering if we could speak to you about Ben Baughman."

She narrowed her eyes. "I have nothing to say. I didn't even know him."

I frowned. "But you did know him. I saw you speaking to him the morning before the fire."

"Yes, I know who he was, of course," she said slowly. "He worked for our company as the night guard. That's all I know about him."

"You gave him an envelope the morning of the fire."

She frowned. "I don't know what you're talking about."

"You gave Ben an envelope, and he put it in his pocket."

"Oh," she said, and waved my comment way. "That was nothing more than his pay for the week."

I wondered if the money had been found on Ben's person. I hoped that if I asked Deputy Aiden, he would give me a straight answer on that. So far, he had been more forthcoming about Ben's death than I knew he was supposed to be. I didn't know how long his candor with me would last.

Flora put the camera strap over her shoulder. "Now, I will have to ask you to leave."

"What are you doing here?" Lois asked.

"Mr. Waller asked me to come to the flea market and take some pictures. He wants to be sure that the insurance adjuster is truthful on his estimate."

"The flea market was insured?" Lois asked.

"Yes. It's not an Amish business. The English have to insure their businesses."

Lois wiggled her eyebrows at me. I sighed. She might as well have held up a sign that said she thought we had another suspect.

Flora frowned at her.

"And how did Mr. Waller and Ben get on?" Lois asked.

Flora cocked her head. "Get on? I don't know what you mean."

"Did they have a good working relationship?"

She put her hands on her hips. "They had no relationship, and I don't understand what you are implying here. Mr. Waller met Ben once in passing. I was the one who hired Ben as the night guard." She looked at what was left of the flea market. "It's clear that I made a mistake. He fell asleep and let this happen. Had he been doing his job, he could have chased away the vandals or, at the very least, sounded the alarm about the fire before it got out of hand. I don't know how he could sleep through it. The flames must have been horribly loud."

"He chased off vandals before," I said.

"So he claimed, but what good does that do me now?" She removed her camera from her shoulder. "If that's all, I need to get these pictures taken and return to the office. As you can imagine, things are very busy at Waller Properties right now, and it's my job to make sure that Mr. Waller gets through this."

Lois and I had been dismissed. I looked at my friend, and she shrugged. I nodded and said good-bye to Flora, and then we walked down the incline to Lois's car.

As we climbed into Lois's car, one of the things that Flora had said stuck with me. She didn't know how Ben could have slept through all the commotion that the fire made. I wondered the same. Even if he was completely exhausted and asleep, I thought that the noise would have woken him up.

But it hadn't.

What if he wasn't sleeping? If that was the case, it was what I had suspected all along.

Chapter Twenty-One

"You're awfully quiet," Lois said.

"I just had a thought. I can't believe Ben just fell asleep. Why wouldn't he have been woken up by all the noise?"

"Do you want to know my theory?" Lois asked.

"Ya, please."

"I don't think he was sleeping. I think . . . he was already dead."

I shivered. "Let's find deputy Aiden to see if he's found out anything new. After that, we can go to the schoolhouse. All the children go home at noon to eat with their families. It would be a *gut* time to catch the schoolmaster at the schoolhouse without any children around."

Lois nodded. "Right. No witnesses."

"We are not going to do anything that would cause us to worry about witnesses." I gave her a stern look.

"Of course not," she said, but she didn't sound like she was convinced. "And don't look at me like that. You remind me of Ruth Yoder when you do." She gave a mock shudder.

"Where do you think Deputy Aiden is?" I asked.

"I don't have his direct number," Lois said. "And I don't think calling the station is a good idea in this case."

"Probably not," I agreed.

Lois snapped her fingers. "I do have the number of someone who keeps tabs on everyone in the village." She set her massive purse on her lap and rooted through it. "Now, where is that blasted phone? I know I threw it in here with the handcuffs this morning."

"Handcuffs?"

"Millie," she said, not looking up from her search. "If we're going to be private eyes, we have to have the gear. We want to be taken seriously, don't we?"

"I never said I wanted to be a private eye. What makes you think I want to be a private eye?"

"Okay, we aren't *technically*. I googled it the other night. To be an actual private eye is a lot of work. You have to apprentice forever with someone who is licensed. Frankly, we are too old to put in all that time. We need to cut to the chase." She lifted her phone out of the bag. "Ah ha! I knew it was in here." She shook the phone at me. "See, it may not look like it from the outside, but I do know what I'm doing, at least when it comes to stocking a purse." She tapped the phone's screen and made the call. "I put it on speaker," she said as it rang.

"Hello, hello, answer me back quickly," Margot Rawling's harried voice came on the line.

"Hello, Margot, it's Lois and Millie."

"Get to it, Lois," Margot said. "I really am in a state."

"We just wanted to ask you—"

"No!" Margot shouted on the other end. "Don't put that table there! It goes to the other side of the square, with the food tables." She lowered her voice. "It's like I'm working with a bunch of people who have never been to one of my events before. Is it a full moon?" Margot asked. "It must be a full moon with all the mistakes I'm running across. Lord, give me strength."

·   "We just wanted to ask—" Lois tried again.

"I can't talk right now," Margot yelled into the phone loud enough for me to hear. "We have a square emergency. If you want to ask me something, you come down here and help." The call ended.

Lois gave me a look. "Do we go?"

I wrinkled my nose. "It does sound like she could use the help, and you are right, she's the most likely person to know where Deputy Aiden is."

Lois set her purse aside and put the car into drive. "It won't be so bad. I don't know about you, but I sort of enjoy it when Margot is discombobulated like this. Let's run over there and save the day."

I nodded and looked out the window. I didn't mind helping Margot. She was just a few years younger than Lois and I, and I had known her since we were all children. However, I knew that if we were going to the square and helping with an event setup, then Uriah Schrock would also be there. As the groundskeeper, he was always on hand when there were big events on the square. I knew, because I will admit that, at times, I had avoided them so as not to run into him. I hadn't yet taken the time to examine my complicated feelings on the matter.

The drive between the flea market and the village square was short. Too short, I would say, since I wasn't fully prepared to speak to Uriah. Lois parked in an open space near her granddaughter's café. It wasn't too close, mind you. Lois was very careful not to take a paying customer's spot.

"I'll just pop into the café and tell Darcy what we are up to."

I nodded and stood on the sidewalk, looking at the square. It was a hive of activity. Margot Rawlings was shouting at the young Amish men who were moving tables and chairs around the square. Her short curls, which were typically so orderly, sprang wildly out of her head. I hoped that she didn't work herself up too much.

I didn't see Uriah, but I knew he had to be there. It was his job to be there.

Lois reappeared at my side. "All's fine in the café. Although Darcy sent Bryan over to the square with a tray of coffees for the workers a little while ago, and Margot chased him off. The poor man still appears to be recovering from the incident."

"Margot can be a little bit excitable. I think for a nervous soul like Bryan, she might be too much."

Lois nodded, and together we walked over to the square.

"Yes, yes," Margot said, clearly frustrated with just about everything she saw. "Those chairs go inside the gazebo with the music stands. That's for the band. They need chairs and music stands. Do you expect them to stand for the entire event?"

The young Amish man she was speaking to shook his head, and when he saw Lois and me walking up to Margot, he took his chance to escape.

"You came," Margot said. "Thank goodness. I could use some help here! I don't know why Bailey King had to be in New York this week of all weeks. She's usually the one I can count on to straighten things out."

"What's the big event you are throwing this time, Margot?" Lois asked.

"This weekend is Octoberfest in the village."

Lois frowned. "I didn't know that Harvest celebrated Octoberfest. Isn't that Berlin's thing, because it's named after the German city?"

Margot folded her arms. "The village of Berlin does not have exclusive rights to Octoberfest in Holmes County. We can do it too. If, after going to that crowded event, people would like to enjoy a real relaxing afternoon in a quiet Amish village like ours, all the better."

"You plan to steal their crowd," Lois said.

"Who said anything about stealing? There is no law that says visitors to the county can't go to both events."

"But you plan to piggyback on their event," Lois said.

Margot sniffed but she didn't correct Lois on that.

"Usually you have things set up in a more orderly fashion. What happened? Where's Uriah?" Lois asked.

"Well, Uriah isn't here! That's the problem. I hired him to take care of this sort of thing, and he is missing in action. It's good luck that I came along when I did. Who knows what this place would look like if I hadn't!"

"That doesn't sound like Uriah at all," I said.

"This is true." Margot shook her head. "It's the first time I have had an event on the square that he's not been here for the setup."

"Do you think he's all right?" I asked. Now I was worried. I had been anxious about running into Uriah on the square, but I'd discovered that not finding him there was worse. I hoped he wasn't in some kind of trouble. Unfortunately, there was no one I could ask. He didn't have any family in Holmes County that I knew of, and he wasn't a member of my Amish district.

"Maybe he's sick," Lois said.

"I would know that if I could find him. I just wish you Amish carried cell phones. If you did, I could call or text him. I can't be running around all of Holmes County trying to find him!"

Lois and I shared a look.

"Is there someone you can call?" I asked. "Does he have access to a shed phone?"

"I don't know," Margot said in a huff. "He's never given me a phone number, and I have never needed one before because he's always been here. It's so aggravating." She sighed. "Now, what did you want from me?"

"We were looking for someone too. Do you know where Aiden Brody is?" Lois asked.

"Now, he has a phone. You could just text him," Margot said.

"I don't have his number," Lois said. "If I did, I wouldn't trouble you for it. You have it, don't you?"

"Of course, I do. I plan most of the events in the village, and I have to have access to the sheriff's deputy at all times. I'm not going through the station with that grump Sheriff Marshall in charge. It's much easier to contact Aiden directly."

"We were thinking the same thing," I said.

"What's his number?" Lois asked.

Margot gave a loud sigh. "I don't know why you are making me look this up. You could walk into Swissmen Sweets and ask any one of them or go to the church and find his mother. She will tell you." Despite her complaints, she reached into her coat pocket and pulled out her phone.

She scrolled through her contacts and then read off a number.

Lois quickly typed the number into her own phone. It was interesting to watch how the *Englisch* did this sort of thing. "Thank you, Margot," Lois said. "Your generosity will not be forgotten."

I wasn't sure whether Lois was speaking ironically or not.

An Amish man ran across Main Street, and I recognized him right away as Uriah Schrock. His face was flushed and looked even redder against the whiteness of his Amish beard. "I'm so sorry," Uriah said. "I had some business to attend to, and it took me longer than I anticipated."

Margot narrowed her eyes at him. "What business could be more important than Octoberfest? You know this is the first time that Harvest has put on this event, and it's essential that we start off on the right foot. If the first one goes badly, people will not come back."

"*Ya*, I know this." He tugged on the collar of his shirt. "I am very sorry. There was . . . I just could not come when I expected to be here. Something urgent came up."

Margot put her hands on her hips and looked as if she wanted to ask Uriah what was so urgent. Before she could do that, I said, "We're glad you are all right." I linked my arm through Lois's. "We were just passing through. Lois, are you ready to go?"

My friend looked down at me. She nodded her head so fast, her large plastic earrings swung back and forth from her earlobes like pendulums. "We got what we needed." She held up the phone. "Thanks, Margot."

"You're welcome." She turned her back to us. "Now, Uriah, there is much to be done."

Lois started back in the direction of the Sunbeam Café. Since my arm was linked through hers, I went with her. As we walked, I glanced back over my shoulder at Uriah. He nodded and pulled on his beard as he listened to Margot's detailed instructions. When he locked eyes with me, his usual teasing expression was gone. Instead, I saw only sadness there.

"I'll call Deputy Aiden now," Lois said.

I spun my head back around. "That's a *gut* idea."

Lois held the phone to her ear and gave me a strange look.

I turned away and gazed through the front window of the Sunbeam Café. Bryan was watching Darcy with studied interest. He glanced out the window and spied me. His face reddened, and he quickly concentrated on his keyboard. I frowned. I had a bad feeling about the tension between Darcy and Bryan. One of them was bound to be hurt. I supposed that I could say the same thing about the tension between Uriah and me.

"Hello, Deputy, this is Lois Henry . . . Yes, Margot Rawlings gave me your number . . . Millie and I have been to the apple orchard and think something is fishy over there. Fishy meaning we think they know more about Ben than they are letting on . . . No, they didn't tell us what it was. If they did, I wouldn't be calling you to check it out. What? No, we haven't been snooping. I had to buy apples for my granddaughter's café. She needs them for all her fall recipes. Yep. You got it. Toodles!" She ended the call, then dropped the phone into her purse.

"What happened?" I asked.

She adjusted the strap of her purse on her shoulder. How she carried it without straining her muscles, I would never know. "Well, Deputy Aiden promised to send Deputy Little over to the orchard—I'm not sure what good that will do—and he also asked us to stay out of the investigation. Since it was the third time, I assume he's just saying it out of habit."

"Maybe he's right. We don't seem to be getting anywhere as far as finding out what happened to Ben. You even said that you think he might have set the fire."

"I don't think he did it. I just don't think we should rule anything out. Let's talk to the schoolteacher. Maybe he can shed some light on this for us."

I certainly hoped that he could because, at the moment, I was very much in the dark about Ben's death.

Chapter Twenty-Two

Stepping into the one-room schoolhouse sent me back sixty years to the time when I was a child in Harvest. I went to school in the very same building for eight years, first through eighth grade, after which my formal education stopped. Kip, Uriah, and Ruth had all been students there at the same time. We grew up together. We learned together. My teacher had been Miss Beachy. I'd heard that she had died while I was taking care of my sister in Michigan.

When I was a child, Miss Beachy seemed so grown up to me, but the truth was she was no more than seven or eight years older than I was. She was a child teaching children. She was the teacher of the school until I finished eighth grade. After my class finished school, she married, and married women could not be teachers in Amish schools. They were too busy caring for their homes and families.

Lois whistled under her breath. "I knew when I came back to Holmes County that a lot wouldn't have changed. It's the nature of the place, but I never expected anything to be exactly the same. This looks just like it did when we were kids."

When we were young, Lois had visited me at the school a few times. Her school and mine had separate holidays. Miss Beachy, who was a kind-hearted woman, always welcomed Lois into the classroom. In fact, I think everyone in the school liked to see her, because Lois, by her very nature, was distracting. When she was around, it was difficult for the teacher and the students to stay focused on their lessons. The only person I could remember who wasn't thrilled when Lois popped into the school was Ruth. Ruth had been prim and proper even when she was a child.

"Can I help you?" a young man asked as he stepped into the school. He was a thick-set man with curly brown hair that didn't appear to take well to the Amish bowl haircut. His curls stood up in all directions. In the pocket of his plain, button-down shirt was a pair of round eyeglasses. He removed those from his pocket and perched them high on the bridge of his nose.

"I hope you can," I said. "We are looking for Isaiah Keim."

He adjusted his glasses and glanced at Lois, who was clearly out of place in this one-room Amish schoolhouse, and then back to me. "I'm Isaiah. Are you here about one of the children in my school? Are you the *grossmaami* to one of the children? The children all have gone home for lunch but should be back within the hour for afternoon lessons."

"*Nee*," I said. "I'm Millie Fisher and this is my—"

"Driver," Lois burst in. "I'm her driver. Been working

the Amish taxi service for several months now. It's the best job I've ever had."

"Oh," the timid man said. He didn't ask, but I knew he must have been wondering why my driver had come into the schoolhouse with me. There were many Amish taxi drivers in Holmes County. When we say Amish taxi driver, we don't mean the traditional yellow cab taxies that someone might see in a big city. Instead, they were *Englischers,* usually retired men, who were on call to the Amish and who trundled them around the county when buggies, walking, and bicycles were impractical. Most of the drivers stayed with the car when the Amish person was at a doctor's appointment or shopping. None that I knew actually went into the final destination with the Amish person.

Isaiah turned back to me. "I know who you are. You're the matchmaker, aren't you?"

"She sure is," Lois said. "She's the best matchmaker in the village, no, in the county, no, in the state!" She pumped her fist in the air as if that helped her make her point.

"Okay, Lois," I said. "I do appreciate the vote of confidence."

Isaiah frowned. "I thought you were the driver."

Lois narrowed her eyes. "Oh, just because I can drive a car, does that mean I don't have a right to give my opinion on Millie's matchmaking skills?"

"I—I don't know," Isaiah mumbled.

Lois had a way of intimidating people. Apparently, that included being able to intimidate an Amish schoolteacher. Knowing Lois, she took great pride in this.

"What's the village matchmaker doing in my school?

My students are far too young to be looking for a match." The schoolteacher pulled at his collar.

Some of his students were fourteen. And although they were too young to be thinking about marriage, he must be kidding himself if he thought that no flirting was happening in his schoolyard. Adolescence had changed quite a bit since I was young, but romance remained the same.

"I wanted to talk to you about Ben Baughman."

The friendly expression dissolved from his face, and I realized my error. Perhaps I should have been less blunt in my approach.

"I don't have anything to say about Ben. I'm sorry that he died, of course, but I hardly knew him. I don't know what you expect to learn about him from me."

"But you know Tess Lieb well," I said. I didn't state it as a question because there was no doubt in my mind that he was interested in courting Tess.

He frowned. "I've known her my whole life. We are the same age and in the same district."

Lois put her hands on her hips. "Did you look at Ben as a rival?"

He blinked at her. "A rival? A rival for what? I told you that I hardly knew him."

"A rival for Tess," Lois said.

He shook his head. "*Nee*. Ben and I were not in competition to court Tess. I will admit that I cared about her, but when it was clear we weren't a good match, I left it at that. That's what all respectable men should do."

"Why weren't you a good match?" I asked.

"Because her family needed her help. Now was not the time for her to be looking for a match. I told her that. When I did, she ran to Ben. The girl is desperate to get married." He sniffed. "I don't find desperation attractive in the least."

"Her family needed her to move to Wyoming to help her aunt."

"I see you already know about it." He frowned. "I respected her father's wishes. I care about Tess very much, but there was no reason to press my attentions on her when her *daed* was against it. In fact, that would be going against everything I believe in. I teach the children in my classroom to respect their parents and do as they are told. They need to learn to mind adults, parents, teachers, and all others who are older and wiser than they."

"I thought the point of education was to help children learn and have critical thinking skills so that they can make their own choices," Lois said.

His face was pinched. "Maybe in the *Englisch* world. The Amish world is different."

"Don't I know it," Lois said.

I put my hand on Lois's arm, hoping that it would warn her not to offend the suspect.

"So Tobias said 'no' and that was that." Lois wrinkled her nose. "Not very romantic if you ask me."

"I will not lie. I did have some hard feelings. It was right after Tobias told me his decision to send Tess to Wyoming. I was crushed. I really was, but I was respectful. That same night I went to a social." His face reddened. "And I saw Ben and Tess holding hands when they were sitting next to each other. How could she tell me that she wanted me to court her and that she wanted to marry me, and then find another suitor so soon?"

"Did you do anything about it?"

"*Nee*, I would never cause a scene. I have to think of

my students first. I can't set a bad example for them. If Tess had so quickly found another man to court with, then that could only mean that she was not my match after all. It only confirmed something I had thought for some time."

"Why were you already suspicious?" I asked. "Did she say something?"

He frowned. "She was just too eager. If she had her way, we would have been married by now. I wanted to take things slower. I also knew that when I married, I would have to give up being a teacher at the school. I didn't want to quit in the middle of the school year. That would be disruptive to the children. The earliest I would marry was next June, when school was finished. She didn't like that idea at all." He looked down. "I suspect that was when she started to look for another suitor."

"Mr. Keim!" a little boy shouted as he ran into the school. "*Maam* sent you some apple cake!"

Another young boy ran into the school, followed by three other young students.

"Now if you will excuse me," Isaiah said. "The children are back." He walked away from us, taking the cake from the boy's hand and thanking him. All of the children crowded around their teacher. It was clear that they loved him.

A little girl walked up to Lois. "How do you get your hair to stand straight up like that?"

"Have you ever heard of Aquanet?" Lois asked.

The girl gave her a confused look.

"Let's leave Mr. Keim and his pupils," I said to Lois. "You enjoy your studies," I told the girl as I pulled Lois toward the door. When we stepped outside, we stumbled into my two grandnephews, Micah and Jacob.

Micah grinned. "Are you here to tell me that I can have the goats?"

Micah had been trying to adopt Peter and Phillip for weeks. Ever since he had begun training them to participate in the goat show at the flea market, his desire to keep the goats for himself had only grown stronger.

"You know that your *maam* would not want the goats at the greenhouse. They would eat all the plants."

He folded his arms over his thin chest.

"*Aenti* Millie," Jacob said. "What are you doing at our school? Is everything all right? We were just at the greenhouse and had lunch with *Maam*."

I patted Jacob's shoulder. He was the oldest of Edith's three children. His father had died four years ago when the children were small. When he was seven years old, Jacob had to take the place of the man of the house. He was a worrier as a result, and moved through the world with responsibility heavy on his slight shoulders. His brother Micah was only a year younger than he but felt none of that strain. At least none that he outwardly exhibited. It was a pity that we couldn't erase that worry from my eldest grandnephew, but his sense of responsibility would serve him well as he grew older. The boy was smart and very attentive.

"Everything is fine, Jacob. Lois and I were just having a chat with your teacher about a friend."

"What friend is that?" he asked with concern.

"I bet it's *aenti's* friend who died in the flea market fire. A lady was talking to *Maam* about it at the greenhouse," Micah said.

Jacob scowled at his brother. "*Maam* said not to mention that to *aenti* because it might make her sad."

I patted the shoulders of both boys. "It's all right. Ben was my friend, and I am sad that he died. Whether or not you speak of it doesn't change anything."

More children came up the path and went into the schoolhouse.

"You had better run. It looks like class is starting."

"Can you stay, *Aenti*?" Micah asked. "It would be so much fun if you stayed with us at school today."

"*Nee*, I would only distract you from your studies," I said. "You need to pay attention to your lessons."

Isaiah stepped out of the school and rang his large school bell over his head, signaling the start of afternoon classes. Jacob grabbed his younger brother's wrist and pulled him toward the school.

"Bye, *Aenti* Millie," Micah called as he went into the school. "Sorry your friend died!"

Isaiah watched the two boys go into the building, glared at Lois and me, and then slammed the school door closed as if to make a point. I believed his point was "keep out!"

Lois frowned at the closed school door. "What's your takeaway from that?"

I glanced at her. "That Isaiah Keim is a *gut* teacher and cares about his students."

She nodded. "I'm thinking the same."

"And I can't see that kind young man having anything to do with Ben's death. Isaiah didn't see him as a threat."

"Maybe," Lois said. "Or he is a great actor. I hate to admit that I liked him. I would be sorely disappointed if he turned out to be a killer. I hate when that happens to nice men."

As we walked back to the car, I couldn't get out of my head what Isaiah had said about Tess just wanting to get married—and that it didn't matter who she married.

"What do you think of him for Charlotte Weaver?" Lois suggested and she unlocked the car.

I blinked at her. I hadn't been thinking about Charlotte at all, so it took a moment for me to adjust my thoughts.

"Charlotte Weaver and Isaiah Keim?" I asked.

Isaiah was a conservative and thoughtful young man. He took his job of teaching seriously, and I knew he would take everything else in his life just as seriously. That might not be a fit for Charlotte. Charlotte was a free spirit and for the last few years had straddled the fence as to whether or not she would be baptized into the Amish faith. Months ago, she'd asked me if I would help her find a match, but I think that had more to do with the fact that she was actually matched very well with Deputy Little, an *Englischer* and sheriff's deputy to boot, than her wanting to marry an Amish man. Charlotte was afraid of her match because of what it would mean for her future. Deputy Little wasn't the ideal match for Charlotte, because marrying him would force her to leave the Amish.

"I don't think that would be very fair to Isaiah," I responded. "And we didn't come here to match Charlotte Weaver," I said.

"No," Lois conceded. "But sleuthing is all about multitasking. That's what I learned from our last case."

I wanted to ask her what she meant by that, but then I thought better of it. Sometimes it was best to ruminate on

Lois's ideas before I said anything. Many times, she turned out to be in the right.

"Where to next?" Lois asked. "I promised Darcy I would be back at the café for the dinner rush."

"Let's make one more stop and then quit for the day. I think we are both tired and have a lot to think about."

"You can say that again," Lois said. "Where are we headed?"

"The lumberyard," I replied.

Chapter Twenty-Three

Lois and I walked toward the lumberyard from the spot where she had parked her car. "I have thought of a cover story for us."

I raised my eyebrows at her. "A cover story?" I asked.

"We have to have a reason for being here, don't we? So you are helping me pick out wood to build a shed in my backyard."

"But you can't build anything in your backyard—you're renting," I argued.

"I know that, but the men working at the lumberyard don't know that."

"Why do we have to have a cover story?" I asked. "Why can't we say we want to talk to someone because Ben worked here?"

Lois sighed. "If that's the tactic you want to go with, fine, but I'm telling you the cover story would be golden."

I shook my head. I was barely able to hear her. The closer we got to the giant building, the louder the noise around us became. There was the sound of large band saws and sanders. I guessed that was how they prepared the wood for sale.

A pickup truck roared up the drive and pulled into the spot right next to us.

Lois jumped back. "Whoa, he needs to be more cautious when he's driving. He could have killed us."

The young *Englisch* man who climbed out of the truck wore jeans and a Miller's Lumberyard long-sleeve T-shirt. Without looking at us, he walked around the back of the truck and lowered the tailgate. The truck bed was full of old barn wood. He began to unload it onto a pallet nearby, piece by piece.

Lois nodded at him and gestured with her head.

I sighed. I understood what she was trying not very subtly to tell me: ask him about Ben.

I walked over to him but remained a few feet away, out of range of the wood he was throwing onto the pallet.

"Excuse me?" I asked.

The man went right on throwing wood onto the pile. He jumped into the truck bed in one leap and began throwing pieces from the bed onto the pallet seven feet away. *Bang. Bang. Bang.* The wood hit the pallet. The noise was terrible.

"Excuse me?" I tried again.

Again nothing.

"Hey!" Lois shouted at the top of her voice.

Startled, he dropped the two by four he held into the truck bed. "Who are you?" he shouted over the din.

"We need to talk to someone about Ben Baughman," I cried over the roaring sound of the saw. I wanted to get it out before Lois could tell him the made-up story about her shed.

He stared at me. "Did Flora send you?"

"Flora?" I blinked. "*Nee.*"

"Wait." He jumped out of the back of the truck bed. "The two of you aren't with Flora."

"Do you mean Flora who works for Ford Waller?"

"Must be my mistake. Flora is the only Amish woman I—I've spoken to. She said that they needed wood to repair the flea market."

"It's going to take a little more than wood to clean up that mess," Lois whispered to me.

"Flora isn't Amish," I said. "She's Mennonite."

He removed his work gloves and shoved them into the back pocket of his jeans. "All the same to me. If you're not here for Flora, I'm sorry, but I can't help you."

"We need to speak to someone about Baughman," Lois said in a cop-like manner.

"Why?" The young man began moving wood again.

"She's his aunt," Lois said. "His only relative in the county, so we came here to collect any personal belongings he might have left at work."

I groaned inwardly. I knew one of these days we were going to get caught in one of Lois's lies.

He tossed another board on the pile. "I didn't know that Ben had any family in Ohio. He said his family was in Michigan."

"Millie moved here from Michigan too," Lois said, going on with her tale.

That was technically true, but I hated it that Lois was resorting to lying to get information.

Lois straightened her back. "And how do you know Ben, young man? What's your name?"

He stared at her. "I'm Jay Kerman. I work here at the lumberyard. Ben and I worked the same shift."

"Do you know who we should talk to about Ben's things?" Lois asked.

"I suppose I can get my boss if you really want to speak to someone about his things, but none of us kept anything here. There's nowhere to put anything. This is an open-air lumberyard. Nobody leaves anything here that he doesn't want to lose."

"We'd still like to speak to your boss."

He tossed one more board on the pile. "Fine."

He went into the building that all the noise was coming from.

"Don't you think it was odd that his first thought was that we were with Flora?" I asked.

"It was because he can't tell the difference between Amish and Mennonites," Lois said as if that explanation was enough.

I frowned. But Jay lived in Amish Country. Even if he didn't know the difference between Amish and Mennonite, I doubt Flora was the only woman of either faith that he knew.

"Who's asking questions about Ben?" an *Englisch* man asked as he approached. The newcomer was as short as he was stocky. The muscles in his thick arms pressed up against the sleeve of his gray polo shirt with the lumberyard's logo embroidered on it.

Lois waved. "That would be us."

He looked from Lois to me and back again. His gaze settled on me. "You must be the aunt then." He pointed at Lois. "No one would mistake her for Amish."

No one would.

"That's a little judgy, don't you think?" Lois asked.

I gave her a look. If we wanted information from this man, it would serve us well not to annoy him.

"I'm Brandon Miller, and this is my lumberyard. I'm sorry to say that I don't have anything of Ben's here. I always tell the men to take their possessions home. There is no way to secure them in the yard."

"Oh, that's a shame," Lois said. "Did you see Ben the day he died?"

He frowned. "He came in for his normal shift that day. I think it was three until eight. I closed up at eight and said good-bye to him. Usually only English men work the late shift like that, but Ben asked for it, so I let him have it."

That was interesting, but I guessed that the other Amish men had farms and families to return home to, while Ben only had Tess. He was working all these jobs to prove his worthiness to Tess's father, but from what Tess had said herself, there didn't seem much point in that. Her father's mind was made up even before she met Ben. She was going to Wyoming whether she wanted to or not.

"I'm sorry that I can't help you, ladies, but there is nothing here of Ben's. We were all saddened when we heard the news of his death. Terrible, terrible thing to have died in the fire like that. He was a reliable worker for me, which at times can be a challenge to find." He shrugged. "If there is a funeral service for him, please let us know."

I nodded. "We will." Even as I said this, I wondered what kind of services there would be for Ben, and whether they would be here or in Michigan. I needed to ask Deputy Aiden if he had been able to get hold of Ben's family in Michigan. No matter the rift that might have happened between them, Ben's father deserved to know the fate of his son.

"Thank you for your time," I said.

Brandon nodded, and then he turned to Jay. "Come inside for a moment. I want to show you where that pallet should go when it's loaded."

Jay nodded and followed Brandon back into the aluminum building, looking over his shoulder at Lois and me as he went. Lois gave him a little finger wave as he disappeared into the building. When the two men were out of sight, she walked around the side of the building, which was in the opposite direction from where she had parked her car.

"Lois," I hissed. "Where are you going?"

"I'm going to do what we came here to do. I'm checking out the lumberyard where Ben worked."

"They said there was nothing to see here. Ben left the lumberyard at eight, as he expected to."

"They say that, but it wouldn't hurt to take a quick peek."

I put my hands on my hips.

"Oh, come on, Millie," she said, sounding like a child. "This could be my chance to use the lock picks."

I rolled my eyes. "Lois, you heard Brandon say that they don't lock anything around here."

"Okay, fine, maybe today is not the day for the lock picks, but we can at least have a look around."

"What if we get caught?" I asked.

"Then we say you wanted to see the place where your nephew spent so much time before he died, just to be closer to him. To those two, we are a couple of tottering old ladies. They will buy our story."

"My *nephew*," I said with a sigh.

"Ben told you and everyone he knew that he viewed you as an aunt. You might not be related by DNA, but you are an adopted relative. In my book, that's just as good." When she said it like that, I could see her point.

She crept around the side of the giant building. It was the only structure on the large cleared lot. Most of the space was used to store the wood that the lumberyard sold to customers and builders. Behind the metal building were rows and rows of wood of every type. There were also giant logs that still had the bark on them and needed to be planked. An Amish man drove a forklift weighed down with freshly cut logs. He was so focused on his task I doubted that he would have seen Lois and me even if we'd run out in front of him waving our arms.

"I really think we shouldn't go out into the lumberyard. They are moving very heavy machinery and piles of boards. It's too dangerous for us and for the men. We could startle them, and that will cause them to make mistakes."

"Fine," Lois said with a sigh. "Sometimes I think this snooping thing sounds a bit more exciting than it actually is."

Butted up next to the building was a pile of pallets that were waiting to be used. A flash of red behind the pallets caught my eye. "Oh!" I gasped.

Lois was at my side in a moment. "What is it?"

"Lois, look at this," I said. I walked around the pallet and grabbed the handlebars of a red bicycle and rolled it out. "It's Ben's."

She stared at it. "Are you sure?"

"I'm positive," I said as I bent over the bike for a better look. "See that dent in the fender?"

She nodded.

"My sister Harriett gave him the bike when we lived in Michigan to thank him for all his help around her farm. This was years ago, when she had still been able to move around and sit outside for a bit." I took a breath as an image of my sister in the last days of her life came back to me like a vivid dream or nightmare. It wasn't easy watching someone die over days, months, or in Harriett's case, years. I swallowed. "There's a dent on the front fender from when Ben ran into a tree when he was thirteen. It was a bad accident, but it could have been much worse. He went over the handlebars and was lucky to break only his arm. He was more upset over his bike than his arm. After the accident, he saved money for months to have the bicycle repaired. He got it back into working order, but there was still a small dent in the front fender that wasn't hammered out. Ben could have replaced the fender eventually, but he never did because he said that it was a *gut* reminder to go slower and think things through."

"What are you two doing back here?" a young male voice asked. "You said you were leaving." Jay stood on the other side of the tower of pallets with his arms folded.

"You said there was nothing of Ben's here. Then how did his bike get behind those pallets?" Lois asked.

Jay scowled at us. "How would I know?"

"How did Ben get from the lumberyard to the flea market the night of the fire?" Lois asked Jay. "There must be twelve miles between the two sites, and he would only have an hour to make the ride. He never would have been able to walk the whole way in that time."

"I told you, I don't know. Why are the two of you assuming that I know anything about Ben? I don't! I just worked with him a few days a week. It wasn't like we were friends. He was Amish."

"Oh-kay," Lois said. "We didn't mean to upset you. And for the record, Millie is my friend, and she's Amish."

He took a breath. "I don't know why the bike is here. He must have left it," Jay said. "Maybe he got a ride with someone or took an Amish taxi."

"Can we take the bike?" I asked, but I had already decided that I wasn't leaving that lumberyard without the bicycle in Lois's car.

He frowned. "I don't see why not. Just take it and go."

Jay watched us as we rolled Ben's bike around the side of the building and into the gravel parking lot where we had left Lois's car.

"How are we going to get the bike in the car?" I asked.

"Oh," Lois said unconcernedly. "We can put it in the trunk, and I can tie it down. I still have the rope from taking that chair home from the flea market."

It took some doing, but between the two of us, Lois and I were able to lift the bike into the trunk of her car, back wheel first. She then tied it down with elaborate knots. "Did I tell you that my third husband had a boat on Lake Erie? I got really good at tying knots while we were married."

I shook my head and wondered what else I didn't know about Lois. Jay kept an eye on us from where he worked at unloading the pickup. It seemed to me that he wanted to be certain we actually left. I couldn't help but wonder why he, in particular, was so worried about what Lois and I were up to when he claimed to have hardly known Ben.

"There!" Lois pulled the last knot tight. "That should

hold until we can get it to your house. That's where it should go, am I right?"

I nodded. "Do you think we should tell Deputy Aiden about the bike?" I asked.

She thought about this as she walked around the car and opened the driver's side door. "That's hard to say. He wasn't that encouraging about our helping out when I called him earlier today."

"Let's wait then. You have to get back to the café, and I have a quilting circle meeting tonight."

"So soon?" she asked.

"*Ya*, Ruth wants to talk about how we plan to replace the quilts lost in the fire. I feel bad for Iris. If I know Ruth, she will make her feel horrible about opening our booth at the flea market."

"Iris couldn't have known that the building would burn down," Lois said to me over the roof of the car as I opened my own door.

I shrugged. "That won't make any difference to Ruth, I'm afraid." I climbed into the car.

Chapter Twenty-Four

As Lois drove to my little hobby farm on the outskirts of Harvest, Ben's bicycle bounced in her trunk. A few times, I wondered if it would fly off the back of the car. Despite having the bike in the trunk, Lois didn't modify her speed and drove as fast as ever. I held onto my seatbelt as if that would help in some way.

As we bumped along, I said, "I think we have done a *gut* job of recreating Ben's last day," I said.

"We have?"

I nodded. "I saw him for a few minutes at the flea market. Then he must have ridden his bike by my house to drop off the note on his way to the village market. After his work there, he only had an hour to get to the lumberyard. He was on time for his shift. I doubt he could have done more than pedal right there. He told me that his shift at the flea market began at ten."

"So basically all he did on the last day of his life was work."

I nodded. "I think so."

"He definitely adhered to the Amish work ethic," Lois said.

"And we know he was alive until eight in the evening," I said. "That's when Brandon Miller closed the lumberyard that night and said good-bye to Ben. What we don't know is what he did when he left the lumberyard. Did someone take him to the flea market? Why would he leave his bike behind?"

"Did he have a friend who would give him a ride?" Lois asked. "If he was the penny pincher that you thought him to be, he wouldn't have called an Amish driver to pick him up."

I thought she was right about that. All Ben talked about was saving money, so that he and Tess could marry. "The only person he was close to would have been Tess, but if she took him to the flea market that night, why didn't she tell us?"

"I don't know how reliable Tess is as a witness. She didn't tell us about Isaiah right away."

"Maybe she was embarrassed to be courted by two young men?" I asked.

"Embarrassed? I would have loved it and worn it as a badge of honor," Lois said.

I smiled. "I know you would, but you're not Amish."

"Nor ever could be, as people continually remind me." She cocked her head. "Really, would I make that terrible an Amish person?" Lois asked.

"Ummm, I think it would be challenging, but I would never doubt you. I think you can do whatever you put your mind to."

She nodded. "Thank you for that, Millie. You really are a true friend to me."

I smiled. "And you to me."

I looked out the window and drove in silence for a few

minutes. We were both occupied with our own thoughts. Finally, I said, "I find it odd that Tess latched onto Ben so fast after she and Isaiah stopped courting. That is not the typical Amish reaction to the end of a courtship."

"But that was according to the dumped boyfriend," Lois said. "We need to take his story with a grain of salt. He could be spinning it to make himself look better."

"Maybe," I said, but I had thought that Isaiah was sincere.

"Well, let's both think this over tonight," she said as she turned into my driveway. The moment the car hit the gravel, Phillip and Peter came running from around the back of the house with their tongues sticking out. Their long ears flew in the air as they ran.

"I wish that someone would greet me with that much joy when I came home," Lois said sadly.

I looked at her. It was the first time my friend had ever hinted to me that she was lonely.

She shifted the car into park, unbuckled her seatbelt, and wagged her finger at me. "Don't you give me that sad face, Millie. We have a good life, you and I, but I doubt either of us thought when we were young that we wouldn't be married and surrounded with family at our age."

My heart constricted because she was right about that.

"Let's get that bike," Lois said, hopping out of the car. Clearly our conversation about loneliness was over.

Phillip and Peter danced around her as she quickly undid the knots, and the two of us lifted the bicycle onto the driveway. Out of habit, my eyes fell on the minuscule dent in the front fender. I didn't even know if anyone else would have noticed it. I did because I knew the story and why it was there. Somehow, I just couldn't stop staring at it.

Lois gave me a hug. "I know all of this has got you down, Millie. You're welcome to come with me to the café. We can always use another set of competent hands. I say competent, because Bryan's hands surely are not so."

"I'm fine. I feel better today. At least we made some progress in finding out what really happened to Ben. I know he didn't set that fire, Lois. I know it."

She nodded. "If you know, then I do too. We are in this together, Millie. Through thick and thin."

I hugged her tight. "I wished that you could come to the Double Stitch meeting tonight."

"Where's it being held? I know it's not at the Sunbeam, or we would be saving a table for you."

"The Yoder farm," I said.

She laughed. "Since it is at Ruth's farm, I know I'm not invited."

I smiled. "It would be quite a surprise for her if you came."

"I would enjoy it, but I did promise Darcy I would help with the dinner rush. She is offering half-priced meatloaf tonight, so the place will be hopping. Bryan will be no help at all. Anytime he has to speak to more than two people in a row, he completely shuts down. I hope the characters in his book are more interesting than he is, or it will be a real snore fest."

I hoped so, too, for his sake.

"Before you go, can I use your cell phone?" I asked.

Lois arched her brow at me. "Is that allowed?"

"In special cases it is, and I need to make a phone call.

Going back to the Raber farm so soon would be a bad idea."

She lifted her giant purse out of the backseat and onto the hood of the car. Lois rooted around in it until she came up with her phone. "There it is! Goodness, how does it always stick to the bottom? It's just like my stapler."

"You have a stapler in your purse?" I asked.

"Technically, it's a staple gun. You would be surprised how many times it has come in handy." She held up the phone. "Who do you need to call?"

I wrinkled my nose. "Ben's father. I tried this morning from the Rabers' shed phone, and there was no answer. I hoped I would catch him."

"Wouldn't Deputy Aiden have told him about Ben's death by now?"

"I'm sure he would have, but the funeral arrangements need to be made."

She nodded, and with her finger poised over the screen, asked, "What's his number?"

I removed my little address book from my pocket and read the number to her.

She held the phone to me. "It's ringing."

I took the phone from her hand and was ready for the machine to click over. This time, I had my message much more planned out than when I'd made the first call on the shed phone, so I was surprised when a female voice answered.

"Hello?"

"Oh, hello, may I speak to Linus Baughman?"

"My husband is not home right now. Who is this?"

This must be Ben's new stepmother. "Stepmother," I mouthed to Lois.

Lois leaned close to me, trying to hear the conversation. I waved her away. I needed to concentrate.

"This is Millie Fisher. I was Linus's neighbor in Michigan for quite a few years. I live in Harvest, Ohio, now, and I'm calling about Ben."

"I know who you are," she snapped. "You're the reason that Ben moved to Ohio, and now my poor husband has to travel there to bury his son."

Her words sucked the wind out of me. I opened and closed my mouth, but nothing came out.

Lois took the phone from my hand. "This is Lois Henry. I'm a friend of Ben and Millie's. When did you say your husband would be arriving in Harvest?" She paused. "Of course. We will be on the lookout for him." She ended the call. "What a rude woman."

"She's not being rude," I said, surprised that I still had the ability to speak. "Her stepson is dead, and her husband had to leave her to deal with his burial. I think anyone would be terse in that situation."

"Terse is one thing. Blaming you for Ben's death is quite another. She should be ashamed at the way she spoke to you."

I smiled at my friend. "I am glad you are on my side, Lois. You are a fierce defender."

She grinned. "Always have been."

"Is Linus in Ohio?"

"His wife said he should be here by now."

I frowned. I didn't know why, but I'd half expected Linus Baughman to get in contact with me just as soon as he arrived in Ohio. He didn't owe anything to me, of course, but he knew that Ben and I had been close. He must know that I wanted to be at the funeral no matter how small it might be.

"I wish there was a way to contact him while he was traveling," I said.

"Saying this not for the first time, but this is the reason I think the Amish should have cell phones."

I shook my head.

"I'm sure we will run into him soon. Harvest isn't that big, right?" She opened her car door, threw her purse inside.

"It's not," I agreed.

I waved to Lois as she drove away, and the goats chased her taillights until they reached the end of the driveway. Then, they turned back and ran to me. I let my hands drop to my sides.

Chapter Twenty-Five

The Yoder farm was one of the largest in my Amish district.

The house was a hodgepodge of sorts and oddly shaped. That wasn't unusual for an Amish farmhouse. As a family grew and changed, instead of moving or building a completely new home, many times the Amish would just expand on the existing one. Even so, I had never seen a house so added onto as the Yoder's. Leah Bontrager from our quilting circle had told me that the Yoder home had been built up so much after Ruth's husband became the bishop. Ruth felt that she had to have a home befitting the importance of his—and her—role in the community.

I turned my buggy from the road onto the Yoder property. The large farm encompassed two hundred acres. The Yoders mostly grew hay and grain, but they also had an impressive herd of cattle. They had one of the most profitable farms in the district but shared their bounty with the community. As aggravating and judgmental as Ruth could be, she was a *gut* person and had a kind heart under her prickly demeanor. I believed most people didn't know that, since she put them off with her sharp tongue so quickly that they retreated from her.

I parked my buggy and Bessie next to the other two buggies that were already there. I recognized Raellen Raber's rig right off. I wrinkled my nose. I wondered what kind of report her husband had given her about my morning visit. I also was surprised that she was there. Roman Raber seemed to be set on talking her into quitting the quilting circle. I didn't know how successful he would be at that. He might want to keep Raellen away from me, but Ruth wasn't going to let a member quit without a fight.

I tethered Bessie to the hitching post. The Yoders had a long one because, more often than not, the district biweekly church services were held at the Yoder farm. If Ruth had it her way, worship services would be at her home every time we met.

After Bessie was secured with a bag of oats under her mouth, I reached into the buggy and pulled out my quilting basket and a plate of oatmeal raisin cookies. One did not arrive at a Double Stitch meeting empty-handed.

As I walked toward the house, I heard a car gun its engine behind me. I spun around and spotted a large SUV speeding down the street going way over the speed limit. I shivered. The Yoders lived on a county road that was way off the normal path for *Englischers*. Even so, sometimes young *Englischers* would come to this part of the county to drive their cars as fast as they could because there was very little traffic. The people traveling that road were usually Amish, and driving so fast by Amish who were on bicycles, buggies, or just walking was extremely dangerous. It was a problem that Bishop Yoder had complained about to Deputy Aiden and the sheriff's department many times.

"Millie Fisher, would you stop staring at the road like a frozen rabbit and get into the house," Ruth Yoder called from the porch. "You are making me let the heat out."

I hurried toward the large house and went inside. The front door opened up to a large room to my left. That was the main room of the house. It was enormous for a living room—almost seven hundred square feet. Ruth had added the room to her home when her husband became bishop. She specifically wanted a large space for church on Sundays. To the right was a staircase leading to the second floor and another much smaller sitting room that opened into the kitchen.

Ruth closed the front door. There were only two buggies out front, but I saw that I was the last member to arrive. Raellen, Leah, and Iris were already there with quilting on their laps.

I glanced around. "Am I late?"

"*Nee*, Millie," Leah said with a kind smile. "We were just early. Iris and I rode in from the village today in my buggy. Iris wasn't feeling well, so I offered to drive us both."

Iris stared at the quilting in her lap although she made no move to work on it.

I set the cookies on the table next to the other desserts made by the ladies. We also had apple bread and cinnamon raisin muffins. It seemed to me that everyone was on a fall baking theme.

I took one of my cookies with me to my seat, an armchair that was nestled between Iris and Leah.

"Now that we are all here—" Ruth said, giving me a look.

"I wasn't late," I complained.

She sniffed. "We need to talk about the stand at the flea market. We lost over four thousand dollars' worth of quilts."

"There's not much we can do about it," Leah said in her practical way, "other than to make the quilts again. Quilts can be replaced. It's the loss of life that is irreplaceable."

"True," Ruth said.

Iris looked up from the folded hands on her lap. "I cannot express how sorry I am over this."

I reached out and squeezed her hand. "Iris, no one is blaming you."

Even as I said this, it appeared that Ruth actually might be blaming Iris.

"What is lost is lost," I said. "The flea market plans to rebuild. In fact, there will be an outside market on Saturday to be held a few hundred feet away from the building."

"We have several quilts that weren't lost in the fire. I think it would be a show of good faith in the flea market if we participated in the outdoor market they have planned," Leah said.

"Why would we do that?" Ruth asked. "After we lost so much."

"Don't forget, we also sold two quilts at the market. Besides, we are a community, and people in a community support each other." Leah gave her a level look.

"We will bring everything that we don't sell home," I said.

"Do you all think this is a *gut* idea?" Ruth asked.

Raellen smoothed the three two-by-two-inch pieces of fabric on her lap. "I do. I think it's the least we can do since Ben was one of us."

"What do you mean by that?" I asked.

"He was the one who caused the fire. We should support the flea market to say we are sorry for what happened."

"I've said this so many times, but I will say it again." I took a breath. "Ben didn't start that fire. There's no proof that he did."

Raellen covered her mouth. "Oh, you don't know."

I frowned at her. "I don't know what, Raellen?"

She looked around the room and leaned forward. "Ben didn't wake up during the fire because he was on drugs."

The word "drugs" was like a slap in the face.

Chapter Twenty-Six

"I knew it. I knew it," Ruth said. "I knew that boy from Michigan would be trouble for the district. You tried to fool me into thinking that he was a *gut* young man, but I should have trusted my instincts. They are never wrong."

"They're wrong in this case, Ruth. Ben was not on drugs. If he was, I would have known," I said.

The other women shared a look with each other. I was certain they were wondering how I could make such a claim. Perhaps I couldn't, but it was still impossible for me to believe Ben would take drugs. "If Ben was on drugs, what drugs was he taking?"

Raellen shook her head. "I didn't hear that part."

I frowned at her. "If you don't know the whole story, then maybe you shouldn't go around repeating it."

She hung her head, and I regretted my sharp tongue. However, that didn't make what I had said any less true. Raellen needed to learn to control her tongue before someone was hurt by it, before she was hurt by it.

Even so, I should not have spoken so sharply to her. "Raellen, I am sorry if I sounded harsh. That was not my intention."

She looked up. "I know that you are just hurting, Millie."

I nodded. "But can you please tell me how you learned about the drugs?"

She swallowed as if she was considering my request. I knew she wouldn't want to give up her news source for fear I would go and talk to that person. I would if I knew who it was.

"I heard it from an Amish driver," she said. "He said that his cousin is a technician at the county morgue. The technician said that there were drugs at the scene and in Ben, too, when they did the autopsy."

I bit the inside of my lip. A morgue technician, I would assume, was a reliable source. "I know Ben didn't start that fire. I just know it."

"Whether or not Ben started the fire," Ruth interrupted, "are we going to participate in the flea market?"

"Let's put it to a vote," Leah said. "Raise your hand if you want to have Double Stitch at the outdoor market on Saturday."

Leah, Raellen, and I raised our hands, and, after a beat, Iris tentatively lifted hers too. Of the group, she was the one most intimidated by the bishop's wife.

Ruth folded her arms. "I see I'm outvoted, but I never said that this quilting circle was a democracy."

"Sure, it is, Ruth," I said. "We voted on that too."

She scowled at me.

"Millie," Iris asked. "Have you heard from Ben's family in Michigan?"

I nodded my head. "I called twice and spoke briefly to Ben's stepmother. Linus, Ben's father, is on his way to Harvest. He might already be here for all I know."

"Oh, he's here," Ruth said. "He was here at the house today, speaking to the bishop about a small service for Ben. He said the police released the body to him."

I stared at her. "And you are just telling me this now? Ruth, you know that I would have wanted to know about Ben's funeral."

"It's not even a full funeral." She sniffed. "Linus only wants a brief prayer at the gravesite."

"Even so, you should have told me."

"I thought you would have known because you are so close to the family," she said hotly.

I took a breath. There was no point in getting angry at Ruth over this. "When's the gravesite service?"

"Tomorrow at the cemetery at seven in the morning. Linus said that he had an Amish driver taking him back to Michigan at eight, so it had to be early."

My heart sank as I realized that Linus had no intention of speaking to me about Ben while he was in Ohio, and I might have missed Ben's service altogether if Ruth had not mentioned it. But I was going to be at the service, and I would make Linus talk to me. I didn't care how he felt about it. Ben was my friend, and I owed him that.

"I'm surprised this is the first time I'm hearing of this," Raellen said.

"You don't know everything that is going on in the village, Raellen," Ruth snapped.

Iris and Leah shifted uncomfortably in their seats.

"Let us quilt and speak of happier things," Leah suggested. "I have a niece who is to be married in the spring. I just heard the news."

And with that, the conversation moved away from drugs and murder onto weddings and family gatherings.

I didn't speak much while the other women compared what they planned to make for the upcoming holidays. An Amish cook can never plan her Christmas menu too soon. However, I was too preoccupied with what Raellen had said. Could it be true that Ben had been on drugs when he died? Would the drugs have caused him to set the fire and then fall asleep in a building that was ablaze? It didn't seem plausible.

Also, why hadn't Deputy Aiden told me? Why, instead, did I have to hear about it from a gossipy neighbor?

The women and I worked on our quilts for another hour, and we agreed that on Saturday, we would take turns at the quilting stand at the flea market in one-hour shifts. Ruth even signed on for an hour. This way the weight of manning the booth wouldn't be all on poor Iris.

At the end of the meeting, we said good-bye to Ruth and walked out in a group.

Raellen stopped me as I untied Bessie from the hitching post. "Millie, I'm so sorry. I should have told you what I knew about Ben and the drugs in private." She pressed her lips together. "Will you forgive me?"

"There's nothing to forgive, Raellen. I know that you don't do these things with the intention to hurt."

"I don't." Her face fell. "My husband is quite angry at me for speaking about the quilting circle and the crimes in the village so much. He would much rather that I just tend to the house and the children."

I frowned. "Did he tell you that I was there very early this morning to use the shed phone?"

She nodded. "He did. He was furious about it. I'm afraid that he blames you for my ramblings."

"I know he does."

"It's not fair of him. I'm curious about these things on my own. I wish he'd understand that, but Roman doesn't have curiosity. He just wants things to be as they always were. I can't be like that, and the older we become, the more stuck in our own ways we become too." She bit her lip.

I was sad to learn that my suspicions were right, and Raellen was struggling in her marriage. I knew that she would never get divorced. It was frowned upon in the Amish community, and she had those nine children to care for. Other than making quilts, she didn't work outside of the home, so it was hard to imagine how she would make enough money to care for the children. I could tell her to speak to the bishop about it, but I feared that he would side with her husband. If he did, that would do little to change things for Raellen. In fact, it might make her feel worse.

"What brought you to the shed phone so early this morning?" Raellen asked.

Despite her husband not wanting her to ask questions of this type, she simply could not help prodding just a little.

"I was calling Lois. I needed a ride." I left it at that. I knew if I said any more, Raellen would spread the news through the district, despite her best intentions.

She nodded. "We should have come together, Millie, just like Iris and Leah did."

I smiled. "Lois and I were out and about until it was time for me to leave, but *ya*, that would be a good idea for next time."

"*Gut*, because now that autumn is here, these roads can be dangerous in the dark." She walked to her buggy.

Frowning, I watched her go. There was something vaguely menacing about her last statement. I tried to put that thought out of my head.

It was getting on to dusk, and it was time that Bessie and I went home. I knew Peaches the kitten and the goats would be looking for me. Perhaps it was something that came with age, but I no longer liked being out after nightfall alone. I felt my eyesight wasn't as reliable as it once had been, and even though I had yellow markers and headlights on my buggy, both of which were allowed by my district, I didn't feel safe on the road at night when a car flew by me. It seemed to me *Englisch* drivers were far less patient with Amish buggies at night, and too many times I had heard about buggy-auto accidents that happened on the county roads after dark.

Bessie seemed to sense my need to get home, and she didn't fight me when I put the bit back in her mouth. I knew that at times it bothered her, so I was careful only to use it when I needed to run the buggy. We were both up there in age. As my father used to say, "getting older wasn't for wimps." Of all the proverbs and lessons that I remembered and recited, I found this to be one of the most true to life. I didn't realize it when I was a child, but that wasn't even an Amish proverb. My father must have heard it from his *Englisch* friends. Surely, the "wimp" part should've tipped me off.

"That's right, girl. Let's go home. Phillip and Peter are anxious to greet you at the barn."

She shook her bridle at that. Bessie just barely tolerated my two rambunctious goats. They tended to hop around a little too much for her liking.

"I know that they can be a pain, but they mean well."

I imagined the horse rolled her eyes at that comment. My, what Ruth Yoder would think if she knew I spoke to my horse in such a way.

It was probably best that Ruth didn't know what I was thinking half the time. And, in truth, it was for the best that I didn't know what Ruth was thinking. We would find each other more irritating if we did. Not knowing exactly what was on each other's minds was indeed a blessing.

Bessie and I turned out of the Yoders' road and made our way home. Despite the misgivings that I felt from Raellen's last comment, we made it home without incident.

There was something about autumn that made it a little more urgent to be safe and cozy inside. The nights grew longer and colder. The chill in the air could trick your mind into believing that there was something afoot. I was Amish and took pride in not being a superstitious person. It was not the Amish way to believe in such things. We trusted in *Gott* to keep us safe. We needed no more security than that.

Bessie turned into my long gravel driveway, and I pulled back on her reins. "Let me get the mail, old girl. I don't want to walk back out here in the dark."

She kicked at the gravel but came to a stop. I hopped out of the buggy and went to my mailbox on the road. I opened it to find a number of bills and one letter from a friend. I was happy to see the letter, the bills not nearly so much.

I was about to climb back into the buggy when there was a scraping sound behind me in the brush that lined the road. I turned but didn't see anyone there. I thought I'd imagined it. Or could it be the goats? I had put them in the barn when I'd left because I knew I wouldn't be back until after dark.

"Phillip, Peter," I whispered. "If that's you, come out and show yourselves."

There was more scraping, and I told myself *Gott* would protect me, but it was *gut* not to be foolish. It was time to go home. I put my hand on the side of the buggy to climb back in.

Wham! A rock hit the buggy just to the right of my hand. It hit the buggy very hard. I gripped Bessie's reins, and thankfully, she did not bolt down the driveway. She was a well-trained horse, and when I pulled back on the reins to keep her still, she didn't budge.

There was a commotion in the brush now, and I saw a figure running away. It was too dark to see if it was man or woman, *Englisch* or Amish, but I got the distinct impression that it was a person.

My breath caught and I hopped out of the buggy again. There was a rock the size of my hand just a foot from the buggy. I bent and picked it up. There was a piece of paper rubber banded to it.

I climbed back into the buggy and directed Bessie to take us into the barn. She didn't wait for me to flick the reins twice.

Chapter Twenty-Seven

Inside the barn, Phillip and Peter cried in their pen. They hated to be so cooped up, and they had been penned for nearly four hours.

I climbed out of the buggy yet again and untethered Bessie. Ben's courting buggy sat in the corner of the barn. It was so new that the black paint shone in the light from the two battery-operated lanterns I turned on. I would have to find a way to return the buggy to Ben's father if I could find him. Before I could do that, I had more pressing problems, like figuring out who'd thrown a rock at me just a little bit ago.

The goats continued to make a fuss.

"You quiet yourselves," I said. "Let me just put Bessie in her stall, and I will come and speak to you."

Phillip let out one final cry to let me know that he wasn't happy with those orders, but then they fell silent.

I led Bessie into her large horse stall and brushed her down as quickly as I could. All the time, the rock with the note wrapped around it felt heavy in my pocket.

Bessie buried her nose in her trough, and I knew she

would be all right. I went out of the stall and latched it closed behind me. Then, I put my hand in my coat pocket and withdrew the rock.

The piece of paper around it was simple, lined paper like the sheets we used in school. I removed the paper from the rock, unfolded it, and read what it said. *Leave things alone if you know what is good for you!* The message was written in a crude scrawl as if the person was trying to disguise his or her handwriting. My hands shook as I gripped the rock for fear of dropping it. I looked around me. I was alone in the barn except for the goats and the horse. If there had been anyone else there, the goats would have let me know.

Phillip and Peter must have sensed something was wrong because they started making a commotion again and no amount of shushing quieted them down.

That's when I realized they were making a fuss because there was a car coming up the driveway. Oh, why hadn't I run to the house before opening the note?

"Shhh," I hushed the goats, and this time they obeyed.

I heard the engine turn off; the car door opened and shut. I shoved the note into my coat pocket for safe keeping and held the rock in my right hand in case I needed to fling it at the intruder. With my free hand, I grabbed the shovel that I used for mucking the stalls.

"Get into the corner of your pen, boys," I whispered to Phillip and Peter.

They did, and I could see them shaking next to each other. They had sensed my fear, and now were afraid too.

The barn door slid open and a flashlight beam caught

me right in the eye. "Millie Fisher!" Lois cried. "Don't you dare whack me with that shovel!"

The goats ran to their pen door and bounced in excitement. They knew friend from foe, and Lois was most certainly our friend.

"Lois, what are you doing here?"

"I could ask you the same thing. You look like you've seen a ghost. I know that the Amish don't believe in ghosts, but you've seen something."

I lowered the shovel and set it against the wall. I loosened my grip on the rock too.

She blinked at me. "A weapon in each hand? What on earth happened here tonight?"

Phillip jumped in his pen. He had gone from terrified to joyful in the blink of an eye. It took a bit longer for me to shift emotional gears.

My shoulders sagged. "I'm sorry if I scared you, Lois."

She put her hands on her hips. "Of the two of us, I wouldn't say I was the scared one. What's going on?"

I put the rock back in my coat pocket and then removed the note and handed it to her. "When I got my mail at the box tonight, someone hurled this at the buggy. It was attached to the rock that I was holding. If it had hit either Bessie or me in the head . . ."

Lois stared at the note. "Whoever wrote this didn't want to knock you out. The person wanted to threaten you. It must be about Ben's death."

I nodded. "That's what I think too."

"You know what this means, don't you?" she asked, holding up the note.

"That we're in danger."

"Yes, that, but also, we are getting close. The perp wouldn't risk being seen by you and throwing this rock if he or she wasn't desperate. We should double our efforts and find out who burned down the barn."

"If only it was that easy. I learned something new about Ben when I was at the Double Stitch meeting tonight." I went on to tell her Raellen's revelations about drugs in Ben's system.

"Drugs! Wow, I would have never pegged Ben as the type."

"I don't think he was the type."

"Everyone who finds out someone they care about is on drugs thinks that," Lois said. She winced when she saw the expression on my face. "I'm not saying that you're wrong. We need to talk to Deputy Aiden."

I nodded.

"We can go in the house, and I will give him a call. It's time that he was honest with us."

"I agree."

I patted Peter between his short horns. "What brought you here anyway? I didn't expect you to come by tonight. I have to say that I'm quite relieved you did though."

"Well, it was the strangest thing. I helped Darcy close up the café and went home. I was there for a little while, and I just had this terrible, nagging feeling that I should check on you. I couldn't call you, of course." She gave me a measured look when she said that. "So the only answer was to come to your farm. When I got here and you didn't answer the door, I decided to check the barn to make sure the goats were here. I never expected you to greet me at the barn door with a shovel."

A feeling of peace came over me. I knew the Good

Lord had moved Lois to come and check on me. It gave me comfort to know this, and the fear I had been holding onto all evening started to melt away. I didn't tell Lois any of this. I knew she would dismiss it, and I was too fragile at the moment to have my comfort in *Gotte's* peace called into question.

I exhaled. "Let's go in the house and call Deputy Aiden as you suggested. I think we all have a lot to talk about."

She glanced at Phillip and Peter. "What about the goats? Should we leave them here if someone is lurking about?"

I bit my lip. "I'm not sure they would behave themselves in the house."

"I was thinking that we might let them loose. They would give any intruder a run for his money. If I was a bad guy and two goats ran at me in the dark, I would mess up my shorts."

I grimaced at the image, but I did think she was right. The goats would guard the house. Besides, I didn't like the idea of them trapped in the barn. "You're right." I lifted the latch to their pen, and they bounded out. Both of them made a beeline for the barn door that Lois had left open behind her. It was as if they were afraid I would change my mind and confine them in the pen again.

I checked on Bessie one more time, and then Lois and I went to the house. When I unlocked the front door, Peaches stood on the threshold and told us what he thought about my coming home so late.

"Wow," Lois said. "He can really meow. Are you sure he's not part Siamese?"

"Not that I know of," I said. "He was born at my niece's

greenhouse. There aren't a lot of Siamese cats strolling around Amish Country."

"True." She removed her coat and then her phone from her pocket. "I'll call the deputy now." Lois put the phone to her ear. "Hello, Deputy Aiden. Yes, this is Lois Henry again. So sorry to bother you. However, Millie and I would like to have a little chat with you ASAP . . . It seems we are getting closer to the killer. Someone threw a rock at Millie's buggy with a threatening message on it. We thought you would like to see it." She held the phone away from her ear and I heard frustrated shouting on the other end of the phone. When the shouting stopped, she replaced it to her ear. "You can come right now. That would be wonderful. We are at her farm. The goats are out, so mind yourself when you come up the drive. Toodles."

I folded my arms. "That sounded like it went well."

She smiled at me. "He's on his way. Apparently, you just have to say 'threatening message' and the cops come running."

I shook my head and went to the far end of the room where my kitchen was. My little ranch house had previously belonged to a family of *Englischers*, so it wasn't set up like a typical Amish home. Instead of a number of smaller rooms, it had an open floor plan, and the living, dining, and kitchen areas were all in one big room. There was a bathroom and two large bedrooms in the back of the house. When I moved in, all the electrical lights had to be removed and the outlets covered. I didn't have all the wires pulled out of the house because there was a very *gut* chance that when I passed on, my niece would have to sell the home to an *Englisch* family. It would be easier for her if the wires were intact. I was at an age when I was beginning to think how to make my own death less troublesome for the loved ones I'd be leaving behind. I had no plans on dying any time soon though.

Headlights turned into the driveway. Lois went to the front window. "That's Deputy Aiden's SUV. Wow, he got here fast, and there is another police car behind his." She covered her mouth as if to stifle a laugh. "And your goats are giving them a proper greeting."

I winced. I hoped that Phillip and Peter would have the *gut* sense not to head butt any of the law enforcement officers.

Lois went to the front door and opened it. A moment later, Deputy Aiden and Deputy Little stepped inside. Deputy Aiden's lips were pressed into a thin line. He wasn't happy, and I thought a lot of that had to do with Lois's phone call. I didn't think Deputy Aiden was the type to make light of rocks being thrown at Amish buggies, and I liked him even more for that.

He nodded at us. "Lois, Millie, can you give me a concise summary of what happened?"

I jumped in because "concise" wasn't one of Lois's strengths, and besides, it was my story to tell. I quickly summarized the events from when I'd left Ruth's home. "When I got into the barn, I unwrapped the rock and found this note." I held out the note and rock for Deputy Aiden to take. I was certain that he wasn't going to allow me to keep either of them. Truth be told, I didn't want them in my home. There was something dark and sinister about them, and I didn't want them in my peaceful house.

Deputy Aiden nodded at Deputy Little, and the younger deputy, who wore plastic gloves, took the rock and put it inside a plastic bag marked EVIDENCE. I swallowed hard when I saw that word. This was a serious situation indeed.

I was more shaken up by the thrown rock than I cared

to admit. I knew it had come close to my hand and there-
fore to my head. I could have been seriously hurt or even
killed.

Deputy Aiden slipped on gloves of his own before he
took the note from my hand and read it. He nodded at
Deputy Little a second time, and the younger deputy
was ready with another, much smaller, evidence bag for
the note.

"Go lock those both in the evidence locker in my car,
and then I want you to search the grounds for any sign of
intruders. Make sure everything is secure. Also, go into
Millie's barn and take photos of where the rock hit the
buggy."

"Yes, Sir," Deputy Little said, and he spun on his heel
and walked out the door, holding the two plastic bags.

After Deputy Little left, Deputy Aiden turned back to
me and put his hands on his hips. "Millie, what on earth
have you gotten yourself into?"

He was over six feet tall, and I was no more than five
feet one, five feet two in my padded sneakers. Even so, I
put my hands on my own hips and stared right back at
him. "Why didn't you tell me Ben had drugs in his system
when he died?"

The deputy sheriff let his arms fall to his sides.

In the kitchen, the kettle whistled. Lois patted my arm.
"I can get that, Millie. You and Deputy Aiden sit down for
a nice chat."

I nodded. I sat on the sofa, and Deputy Aiden perched
on the edge of a rocking chair with care. I could see why
he was afraid it might break. The rocking chair was over
one hundred years old and had belonged to my husband's
grandmother, but it had survived for so long because it
was sturdily made. The rocking chair wasn't going to break

anytime soon, if ever. I suspected it would outlast me, my niece, and her children.

"Millie," the deputy began again.

I wasn't going to allow him to lecture me. "Deputy Aiden, I respect you. You're a *gut* man and a fine sheriff's deputy. Everyone in the Amish community knows that if we have trouble in the county, you are the one we should go to, but you didn't tell me about the drugs. Instead, the news took me by surprise."

He leaned forward in the chair and it rocked slightly. He straightened up. "I'm so sorry, Millie. That was classified information. I don't know how it leaked out of the department. I didn't tell you and I didn't tell anyone outside of the department."

"What happened?"

"At the scene, the evidence team gathered a quarter of a tray of brownies that were near Ben's body on the floor. They were taken into evidence. When they went to the lab to be tested, it was discovered that there was THC in the brownies."

"What's that?"

"Marijuana, pot. A common drug and easy to come by. It's even more so now with medical marijuana being legalized in Ohio. As a law enforcement officer, I'm not really worried about marijuana. What we do worry about is when it leads to more dangerous substances."

I swallowed. "Were there more dangerous substances evident in Ben's body?"

He shook his head. "No."

Lois handed me a cup of tea. "Would you like one too, deputy?"

"That's very kind, but no, thank you."

Lois sat beside me with her own cup of tea. I smelled

honey and whipped cream in hers. She'd made mine just the way I liked it: black. No sugar. No cream.

I didn't sip my tea. I only held onto it for the warmth it provided. It was a cool night, and there was a chill in the house. I hadn't yet fired up my wood-burning stove for the season. Perhaps I thought I could hold onto the warmer days if I held off.

"How did Ben die then?" I asked. "Were the brownies involved?"

"The coroner still says that Ben died of smoke inhalation, but the brownies are what knocked him out. It is very possible that he never heard the fire as we thought. He was passed out. If he was the one who ate almost an entire nine-by-twelve-inch tray of brownies, and if, as I suspect, he wasn't someone who had used drugs before, it could easily have incapacitated him enough that he wouldn't have been woken by the fire."

I shook my head. "I can't believe that Ben would knowingly take drugs. He was working too hard and had too much to live for. He was trying to prove to Tobias that he should be allowed to court Tess. That doesn't sound like a young man who would be so careless, does it?"

Deputy Aiden shook his head. "No, and I tend to agree with you. It's my theory, although not everyone in the department agrees with it, that someone gave those brownies to Ben, wanting to knock him out so they could start the fire."

I shivered. "In that case, the person who gave him the brownies would have known that Ben was inside the flea market during the fire. That's so cold blooded."

Deputy Aiden nodded. "It's cold-blooded murder."

Chapter Twenty-Eight

Peaches walked around the perimeter of the room as if he was taking stock of the sheriff's deputy. Deputy Aiden must have passed some kind of test, because a moment later, the kitten walked over to the deputy and rubbed his lithe body along Deputy Aiden's pant legs. He left white and pale orange fur behind before he sauntered over to Lois and me on the sofa and settled down between us.

"Deputy Aiden, Flora from Waller Properties told me that she paid Ben the morning before he died. I saw her give him an envelope. She said that was his pay. Did you find anything like that with his body?"

His brow furrowed. "There was an envelope with cash on his person. We didn't know where it came from. I will speak to Flora about that."

"If someone killed him, wouldn't they have taken the money?" I asked.

"One would think so," Aiden said.

"Where would he have gotten the brownies?" Lois asked.

"That's what I would like to know," Deputy Aiden said. "I think once I find that out, we will find the killer."

I stared out the window. Deputy Little came back out of the barn. Through the window, I saw the beam of his flashlight move back and forth over my lawn. There was something eerie about the yellow beam flashing over the dry grass and tufts of fallen leaves. Suddenly, the beam began to bob at a fast pace across the lawn, and even through the glass, Deputy Little could be heard yelling, "Back, goat!"

"Millie?" Deputy Aiden asked in a way that told me it wasn't the first time he had tried to get my attention.

I looked at him.

"Millie, I want you—and you too, Lois—to stay out of this. If someone was cruel enough to give Ben drugs with the intent of burning him alive in a fire, that is not a person to mess with. Also, that rock he or she threw at your buggy was a warning. Next time, I'm afraid there won't be a warning, and I will be solving your murders too."

Lois finished her tea and set the cup and saucer on the side table next to the sofa. "That's very dark, Deputy."

"That's very realistic. I don't want anything to happen to either of you. Promise me you will stay out of this case."

Lois sat up straighter in her seat. "We most certainly will not—"

"We will," I said, interrupting my friend.

Relief flooded the deputy's face, but I didn't know how long it would stay there after what I said next.

"We will, if you promise me that you will prove that Ben is not behind this, and you will clear him of all blame."

"I will do my best," Deputy Aiden said.

I shook my head. "*Nee.* You must promise, and if you can't do that, Lois and I still have to be involved. I will not let whoever killed Ben ruin his reputation too. He was a kind young man who was in love. He was in the prime of his life. He was doing everything right. He was baptized in the church and was working to earn enough money to support a family someday. He should be remembered that way."

"Millie," Deputy Aiden said, as if just saying my name caused him pain. "I can't promise that. I'm in a tight spot. The sheriff wants this case tied up, and he wants the flea market opened again. He and the owner, Ford Waller, are friends. Ford wants to put this behind him and rebuild. The sheriff already agreed to let the flea market reopen outside on Saturday. That's much sooner than I would have liked it to happen. Fire scenes are very tenuous. I don't want a lot of people poking around there during the market. It could compromise the evidence."

"Deputy Aiden, I understand the tough position you're in. I respect that. You might be asked to give up the case, but Lois and I won't until Ben's name is cleared."

Deputy Aiden nodded. "I won't either, Millie, I can promise you that. Even if the sheriff asks me to drop the case, I will work on it on my own time. However, there is every possibility that Ben did set the fire, perhaps accidentally. The flames were caused by a broken lantern. The fire investigator determined that. Ben could have been careless and high and dropped the lantern. Maybe we will learn that it wasn't so much a crime as an accident."

Perhaps, but that didn't explain why someone would threaten me. And from Deputy Aiden's expression, he realized it too.

Deputy Little came into the house, and he was panting as if he had just sprinted around the entire property twice. There were telling hoof marks on the front of his trousers.

It seemed to me that I would have to give those goats a talking-to about manners. A good host does not chase a guest around their property.

Deputy Little caught his breath, swallowed, and then said, "The area is clear, sir."

Deputy Aiden stood up from the rocking chair and it careened back on its rails. He caught it before it could topple over and then smoothed out the shirt of his uniform. "Good. I'm glad to hear that. What about the buggy?"

"I saw where it was hit. There is a dent in the wood and a nick in the paint. Whoever threw that rock gave it all he had."

Lois put her hands on her hips. "Why do you assume it's a he? Women can throw hard too."

"I'm well aware of that," Deputy Little said.

Deputy Aiden folded his arms. "We might need a police presence here tonight."

I stood up and set my own teacup and saucer on the table as Lois had. "That won't be necessary. Whoever threw that rock is long gone now. I told you I saw the person run away. Deputy Little or the goats would have found him by now if he was on my farm."

Deputy Little cleared his throat. "I think she's right, sir. The goats seem to be patrolling the grounds with marked attention."

"That's one way to describe what they are doing," Lois said with a laugh.

"What are your plans for the night, Millie?" Deputy Aiden asked. "I don't like you staying all the way out here by yourself."

"I can't leave," I said. "I have my animals to worry about. I'll be fine here. The goats are outside, and they can scare almost anyone away. I'll lock all the windows and doors."

Deputy Aiden looked as if he wanted to argue with that plan until Lois said, "And I'm going to stay the night with her. I studied karate back in the day. I only got to a purple belt. I wasn't so good with the focus and concentration aspect of it. All that slow breathing made me want to take a nap. I feel the same about yoga. Put me in Savasana and you might as well knock me out with a two-by-four . . . there is no way I'm staying alert under those conditions." She took a breath.

Deputy Aiden stared at her. "All right," he said. "But keep the house locked, and if anything strange happens, I want you to call 911 and then me right away. Don't go outside and check it out yourself for goodness sake!"

"We won't," I said.

Deputy Aiden shook his head and turned to the young deputy. "Let's increase patrol over the next two days on Millie's street. That will make me feel a touch better about all this."

Deputy Little nodded. "Yes, sir."

The deputies said their good-byes and went out the door. Phillip and Peter were waiting for them, and the two goats took great pleasure in chasing Deputy Little straight to his cruiser.

Lois held the door open and watched. "It seems your goats have taken a real shine to Deputy Little. Poor man." Lois closed the door as the two police vehicles drove away, and then she sniffed. "Sheesh, it's almost like he doesn't trust us to stay out of trouble. We are two very respectable women." She paused. "Okay, *you* are a very respectable woman. I'm the fun one. Anyone can see that."

"We both are respectable in our own way," I corrected her. "And he just wants us to be careful. I, for one, have no desire to go out in the dark again tonight."

"Me neither," she admitted.

"Are you sure you want to stay here for the night? You don't have any of your things with you."

"Oh, I can get by for one night just as I am. My first husband was in a rock band, and many times I had to sleep in my clothes on the road. This will be a lot more comfortable than sleeping on the floor of a dirty cargo van."

I made a face. "I should hope so."

"And I can protect us. My second husband was the one who got me into karate. He taught me some self-defense moves. I never forgot them." She kicked her leg in the air, hitting a lampshade in the process. If I hadn't been there to catch it, the lamp would have been in pieces on the floor.

Peaches ran out of the room as if his tail was on fire. I knew he would be hiding under my bed.

"Careful. You are going to hurt yourself if you keep doing that."

"Naw," she said. "Working at the Sunbeam Café has kept me young. I think I forgot how hard restaurant work is. I haven't felt this fit in decades."

"Let me show you to the guest room. It's not fancy."

She smiled. "You're Amish, Millie, I'm not expecting the Four Seasons. And this will be fun, like old times when we used to have sleepovers in your father's barn, but we won't wake up with cows in our faces. At my age, sleeping in a cozy bed is much more appealing than in a barn."

I showed Lois the guest room and brought her a fresh towel and a bar of homemade lavender soap. When I came back with the towels and soap she was already under the quilt.

Lois snuggled down in the bed. "I don't know how you did it, but this house smells just like your childhood home. When we were young, I loved spending the night at your house. There was so much love and so much going on. It was much more exciting than my house. That's why I liked being over there so much." Her voice trailed off.

Lois's father was a harsh man, and Lois had avoided him as much as she could. It wasn't uncommon for Lois's mother to walk over to our farm and ask Lois to come home. At the time, I had the feeling that neither Lois nor her mother wanted to go back, but they did so out of duty. Perhaps, had her mother lived in today's world, she would have divorced Lois's father. But as far as I know, that never came up.

Lois sat up against the pillow with a faraway look on her face. "Spending time with you has brought back memories from my younger days. A lot of them are good." She paused. "But not all of them. I know that I have bad taste in men because of my father, although I never was attracted to harsh men like him. With the exception of my third husband, I chose weak men. I thought I was safer that way. My father was so strong and fierce, and I wanted no one like that. If I was the stronger person in the relationship, I could protect myself from being hurt. Over time, I found that a weak man wasn't the answer. What I needed was my equal. I found that with my third husband, but as fate would have it, he died too soon. I guess I thought that all I deserved was a weak man, and that got me into my fourth disastrous marriage." She smiled sadly. "You knew from the very beginning you needed an equal partner, Millie, and you had that in Kip. You don't know how lucky you are to have found him so young."

"I'm sorry, Lois." I didn't know what else to say.

"It's quite all right. I found my way out of it all, and I'm happy even if my happy means being alone." She snuggled down in the covers. "Now, we'd both better get to sleep. I don't know about you, but I plan to catch a killer tomorrow."

I laughed. "Good night, Lois."

"Good night, Amish Marple," she said drowsily.

I smiled as I closed the door.

Chapter Twenty-Nine

The next morning, I woke up before dawn just as I always did. Peaches was curled up at the foot of my bed. After getting myself ready for the day, I knocked on Lois's door. There was no answer, and I peeked inside. She lay in the middle of the bed on her stomach with a pillow over her head.

Peaches was at my feet and he meowed up at me. "She should sleep a bit longer," I whispered. "She can be a real bear if woken up too early."

I went outside to check on the goats. The pair of them were curled up together in the front yard. When they saw me, they got up, but they didn't bound and jump as they usually did when greeting me. But then again, they were not morning goats. However, when I made my way to the barn, they galloped behind me.

"I suppose the promise of breakfast will get you moving," I told them.

Inside the barn, I fed Bessie and the goats and cleaned all their stalls. There was something about doing the daily chores that gave me calm. I could never say I didn't have a reason to get up in the morning. These animals needing my care were my reason. They weren't my only reason, of course, but it was good to know someone depended on me to start the day.

After the stalls were cleaned, I went and looked at the buggy. I saw the footprints of Deputy Little on the barn floor beside it. On the dusty concrete floor, I could see the exact place where he'd stood as he examined the buggy. The dent and nick in the paint he had described were there. I realized that the mark was just at the level of my head. It had been a miracle that the rock had missed me.

"Millie," a voice whispered.

I jumped and spun around. Wrapped tightly in a black cloak, Tess Lieb stood in the opposite corner of the barn. She had straw in her hair and her prayer cap was slipping off her head.

"How long have you been there?"

She swallowed. "Since the police left your house last night."

I shivered. "You were in the barn and watched me muck the stall without saying a word?"

She blinked away tears. "I'm sorry. I was trying to build up the courage to speak to you."

I removed my work gloves and hung them on the nail by the goats' stall. "It seems that you have been able to."

She nodded. "I'm trying so hard to be brave."

"Just being here makes you brave in my book."

She looked down at her hands, and tears fell to the concrete floor.

I looked away, giving her a moment to collect herself. I eyed the goats. "Some security you two are." They were so concerned with breakfast, they didn't seem to think they should tell me that someone was hiding in the barn.

"The goats slept with me last night," she said. "It was comforting to have animals nearby. They are very sweet."

I smiled. After the rock throwing incident the night before, I had left the barn door open so the goats could come and go as they pleased and scare off any possible threats. It seemed they did not view Tess as a threat. "They are, and they can be gentle, especially when they sense someone is hurting." I peered at her. "Are you hurting, Tess?"

"I—I'm just so confused. I don't know what to do. Do I go to Wyoming or leave my family? It's the hardest decision I've ever had to make. I—I almost feel like I need to go to Wyoming now because it's what I deserve. My *daed* says that I'm ungrateful for all he has done for me. Maybe he's right. All this time, I thought he didn't care about me, but maybe Wyoming is what I need."

"What can I do for you, Tess?" I asked.

"I—I don't know. You were so kind to Ben. He spoke of you often." She took a breath. "I still can't believe that he's gone. He was my way out."

My forehead wrinkled as she said this. I didn't believe that thinking of a man as a way out of a tough situation was the right way to go into a marriage. I thought of what Isaiah had told Lois and me in the school the day before. He believed that Tess just wanted to marry to escape her family, not because she loved him or Ben.

In my way, I understood how she felt. Every Amish young person had their own version of rebellion. I had gotten into my fair share of trouble. My parents thought I had made mistakes because of my friendship with Lois. However, I knew that wasn't it at all. I might have been drawn to Lois as a friend because I loved to watch her push the boundaries. I was a rule follower, and it was exciting to be around someone who didn't care about the rules and had another version of right and wrong. When I married Kip, some of the rebellion fell away, but he always said that he loved my inquisitive nature, for which I was grateful. It would have been impossible to snuff it out completely.

Tess walked over to the courting buggy in the corner of the barn. "That's Ben's, isn't it?"

"How did you know?" I asked.

"Because it looks like the buggy he was having made for us. It's the prettiest buggy I have ever seen. He saved all his money and had it made to impress my *daed*."

"I thought it might have been something like that."

"He just wanted to prove that he could provide for a wife and family. I told him that nothing would impress my *daed*. Ben would have done better saving his money rather than spending it on a lavish buggy."

I studied her as she touched the buggy. I was just about to ask Tess how she really felt about Ben when I heard Lois push open the barn door. "What are you doing up at this ungodly hour? It's not even seven in the morning." Lois's loud voice preceded her into the barn. "It's so cold this morning, I definitely need to go home and grab my coat. Not to mention, my hair looks a fright. I'm guessing you don't have a flat iron." She stepped into the barn, her red/purple spikey hair standing up in all directions. She wore no makeup, and she had a mark on her cheek from where it had pressed up against the pillow.

"Lois, we have a guest," I said.

She blinked at me. "The goats aren't guests."

I turned around and saw that Tess was gone. She must have slipped out the back door that led to the small pasture where Bessie grazed on quiet days. I hurried to the door just in time to see her climb over the wooden rail fence and run up the hill in the direction of the Raber farm.

"Who was that?" Lois asked with her mouth hanging open.

"It was Tess," I said. "She said she spent the night in the barn."

Lois turned back to the goats. "What is it with you two? You're supposed to tell us if someone is here."

The goats hung their heads.

I walked over to the goats and scratched them each between the ears. "Tess said that they spent the night with her. I'm proud of them for providing comfort to such a troubled young woman."

"And a fast young woman," Lois said. "Did you see how she leapt over that fence and ran? She should really be on a track team of some sort. What did she want?"

"She's still torn about going to Wyoming, and I think she was about to tell me something when you came in."

Lois winced. "Sorry about that."

I patted her arm. "You couldn't have known."

"Wasn't her father going to put her on a train to Wyoming today?"

"That's what she said yesterday. I'm kicking myself that I didn't ask Deputy Aiden about it when he was here last night."

"You had other things on your mind," she excused. "Like almost being killed."

"I don't think whoever threw that rock was trying to kill me."

She shrugged. "Maybe not right then, but he or she—I'm an equal opportunity accuser here—wouldn't be broken up if you died either."

I pressed my lips together.

"Are we going to go to the orchard to track Tess down?" Lois asked.

I shook my head. "That would be a bad idea. Her father is already suspicious of us, and I believe it would just make things worse for Tess."

"I do too," she agreed. "I need to get home and do something with my hair. How about I drop you off at the Sunbeam Café, and you hatch a plan while I get ready?"

I eyed her. "How long will it take you to get ready?"

"Just an hour." She touched the wilted spikes on the top of her head. "Maybe two."

I followed Lois back to the house. "Do you have a hat in your purse?" I asked.

She looked over her shoulder. "Do I have a hat in my purse? Of course, I have a hat in my purse. You never know when you will need one."

"*Gut*, because we have to make a stop before the Sunbeam Café, and we have to be there at seven sharp."

"It's six-thirty now. That doesn't give us much time. What's the stop?" she asked.

"The district cemetery." I paused. "For Ben's funeral."

Chapter Thirty

I was grateful when Lois didn't argue with me about going to the funeral. Not that I thought she would. And she spoke the truth when it came to the hat too. We were in her car driving to the cemetery when she reached into her purse and tossed two hats onto my lap. "Which one should I wear? I didn't know that I would be going to an Amish funeral today, or I would have brought something black."

The first hat was a bright pink crocheted beret, and the second was a multicolored cloche covered with felt flowers.

"The beret?" I said.

"You don't sound too certain about that." She glanced away from the road for just a moment to look at me.

"That's because I'm not."

"Okay. I'll wear the pink one. It's more sedate."

If she said so.

The district's cemetery was at the top of a hill in a secluded part of the county. A lone sycamore tree stood at the top of the hill in the middle of the plain funeral plots. I sucked in a breath as soon as the tree came into view.

"Are you okay?" Lois asked.

"Kip's buried under that tree," I said. "I have been meaning to come back and visit since I moved home to Holmes County but haven't yet. It's just such a shame that Ben's death was the event to bring me here."

She squeezed my hand. "You've told me before that the Amish believe that when a person dies, they are no longer on this earth. Not visiting Kip's grave doesn't mean you love him any less."

I smiled at her. "I know that, but perhaps I should have come here for me. For some type of peace or closure, as you *Englischers* call it."

Lois looked as if she wanted to ask me more about that, but I wasn't sure I was prepared to answer her questions. I was saved by pointing out the only other *Englisch* car parked along the road near the cemetery. It was Deputy Aiden's departmental SUV. "We have company."

"He did mention that he was coming to this last night," Lois said.

"*Nee*, he did not."

Lois parked the car and we both got out. If Deputy Aiden was surprised to see us, he didn't show it. The deputy stayed outside the weathered rail fence that surrounded the cemetery. He leaned against his vehicle.

Inside of the fence, a small group of mourners stood around a fresh grave. It was a quarter to seven, but it looked to me as if the service was about to start early.

"Are you going inside, Deputy Aiden?" Lois asked.

He shook his head, and then, looking at me, he said, "I'm very sorry for your loss, Millie. I truly am."

Something lodged in my throat, and I couldn't answer. I only nodded.

Lois took my arm as we walked through the opening in the fence. There was no gate.

Among the mourners, I saw Bishop Yoder, Ruth, three other elders from the district, and Linus Baughman. Linus was a tall, lanky man. His face was perpetually tanned from working hours in the sun on his farm. He wore a pair of round glasses that were perched high on his nose, and he frowned at me.

"It seems to me," Bishop Yoder said, "that everyone we expected to come is now here. Shall we begin?"

Linus gave a slight nod.

Bishop Yoder led us in a short prayer, and then Ruth began to sing a hymn as we each threw a handful of dirt onto the coffin. Ruth's voice was a clear and strong alto. Beside me, I heard Lois sniffle. I didn't look at her. I knew if I did, I would break down as well.

After Ruth's song, the bishop said another short prayer, and then it was over. Bishop Yoder and each of the elders spoke to Linus in turn. He nodded at their words.

Ruth walked over to where Lois and I were standing. "I expected you to be here, Millie." She wrinkled her nose. "But not you, Lois."

Lois cocked her head. "Ben was my friend, too, and I came to pay my respects."

"You're not Amish," Ruth shot back.

"I have no idea why you continually feel the need to point that out to me," Lois said. "I think my first clue that I wasn't Amish was when I was born in a hospital."

Behind them, Linus began to walk with one of the district elders to the cluster of buggies. This might be my only chance to speak to him. I left Ruth and Lois bickering at the edge of the cemetery and hurried after him. "Linus! Can I speak to you for a moment?"

He turned and looked at me and then spoke quietly to the district elder. The elder nodded and walked the rest of the way to his buggy.

Linus waited for me just on the other side of the fence. "Millie," he said.

"I'm glad that you are here. I'm so very sorry about Ben."

He pursed his lips. "*Danki.*"

"I tried to call you a couple of times about all this, but you must have already been on your way here."

"I came as soon as the police told me," he said.

"I just want you to know that Ben was doing very well in Holmes County. He was happy."

He nodded but said nothing. Linus was not making this conversation easy for me. Not that I expected he would. He was a stern man, and as far as I knew, had always been so.

"I know it must have been difficult for Ben to choose to move to Ohio, but he was doing very well. He had several jobs and was extremely responsible."

"I am glad he moved. I told him he needed to find a place to go. This was as *gut* as any other place."

I raised one brow. This was not what I'd expected him to say. I'd thought he would be angry because Ben had chosen to move so far away from his home district. "You approved of his moving here?" I asked.

"I'm starting a new family with my new wife. It would not do to have my adult son hanging about. He needed to make his own way. Since he was showing no motivation to leave on his own, I encouraged him to go."

I frowned. To push one's child out of the nest wasn't a very Amish practice. Typically, young Amish men and women lived with their parents until they were married. I wondered if Linus's new wife had asked Linus to make Ben leave because he was a reminder of Linus's old life. I hoped that I was wrong in that suspicion.

I shook my head. It was not my place to judge the choices that Linus and his wife made about raising their family. One of my proverbs came to mind. "It is better to hold out a helping hand than point a finger."

I took a breath. "Is there anything I can do for you? Ben was a great help to me when my sister was ill. I would like to help you, too, if I can."

"I think you have done enough, Millie." He said this in a way that suggested I had done too much and none of it was *gut*.

As much as it hurt me to hear that, I did not argue with him. No matter what his relationship with his son had been, he had lost his child. That was something I had never been through and, as a childless widow, would never be able to fully understand. Even so, I said, "I do have some of Ben's belongings. You should take them."

"The police gave me some of his things."

"There is also a courting buggy that he paid for. It's in my barn." I swallowed. "It was never used. He was court-ing a young woman named Tess Lieb, but he died before the buggy was completed. It's rightfully yours."

"I don't want the buggy," Linus said.

"You could sell it, or I could sell it for you and send you the money," I offered.

He scowled at me. "I don't want the buggy or the money."

"But—"

"But nothing," he snapped. "I have made my decision. Please respect that. I do not care what you do with the buggy."

My heart sank.

"Now, I must go. I have an *Englisch* driver waiting for me in Millersburg to take me back to Michigan." He walked away.

I took a step after him and then stopped myself. He'd made his choice.

He paused and looked over his shoulder. "*Danki* for taking care of my boy while he was here."

Before I could respond, he walked to the waiting buggy and climbed in.

Lois joined me. "That didn't look like it went so well."

I gave her a sad smile. "I would say that it didn't."

"What did he say about the courting buggy?"

"He doesn't want it. Doesn't want to sell it for the money either."

"I suppose that makes it yours now."

I frowned, unsure how I felt about that.

Deputy Aiden joined us at the fence. "It was a lovely service even if it was brief and I couldn't understand the Pennsylvania Dutch. There was a serenity about it."

"I couldn't agree more, Deputy," Lois said.

"Why didn't you come into the cemetery?" I asked.

"I promised the bishop that I would just observe from outside the fence. He did not want law enforcement at the service."

"You didn't stop Linus to talk to him. Didn't you want to question him about what he might know of Ben's death?" I asked.

"I spoke to him yesterday when he arrived in Holmes County. He came down to the station and was there for a couple of hours. I'm sorry to say that he had little contact with his son after he left Michigan, so he wasn't much help in the investigation."

"If you already spoke to Linus, why come to the funeral at all?" I asked.

He frowned. "In the middle of a murder investigation, we usually go to the funeral to see who shows up—or doesn't. It can be telling at times."

"What did you learn?" Lois asked.

Deputy Aiden folded his arms.

"I am glad that Linus had the service, no matter how small it was. Ben deserved a Christian burial and he would have wanted his *daed* to be there," I said.

Deputy Aiden nodded.

"It's clear to me that Linus had nothing to do with his son's death," I added.

"I don't see how he could. He was in Michigan when Ben died, nowhere near the fire. We know he was there because I called the sheriff's department in his county, and an officer went to Linus's farm to tell him about his son. I know it is difficult to get hold of the Amish on their shed phones, and this was certainly not a message I wanted to leave him over an answering machine."

I had felt the same way when I left my first message at the Baughman farm after Ben's death.

"Where does that leave the investigation?" Lois asked.

Deputy Aiden rubbed the back of his neck. "Pending.

The sheriff is tired of so many resources being used for this case when there is no factual evidence of foul play. All that we know for sure is that Ben ate brownies laced with marijuana and fell asleep. The fire was caused by a broken lantern. We do not know if that lantern was broken on purpose or accidentally. It is possible that Ben knocked over the lantern unwittingly when he was high from the drug."

"Are you telling us that you are giving up on the case?" Lois asked.

He frowned. "No, not yet, but if I don't find something to prove there was foul play involved, the sheriff might just take the case from me and close it. Permanently."

And Ben's reputation would remain tarnished forever.

Chapter Thirty-One

After Lois and I said good-bye to Deputy Aiden and the bishop and Ruth, we climbed into Lois's car. We hadn't even been at the gravesite for a half hour by the time we left.

Lois removed her pink hat, and her hair sprang up in all directions. "How does my hair look?"

"Ummm . . ."

She groaned. "I need a flat iron, stat. I'll drop you at the café like we planned and then go deal with my hair."

I nodded but didn't say anything more. I was too preoccupied by my conversation with Linus Baughman. I realized that I needed to make peace with it. In the end, he had thanked me for being there for Ben. It was possible that he could not give me anything more than that, and I should not expect anything more.

Lois drummed her fingers on the steering wheel. "There's just one thing that seems odd to me."

I glanced at her. "Just one?"

"All right. More than one, but one in particular stands out. Where was Tess Lieb? If she really loved Ben and was going to marry him, wouldn't she come to his funeral?"

"Perhaps her father didn't let her, or she couldn't get away."

"But she got away last night to hide in your barn."

"Maybe she didn't know about the funeral and when it was. I just found out last evening, and I wasn't able to tell her this morning before she disappeared."

"Maybe," she said, but her tone suggested that she doubted that was the real reason.

Twenty minutes later, I climbed out of Lois's car in front of the café. She had a scarf wrapped around her head in addition to her hat and large sunglasses over her eyes. So that no one would see her with bad hair and no makeup, she had told me. She reminded me of the women who used to walk to the *Englisch* salon to get their hair set in Millersburg when we were children.

Lois tooted the horn as she drove away. I waved and stepped into the café. It was close to eight now. There were several tables full of people sipping coffee and reading. Bryan was absent. That was a surprise. It might be the first time I had come into the café when he wasn't sitting at his table by the window with his laptop.

"Where's Grandma?" Darcy asked, sounding concerned, as she walked by me with a tray of coffees. She put the coffees on the table for the customers, asked them if they needed anything else, and came back to me at the counter, seemingly all in one breath.

"She had to run home. She said she had a hair emergency," I said.

She set her tray on the counter. "Oh." Darcy nodded. "I know what those are like. We will see her in a couple of hours."

I frowned. I hoped that it wouldn't take nearly that long. We had a case to solve.

Darcy grabbed a mug from the shelf behind her and poured a coffee for me from the carafe. She set it in front of me. "You might want to have a seat, Millie. You might be here for a little while if you're waiting for Grandma."

I slipped into the sole seat at the counter. I was so short that my feet didn't quite reach the stool's rails. I sipped my black coffee. Since Lois wasn't there, Darcy had actually given me what I ordered, instead of Lois giving me what she thought I should have. Her thoughts tended toward sugar and fat. Black coffee was just fine with me. The sharp bitter taste kept me alert and gave me clarity of thought.

"Millie, can I ask you a question?" Darcy asked.

"Of course, *kind*."

She leaned forward. "It's a matchmaking question. Do you ever match non-Amish?"

I shook my head. "*Englischers* are not typically look-ing for help from an Amish matchmaker, so I can't say I ever have."

She frowned and thought about this. "If I speak to you about something, can you promise not to tell anyone, not even Grandma?"

I cocked my head. "If it puts someone in danger, I can't promise that."

"Oh!" she exclaimed. "No, it's nothing like that."

I nodded for her to go on.

"What do you think about Bryan?"

I sipped my coffee to give myself a bit of time. I wasn't that surprised to hear her question. Bryan had been attracted to Darcy from the moment he'd stepped into the café the first time. It was all over his face.

When I didn't say anything, she went on as she looked around the café to make sure that none of her customers needed anything. "You see, yesterday afternoon when it was slow and we were the only two people in the café, he asked me on a date. He looked like he might pass out when he said it. The first time he asked, he was so garbled that I didn't even know what he was saying until he repeated it. Now, I'm not sure what to do or how to act around him."

"What did you say?" I asked.

"That I had to think about it."

"That was a *gut* answer," I said.

She smiled.

"And act around him as you always have. There is no need for you to change your behavior."

"The thing is, he's changed his. He left right after I said I needed time to think about it, and he hasn't been back. Usually, he's the first person in the café every morning, but he's not here." Her face fell. "I'm afraid I hurt his feelings."

"He might be hurt some, but that's not your fault. You need to sort out how you feel about him. He can't expect you to know right away. If he changed his behavior because you asked for time, I think that's telling, don't you?"

She nodded as she thought this over.

The front door of Sunbeam Café opened, and in stepped Lois with perfectly spikey hair, a black and red tracksuit, and full makeup. Lois pulled Bryan into the café after her. "Look who I found writing on a park bench on the square like it was a summer day. It's cold out there."

Bryan had his messenger bag in the crook of his arm and gripped his open laptop with both hands. It looked to me as if Lois had yanked him from the bench and dragged him along behind her.

She let him go, and, without looking at any of us, he went to his table by the window. Darcy and I shared a look, and Darcy's brow wrinkled in concern. I hoped she wouldn't confuse sympathy for him with attraction. She wouldn't be the first woman to fall into that trap though. Despite my advice, this might be a lesson Darcy would have to learn on her own.

"Ready to go?" Lois asked me.

Before I could answer, she cried, "Oh, what's that you're drinking?" She pointed at my almost-gone mug of black coffee. "Darcy, how can you serve my best friend such stuff?"

Darcy smiled at her grandmother. "It's what she ordered. Unlike you, I give customers what they ask for. I have found that it's the best way to keep my business afloat."

"Clearly, I have taught you nothing," Lois muttered.

I took one last sip from my coffee and stood up. "I'm ready to go."

"Where are the two of you headed?" Darcy asked.

Lois opened the door and ushered me out. "Just a little snooping, granddaughter. Nothing for you to worry about."

Darcy's mouth fell open, and she looked as if she wanted to say something in response, but Lois had already closed the door behind us.

Chapter Thirty-Two

"Where to?" Lois asked after we got into the car.

"Waller Properties. I think we need to have a cover story to get in."

"We do? Do tell." She clapped her hands.

"Well, if the flea market comes back on Saturday, Double Stitch would like space. I need to speak to them about that."

"Don't tell me. You convinced the quilting circle to rent space so that you could check out Ben's boss, didn't you?"

I settled back into my seat. "Okay, I won't tell you that."

I didn't know how to get to Waller Properties, but Lois tapped the address into her little phone and a very prim and proper woman gave us directions. "How does she know where we are going?"

"It's GPS. It's great when you're lost, but there is the catch that the government can track you down at a moment's notice."

I blinked at her. "Not me."

"Not you. That's a perk of being Amish." She grinned at me.

Waller Properties was housed in a large office building a block from the Holmes County Courthouse in Millersburg. The façade was tan brick and the windows were large and double plated. The only building I'd ever seen that had been somewhat similar to this was the hospital where my dear sister Harriett was treated over the years.

Lois parked in the large lot next to the building. I stared at all of the vehicles in the lot. "Are all these cars here for Waller?"

She shook her head. "I don't think so. This is one of those office buildings with dozens of offices in it. See, it says on the side there that there are attorneys, doctors, and even a graphic designer."

We got out of the car, and I let Lois take the lead into the building. We stood in a large glass atrium, and Lois walked over to the building directory. I looked around, already feeling claustrophobic. I didn't think I could work in a place where there were so many small offices smooshed together. Even though it was a large building, it felt small to me because it had been chopped up into so many little pieces.

"He's on the second floor," Lois said. "Elevator or stairs?"

"Stairs," I said without even considering the elevator. I had ridden in one before in the hospital, and I tried to avoid them when I could.

Lois went to the stairs. On the second floor, there were five different offices, but it was easy to find the one we were looking for. A sign above the door said, WALLER PROPERTIES.

Lois whistled. "This is a serious kind of place. I think

his sign is plated in real gold." She opened the door and stepped inside. I went in after her. Flora Kimble sat behind the front desk, and she didn't look the least bit pleased to see Lois and me in front of her.

"I'm surprised to see you using a computer, Flora," Lois said.

Flora frowned at Lois. "I'm Mennonite. Not Amish. There's a difference."

"You bet there is. You can have a car," Lois said, not even fazed by her mistake. "And you can type."

I groaned inwardly. We had only just arrived, and it was very possible that Lois had just insulted the person who had the best chance of giving us access to Ford Waller.

Flora folded her hands on the top of her desk. "What may I help you with?"

I cleared my throat. "We'd like to speak to Mr. Ford Waller."

"Why?" Flora asked with a frown on her face.

"We'd like to sign up for a booth at the flea market on Saturday," I said. "I'm a member of Double Stitch. If you will remember, we spoke briefly at the flea market yesterday."

"I remember," Flora said.

"We'd love to sell the quilts that we didn't lose in the fire. I think a big crowd will come out for the market because of all the talk and news coverage about the fire."

"If you have an existing booth in the flea market, you have already received a call, asking if you'd like to participate in the open-air market on Saturday." She tapped on a computer. "I called a woman named Iris and left a message for her." She looked at her computer again. "Iris Young called the office earlier this morning to claim your spot. It seems to me that there was a miscommunication between you and your friends. You are already set to go. There's no reason for you to be here."

I looked at Lois.

"That's a shame," Lois said. "I hate it when wires get crossed like that. Don't you? Even so, we would really like to talk to Mr. Waller. We came all the way down here. Maybe we can pick his brain about what it takes to have a successful booth at the flea market."

"Are you a member of the quilting circle too?" Flora asked dubiously.

"Sure am. I'm just starting out. I'm learning to quilt, really. In the past, I have done most of my sewing on the machine, but there is something special about working by hand."

Lois was an honorary member at best, and I doubted that Ruth would even be willing to give her that title.

"I'm sorry, but Mr. Waller is a very busy man, and he doesn't have time to give advice like that." She leaned over and opened a file drawer. She straightened up again and handed Lois a piece of paper from the drawer. "We get this question often, so I have typed up some tips to help you make the most of your booth."

The number one note on the list was "advertise." That seemed vague, I thought. Every business had to advertise.

"Are you sure Mr. Waller can't spare two minutes?" Lois asked.

I had to hand it to my friend. She was persistent.

"No," Flora said. "Mr. Waller isn't here today. He's dealing with some—" She paused. "Some complications with one of his properties."

"Would that be the flea market?" I asked.

"Yes, since it burned down, the flea market has had a number of complications, but it should not matter to you where he is." She stood up and folded her arms. "What are you *really* doing here? Double Stitch already knows how to sell quilts. They were doing it long before they had a booth with us."

"I wanted to talk to Mr. Waller about Ben Baughman," I said.

She pressed her lips together. "He has nothing to say on the matter. I can assure you of that."

"Maybe Mr. Waller should be the one to answer that question," Lois said. "Would your boss really want you to be answering for him?"

Flora glared at Lois. "Part of my job as Mr. Waller's office manager is keeping unnecessary people out of his way so that he can do his job."

"Are you calling us unnecessary?" Lois put her hands on her hips.

Flora moved an envelope from the corner of her desk to the top drawer. She closed the drawer after it. As she did that, something stirred in my memory. The morning I'd met Ben at the flea market, Flora had given him a similar envelope and he had put it into his pocket. What had it been? And what had happened to it?

"You gave Ben an envelope the morning of the day he died. What was in it?"

She scowled at me. "I see no reason to answer that question, but I will because I have nothing to hide. I was paying him for the previous week." This was the same response she'd given me when I'd asked her about it earlier.

I doubted she was telling the truth, but before I could ask her further about it or for some sort of proof, the office door was flung open. "Flora, I need—" A young man pulled up short when he came into the room and found Lois and me standing across from Flora. "What are you two doing here?" asked Jay, the young *Englischer* we'd met at the lumberyard the day before.

"You know each other?" Flora asked.

"We popped in at Miller's Lumberyard yesterday. Jay was kind enough to show us around."

Jay had done no such thing. He hadn't wanted to help us at all, and he most certainly hadn't wanted to talk about Ben's death.

"What were you doing there?" Flora asked with a concerned voice. "You don't need lumber to make quilts."

"*Nee.*" I shook my head. "You don't, but we were there because it was the last place Ben went before the flea market on the night of the fire. We wanted to retrace his steps."

Jay glared at us. "So you're following me?"

Lois put her hands on her hips. "We didn't know you would be here. We have business with Waller Properties."

"And so do I."

"What business?" I asked.

He narrowed his eyes. "None of your business."

Flora folded her arms. "I think it's time for you ladies to leave. I've told you what I can about the flea market on Saturday."

Lois and I shared a look, and I gave a slight nod. It was apparent Jay wasn't going to say anything to Flora as to why he was really in the office as long as we were standing there.

Lois opened the door, and I went out.

"We'll see you at the flea market." Lois closed the door after us.

On the other side of the door, she waited a beat and then put her ear next to the wooden panel. "What are you doing?" I hissed.

"Hush. I'm trying to eavesdrop. It's not easy. This door is a lot thicker than it looks. I wish I had a glass to put up to my ear. A glass is one thing I don't carry in my purse. It could break too easily, and there would be glass all over the bottom of my purse until I took the time to clean it out, which would be approximately next to never."

"How are we going to eavesdrop?" I asked. "The door is closed. There's not even a window to peek into from the hallway."

Lois pressed her ear harder against the door. "I can hear them speaking."

"What are they saying?" I asked.

She shrugged. "I can't hear that well."

"We need to leave before Jay or Flora comes out and catches us listening in."

With her ear pressed up against the door, Lois said, "Listening in? I'm not listening in. I can't be listening because I can't hear anything."

"If you can't hear anything, then stop."

She ignored my request, saying instead, "Millie, those two are in cahoots. It's as plain as day to me."

"Why would a young *Englisch* man be in cahoots—as you say—with a Mennonite woman at least ten years older than he?"

"Darned if I know, but that's what's going on here. I'd bet my new orange chair."

Lois really loved that gaudy orange chair, so I knew she was serious.

"Do you think we should tell Deputy Aiden about it?" she asked.

"Maybe Jay works for Waller too," I suggested.

"He's already working for the lumberyard."

"Two jobs?" I asked.

"Maybe . . ."

The door opened, and Lois, who still had her ear against it, fell into the office. She lay on the industrial carpet.

"Lois, are you okay?" I asked.

She was on all fours on the office floor, and Jay stood over her. Flora leaned across her desk to see what was going on.

I started to help her up and Jay did too. Between the two of us, we got her to her feet, and she gripped my arm for support. "Oh my. I was leaning on the door there and when you opened it, down I went. I should have known better than to lean on a door like that." She tapped herself on the forehead. "When will I ever learn?"

"Why were you leaning on my door?" Flora asked.

"Millie and I were talking about where we wanted to go to lunch. It's always such a difficult decision, and places are busier on Friday than on other days of the week, aren't they?"

"It's ten in the morning," Flora said.

"That's right," Lois said, holding onto my arm. "It's never too early to plan my next meal. I take eating very seriously."

"Are you hurt?" Flora asked.

"No, the carpet was soft-ish, and I bounce right back. I might not bounce as easily as I did in my twenties, but I still got to my feet."

"We will just be on our way," I said and tugged on Lois's arm. "It was so nice to see you again."

"Bye!" Lois called before we went into the stairwell.

Chapter Thirty-Three

"I wish we had been able to speak to Ford Waller," Lois said as she parked in front of the Sunbeam Café.

"I was just thinking the same," I said. "I think he could clear up some things about the flea market."

"And he's a suspect. You can't tell me that he didn't have insurance out on the flea market."

I unbuckled my seatbelt. "Don't you think Deputy Aiden must have already looked into him?"

She nodded. "That is a good point. If the deputy could prove that Ford Waller was making money off the fire, I think he would have arrested him by now."

"But we can't forget what Deputy Aiden said about Ford Waller and the sheriff being friends."

"Oh my! It could be arson and police corruption," Lois cried.

I wasn't nearly as excited about it as Lois was. I didn't know anything about police corruption or what I could do about it. I stepped out of the car and looked over at the square across the street. Despite Margot's complaints, Harvest was ready for Octoberfest. There were dozens of straw bales all over the grass to provide extra seating, and booths that held signs like BRAUTS!, STRUDEL!, and SCHNITZEL! The pretzel shop had a booth, of course, as did Swissmen Sweets. The only thing missing from Octoberfest was beer, because the village had a no-open-container alcohol policy. I wondered how long it would be before Margot convinced the village council to make an exception. She would have it done before the next Octoberfest. That much I was sure of.

"There's Uriah," Lois said and started to wave. "You should go over and talk to him." She kept waving.

"Why?" I asked.

"To be neighborly. Aren't the Amish into being good neighbors?" she asked.

"Of course we are, but I don't want to talk to him right now because—"

I didn't get a chance to tell her my reasons, because Lois was already crossing the street and making a beeline for Uriah.

Lois made it across with no problem, but I had to wait on the other side of the road while an Amish wagon rolled by followed by an Amish man on a large tractor. Finally, they both passed, and I made it to the square.

"Octoberfest is likely to be one of the biggest events in Harvest," Uriah said. "I'm not just saying that because it's what Margot would want either. It's a *gut* fit for our village. The Amish are of German descent, after all, and we still read High German in church, or at least the bishop and the church elders do. I never applied myself to my studies enough to learn it." He smiled at me as I approached. "I wouldn't be surprised if Millie could read German though. She was always at the top of our class in school."

I shook my head. Not always.

"All right. You flip-flopped with Kip then. It was no wonder that the pair of you married. You were smart enough for each other." He looked at Lois. "I didn't stand a chance when Kip was my competition."

"Kip Fisher was a fine man," Lois said.

"He was. He was always kind to me, even when . . ." he trailed off and shook his head as if displacing a bad memory. "It's no matter. Will you ladies be at October-fest?"

"We'll come this evening, I think. Doesn't that sound like fun, Millie?" Lois asked.

"It does," I agreed. I felt myself blushing and my face heated even more from the embarrassment of it. I was a mature woman. I shouldn't be blushing over any hand-some man.

"You should come tonight and on Saturday. It's going to be quite an event. Margot wants to go bigger and better with every single square celebration."

"We can't come Saturday," I said. "The flea market is open that day. Not the building, but there will be an open-air market. Double Stitch has a booth there."

"Already?" he asked.

"It's not the full market," I said.

"Oh, I think I see my granddaughter. I will let you two chat." Lois skipped away.

I sighed as I spied Darcy sweeping the doorstep of the Sunbeam Café. I knew spotting her granddaughter wasn't the reason Lois was scurrying across the green. I should have known when she suggested that we talk to Uriah that it was not to be neighborly but because she wanted me to speak to him. My friend was a hopeless romantic. I was not.

"Lois can really walk fast," Uriah said.

I folded my arms. "When she has the right motivation, she can."

"What motivation is that?" he asked.

I shook my head. I wasn't about to answer that question.

When I didn't say anything, Uriah put his hands in his trouser pockets and rocked back on his heels. "I'm happy for Ford that the flea market will reopen so soon. I know he was heartbroken over the fire."

I blinked. "Do you mean Ford Waller?"

"Sure do."

"You know Ford Waller?" I asked.

"I do. He and I worked together at a warehouse when we were teens. I always knew he would be a successful businessman. He looked at every problem with a desire to make things more efficient and better. He had an eye for that sort of thing. He's a *gut* man and a hard worker."

This was news to me and not at all how I imagined the owner of the flea market. I thought he would be another *Englisch* developer who was just interested in making money. I'd prejudged him, and even if I was the only one who knew it, I was not proud of that.

"Have you seen him since the fire?" I asked.

Uriah shook his head. "*Nee*, but I'm sure that it's been hard on him. When I first heard about the fire, I didn't realize the flea market was his building. If he's like the Ford I remember, he will do what he can to take care of the vendors who lost everything. He was just that kind of man."

"I'm very glad to hear that. Thank you, Uriah. I think you cleared something else up for me too." I started to move away.

He took a step after me. "Millie, would you like to go for a buggy ride sometime?"

I stared at him and opened and closed my mouth. "A buggy ride? Why would we do that?" The words came out of my mouth before I took a second to consider them.

His face fell, and instantly I regretted my quick reply. "I can't even compete with Kip when he's gone, can I? I have no chance against his memory."

"I'm sorry, Uriah. I didn't mean it like that. You surprised me. I'm sorry if my response came out wrong."

He put his hands back into his pockets. "Did I really startle you?"

Before I could answer, he went on to say, "Millie, you have to know that I admire you. I don't think I have ever stopped since we were young."

I stared at him. He was right. I wasn't surprised that he'd asked the question. Maybe I was startled by his timing, but part of me had known an invitation was coming all this time. Even so, I didn't know what to say.

"*Ya*, well, maybe you're right. The business I came here to settle will be over soon, and I can return to Indiana."

My heart twitched again. It felt something like disappointment. I pushed the feeling aside. I had made my choice; there was no going back. "You said that you were in Holmes County for business. All is well now?" I thought of the day before, when Margot was so angry he was late to work and he said he had business to deal with. Was it this business?

A strange look crossed Uriah's face. "I have been here

much longer than I thought I would, but *ya*, all is well now."
He took a breath. "At least as well as it can be. Time will
tell. It always does."

I wanted to ask him more, if there was anything I could
do to help, or what the problem was. But I couldn't. It
wasn't the Amish way to pry.

If Lois had been there, she would have asked. I had
learned that she was a *gut* person to have around because
she was willing to ask the questions that I couldn't bring
myself to utter.

"Millie!" Lois called as she power walked across the
green. "Millie!"

Uriah stepped back. "You should go. Your friend
wants you."

"Uriah, I . . ."

He shook his head and walked away, back toward the
small crew of Amish men who were putting the final
touches on the Octoberfest decorations on the square.

"Millie, I have great news."

I tore my eyes away from Uriah's back and forced a
smile. "What's that?"

"The ladies' auxiliary from the church is going to Lieb
Orchard today to pick apples, and we have to go." She
clapped her hands once for emphasis.

"But you don't go to the church," I said.

"I know I don't go there regularly, but I've been to a
service or two. And Juliet, who was just in the café picking up a coffee for Reverend Brook, invited me, which
means you can come too."

"Don't you think Tobias Lieb will see us and be suspicious?"

"Probably, but don't you want to speak to Tess and find
out why she slept in your barn last night?"

I did. "Okay, let's go."

She pumped her fist in the air. "That's the spirit." As we walked back toward the café, she asked, "How was your chat with Uriah? Did he ask you out on a date?"

I gave her a look. "The Amish don't date."

"Fine, fine, did he ask if he could court you? That's the right terminology isn't it?"

"Amish women of my age don't get courted."

Lois put her hands on her hips. "Why not? You're not dead yet, and you're a catch. I mean, I would kill to have your skin, and you don't even put anything on it. Do you know how much I have to spend on my beauty regimen to look like this?" She pointed at her heavily made-up face. Today she was wearing red eyeshadow that was the exact shade of her dyed hair. The image was a little bit startling if you looked too closely.

"But Kip . . ."

She stopped in the middle of the green and grabbed my hand. "I'm only saying this because I love you. Millie, Kip has been dead for twenty years. You have done enough for your family in the time since his death—more than enough. It's time to move on and find another happily ever after. It doesn't have to be the same one. In fact, it can't be. You're a different person than you were when you married Kip. You have to be. I hope none of us are the same as we were when we were nineteen. I certainly hope I've changed and learned a thing or two about life along the way."

I wanted to say she didn't understand because she had been married four times. She had always been willing to take risks in love. I never had to. I met Kip when I was a child. It was love from the start. I couldn't say any of that though.

"You should at least recognize, as a matchmaker, that you and Uriah have a spark. If I can see it, I know that you can see it too. Can't you?"

"*Nee*," I said, and it was the first time that I ever lied to Lois in sixty-seven years.

Chapter Thirty-Four

"I'm just so tickled that you could join us, Lois and Millie!" Juliet Brook beamed at us as she held her black-and-white-spotted potbellied pig, Jethro, close to her chest. "This is going to be the most wonderful outing for the women's auxiliary!"

Lois and I stood with Juliet and Jethro along with fifteen other women from Juliet's church, waiting for our tour around the orchard.

"We're so happy to be here," I said.

Juliet smiled. "Let me go see about the tour."

I leaned in close to Lois. "You didn't say anything about a tour. Tobias is definitely going to know we're here if there is a tour. He might even be leading the tour."

"He would never lead the tour," she argued. "You have to be friendly to be a tour guide. No one mistakes Tobias for friendly."

She had a point.

"Ladies, I found our tour guide!" Juliet announced as she came out of the apple shack followed by none other than Tess Lieb. When Tess saw Lois and me standing among the other women of the church, she swallowed hard.

Juliet smiled, completely unaware of what was happening. "Tess?" she asked.

Tess broke eye contact with me. "I'm sorry. *Danki* for coming to Lieb Orchards," Tess said. "When Juliet suggested this event, we were more than happy to do it. Like all the Amish in Holmes County, we are so grateful for the close relationship that the church has with the surrounding Amish community. I'll be your guide today, and we will start out in the shack, where I will tell you about our apples and the different varieties. After that, you will have time to pick a few apples yourselves. The Golden Delicious just came into season, and that's a favorite with bakers. If you will follow me . . ."

The group of women dutifully trooped into the apple shack. It was early afternoon on a Friday. There were a small number of customers in the shack, but not nearly as many as would be there on Saturday.

Tess cleared her throat. "We grow five kinds of apples on the orchard. Ohio is a great place to grow apples because of the rain and change of seasons. All of which help the crops." She pointed at a table where five apples were lined up as if they were on some kind of drill line. "Listing our apples from tartest to sweetest, we grow Granny Smith, Cortland, Honeycrisp, Golden Delicious, and Gala. So we sell the five most popular kinds of apples for eating and baking. Of course, the Granny Smiths will be the tartest, and your Gala will be the sweetest. People tend to bake with the tarter apples and eat the sweeter ones." She took a breath. "Lieb Orchards was established sixty years ago by my grandfather. Ever since the beginning, it was a family-run business. We—"

Jethro wiggled out of Juliet's arms, jumped on the table and ate the Honeycrisp apple in three bites.

Tess and the church ladies stared openmouthed at the pig, and since no one moved to stop him, he ate the Gala next.

"He's a smart pig," Lois said. "He went for the best ones in the bunch."

"Oh my!" Juliet exclaimed. "Tess, I'm so very sorry! Jethro has never done anything like that before."

I didn't think anyone on the tour believed that.

"Could you move your pig?" Tess asked.

Jethro munched on the Cortland apple next.

Juliet laughed. "You would think I didn't feed him lunch, but I did."

"He's a pig," Lois said. "No one is surprised that he eats apples."

Juliet blushed. "I know. Usually he's so well mannered."

I didn't think anyone believed that either.

Once Jethro was tucked safely in Juliet's arms, Tess went on with her description of the history of the orchard. She told us how her grandfather started it, planting strictly apples. Tess's father was the one who expanded it to other fruits, too, so they would have produce to take to market throughout the growing season. During all the time she spoke, she refused even to glance at Lois or me.

At the end of her talk, Tess took a big breath. "Now, we have pull wagons and half-bushel bags for all of you to go out and pick some apples. Today we have Golden Delicious and Granny Smith in season."

The women talked excitedly among themselves as they each took a bag from Tess and then grabbed a wagon. Juliet put Jethro in her wagon, and he lay down as if he was used to being pulled around all the time. I suspected that he was.

I held onto Lois's arm, and we were the last in line to accept our half-bushel bags.

"Here's your bag," Tess said, not meeting our eyes. "I hope it's okay if the two of you share a wagon. It seems that all the others are taken."

I accepted the bags. "Tess, we need to talk about what happened this morning."

"I can't," she whispered.

I would not be deterred. "You were going to tell me something."

"I don't know if I can," she said, just above a whisper.

"We want to help you," Lois said.

"I need to think about it, but I can't tell you here. My *daed* could walk in at any moment. Can we talk tomorrow at the flea market?" She looked around the apple shack as if to make sure no one was watching us. "I'll be working the booth at the flea market alone. We will have a much smaller presence there than we did when it was inside the building."

"I thought you were being shipped out to Wyoming today."

"My *daed* wanted to send me, but the police said I am not allowed to leave the area until the investigation into Ben's death is over and done with." Tears gathered in her eyes.

Lois nodded to me. "See? Didn't I tell you that's what would happen?"

"All right," I said. "I will talk to you tomorrow, but you have to be willing to talk. Whatever it is, it can't be that bad. We can help you."

She shook her head as if I couldn't possibly understand her situation.

An Amish woman, most likely a relative of Tess's, watched us curiously from the cash register. Lois and I noticed her marked attention at the same time.

"Thank you so much for the wagon," Lois said in a too-loud voice. "That's all we needed, thank you. You gave a fine lecture on the history of the apple."

Lois pulled the wagon out of the apple shack into the orchard and headed toward the rows of apple trees.

I stopped her. "You're going to pick apples?"

"Why not? That's what people do at apple orchards, isn't it?"

"*Ya*, but you bought two bushels of apples for the café already."

"This is just a half bushel more, and my granddaughter can experiment with all the extra apples. Maybe I'm helping to find her next great recipe."

"Let's hope so," I said. "Because I don't know how she is going to feel when she walks into the café to see you got even more apples."

The ladies from Juliet's church were already in the process of picking apples. They laughed and made careful selections. Jethro ran up and down the row eating as many of the fallen apples as he could. Despite the trouble he might have caused, I hoped the little pig didn't gorge himself on too many apples. Also, I wasn't the one to criticize Juliet for having a pet that was difficult to control. I had two: Phillip and Peter.

"They have ladders," Lois said. "That's what I'm going to use to pick my apples. These ladies are too afraid to go up the ladder, so I have a better chance of getting a real winner apple up high."

The ladder was seven feet tall and was made of weathered wood. Although it appeared to be solidly constructed, I was nervous for her. "Are you sure that it's safe?" I asked.

"Don't be such a worrywart, Millie. I will be perfectly fine."

Despite my misgivings, Lois climbed up the ladder and began putting apples one by one into her half-bushel bag. I grimaced as I watched her up on the ladder.

"Lois is a hoot." Juliet pulled her empty cart along the bumpy ground while Jethro ran around the tree aisle, barely able to contain his excitement or appetite for apples.

I turned away from Lois and the ladder. "She is that," I agreed.

"Ahh!" There was a scream, and when I turned around again, I found Lois on the ground in the middle of the apple rows.

"Oh no!" Juliet cried. "Lois fell off the ladder. Do we need a medic?"

I ran over to her. "Are you okay?"

She grunted. "Sore, but I will be all right. Can you help me up?"

"What happened?"

"There was a bee the size of a semi coming after me. I tried to swat him away, and I swatted myself right off the ladder."

I shook my head. That sounded exactly like something Lois would have done. "Are you sure nothing is broken or sprained?"

She struggled to her feet and accepted my arm when it was offered to her. "I'm fine. A bit winded, but I got off better than I might have. I got lucky. I know. It's not like falling when I was younger. I'll be sore tomorrow. If only young folks knew how easy they have it."

"Let's go home." I rubbed her arm and looked her over for any sign of injury. "You picked another half bushel already. Darcy will have apples coming out of her ears."

"I think we have enough apples. My granddaughter will love these. She makes the very best apple crisp you have ever eaten in your life. Even though you are Amish and know some great Amish bakers, I stand by my claim that they don't bake better than my granddaughter."

"Don't say that in front of Ruth Yoder if you know what's *gut* for you," I advised.

"Aww, Ruth is a softie when it really comes down to it."

Juliet hurried over to us. "Lois, are you okay?"

Lois held onto my arm. "I'll be okay. Millie and I should leave though. We plan to go to Octoberfest tonight in the village. Will you be there?"

"Of course I will. I bought Jethro lederhosen to wear."

"Seeing that will be worth the price of admission," Lois said.

"Octoberfest is free," Juliet said.

"Then it's a steal," Lois said.

I shook my head.

Lois paid for her apples in the apple shack. Tess was nowhere to be seen, and we rolled the apples to the car in the wagon.

When we were in the car, I buckled my seatbelt before saying, "Lois, that is the second time you've fallen today. Are you sure you're all right?"

"If you're worried about my balance or any of that, don't be. I'm fine and could walk across a balance beam with my eyes closed if the need should arise."

I wasn't so sure about that, but I didn't correct her. Something else was going on. "Did you really get scared off that ladder by a bee? I've never known you to be afraid of bees."

"I'm not." She started the car. "I fell off the ladder because I was trying to get a better view."

"A better view of what?" I asked.

"Of Flora from Waller Properties talking to Tess Lieb."

Chapter Thirty-Five

"Why would they be talking?" I asked. "I didn't even realize they knew each other."

"It's a small village. They probably know each other, and both are involved in the flea market," Lois said.

I pursed my lips. "They seem like an odd pair of friends. Flora is Mennonite."

"And I'm English, and you are Amish. Does that make us an odd pair of friends?"

"*Ya,*" I said with a smile. "Ask Ruth Yoder."

Lois grumbled something under her breath.

"But that's not the only reason that they are an odd pair. Flora is at least ten years older than Tess."

She glanced at me out of the corner of her eye. "Millie Fisher, are you an ageist?"

"*Nee,*" but you have to admit it's odd." I touched my finger to my cheek in thought. "I suppose that Flora could have been there to talk about the open-air flea market tomorrow, but she said she had already called every vendor. The Liebs have a phone in the apple shack. I noticed it when Tess was telling us the history of the orchard."

"You're probably right." She tapped the heel of her

hand on the steering wheel. "If only I hadn't fallen out of that tree. I might have heard what they were saying."

"You're lucky you didn't hurt yourself. I worry about you putting yourself at risk, Lois. I don't want anything to happen to you."

She eyed me and then concentrated on the road. "That's funny coming from the woman whose buggy was attacked last night."

"It wasn't exactly attacked," I said.

"No, it's no big deal that someone threw a rock at your buggy." She shook her head.

I rolled my eyes. It was a habit that Lois had had when we were teenagers. As I expected, the eye rolling made her laugh.

"We need to think over who might have set that fire," I said.

"Right," Lois said more seriously. "Who do we have for suspects?"

"Tobias Lieb," I said.

"Motive?"

"He's Tess's father and wants her to go to Wyoming to help his younger sister."

"Yeah, with the triplets. Sounds horrible. It would have been my worst nightmare at Tess's age. In fact, it's my worst nightmare now."

I glanced at her. "He might have started the fire to kill Ben, so she didn't have a reason to stay."

She raised one penciled-on eyebrow. "And gave him pot brownies too?"

I shrugged.

"I like him for it though," she said. "He had the means,

motive, and opportunity. That's legal talk for he could have done it."

"I know that." I frowned. "But he lost his booth, too, and the hundreds of apples that were inside it."

"Who else do you have?"

"The owner of Waller Properties, Ford Waller. We can't forget that he might get some money from insurance. I would think that Deputy Aiden would have already ruled that out, but we can't clear him until we know for sure. And we can't forget he's friends with Sheriff Marshall Jackson. I could see the sheriff looking the other way, or asking his deputies to, if a friend of his was in trouble."

"I can, too, and insurance money is an excellent motive. Someone with as much money as Waller has would have no problem finding drugs to make Ben fall asleep," Lois said. "Next?"

"Flora Kimble is another suspect for the same reason. She works for Waller, so maybe she was his accomplice."

She nodded. "Anyone else?"

"Isaiah Keim, the schoolteacher," I said.

"Aww, I would hate for it to be him. I really thought he was a good guy."

"I did too, but maybe he was lying about being over Tess. He may have, in fact, viewed Ben as a romantic rival."

"If that were true, why doesn't he make a move on Tess now that Ben is dead?"

"Maybe he's waiting for an appropriate amount of time to pass first."

She cocked her head. "You know, Millie, the more time you spend thinking about murder, the more devious your brain is becoming. I like that. You might be carrying lock picks in your apron pockets soon. Anyone else, or have we come to the end of our list?"

I sighed, not waiting to state the obvious. "Ben Baughman. I don't think he killed himself, but it could have been accidental. If he ate the brownies either knowingly or unknowingly, he could have knocked over the lantern without even realizing it."

She squeezed my hand. "It might come to that, Millie. I really hate to say it, but it just might."

I folded my hands in my lap. "If that's true, all this running around trying to find out what happened to Ben was a waste of time."

"No, no, it wasn't," she said. "You were trying to find out what happened to your friend and wanted to save his reputation. That's what any true friend would do. I know if I were to be killed, you would stop at nothing to find out who did it."

"Lois! Don't say something like that. I can't bear to think of losing you."

She grinned. "Who would want to off me?"

I shook my head. "Can we just have a nice evening at Octoberfest with no more talk about murder and death?"

"I find it to be quite an interesting subject, but if that's what you want, then you shall have it. We will have strudel and brats, and maybe you can have a nice private chat with Uriah Schrock too." She winked at me.

I rolled my eyes for a second time.

Margot Rawlings didn't disappoint. That evening, when Lois and I walked over from the Sunbeam Café to see what was happening at Octoberfest, the square was buzzing with activity. There was a scarecrow-making station, pumpkin painting, strudel-baking lessons, and so much more. It was overwhelming, the number of things she had been able to fit on that patch of grass in the middle of the village. A German band, complete with accordion, played in the gazebo. And as promised, Jethro the pig walked around the festivities in lederhosen. Tourists stopped Juliet and Reverend Brook, who were walking the pig on a leash, so that they could get photos with the pig. I overheard as Juliet said, "This is Jethro. I'm sure you've seen him on several episodes of *Bailey's Amish Sweets* on Gourmet Television. He's famous!"

Bailey King waved to us from the Swissmen Sweets booth. Lois and I made our way over.

"It's nice to see you," I said. "I thought you were in New York this week."

"I was." She smiled. "But I knew that I had to be back for Octoberfest. Margot would never let me hear the end of it if I missed the festivities."

Lois pointed. "Is that Jethro in lederhosen? I thought Juliet was making a joke about dressing up the pig."

A pained expression crossed Bailey's face. "Juliet never jokes when it comes to Jethro. Trust me." Her face softened. "Millie, I was sorry to hear about Ben Baughman. Aiden said he was a friend of yours. It's a terrible thing that happened."

I nodded. "Thank you." I looked down at her table. There was a row of chocolate pumpkins.

"Would you like a chocolate pumpkin truffle? I made them for the last episode that I filmed for my television show and thought they would be a nice fall addition to the shop."

"I would," I said with a smile. "How much?"

"No, no, just take it. You've been through enough this week. Chocolate always helps. If it's a truffle in the shape of a pumpkin, it helps more, or so I've been told." She winked at me and went to help the next customer in her line.

I hadn't realized that while I was standing there chatting with her, a long line of people had gathered, eager to meet Bailey because of her television fame. They were impatiently waiting. Not once had Bailey made me feel rushed or given me the impression that I was holding up business. She was a kind woman, and the perfect match for Deputy Aiden. I wondered what was keeping them from walking down the aisle. I knew I wasn't the only one in Harvest who wondered the same thing. Juliet would be first in line. The way she told it, Bailey and Deputy Aiden were already engaged, but I knew they weren't.

"I think I'll get myself a soft pretzel, and I promised to bring Darcy a piece of strudel too. She can't get away from the café, poor thing. She is overrun with customers from Octoberfest. It's a good problem to have for the business, but exhausting," Lois said. "She's already called in her two other part-timers, and Bryan is there, too, of course, if she's desperate. How he can write with all this commotion going on across the road is beyond me."

"I think I will just walk around and take a look at everything before I decide what else to eat. That truffle took care of my sweet tooth."

She nodded. "I had better get in line. Looks like there is a long wait for just about everything."

Lois walked away, and I wandered around the square, taking a moment to listen to the band and smile at district members and neighbors while I moved about. No one stopped me to chat, and I was grateful for that. My mind was so filled with all that had happened over the last few days, it was nice to relax and not be preoccupied with death and murder.

I was watching the band when Uriah Schrock came around the other side of the gazebo. He smiled at me, and I waved back. Then, like a coward, I quickly walked away as if I had seen someone else I needed to speak to.

I was halfway across the square when I chided myself for being childish and ridiculous. Uriah and I were two adults. In fact, we had been adults for quite a long time. I should act my age. An Amish proverb came to mind. "Faith gives us the courage to face the present with confidence and the future with expectancy."

It was a *gut* lesson, especially for me.

I was about to turn around and go back to the place where I had last seen Uriah when another man, a much younger man, caught my eye. It was Jay from the lumber-yard. He was walking around the square, looking every which way as if he was being followed. He was making his way toward Main Street.

Lois wasn't anywhere to be seen. I knew she must be in one of the extra-long food lines, waiting for a pretzel or strudel or some tasty delight. I couldn't let Jay walk away without trying to talk to him again.

I wove through the crowd and lost sight of him once, but then spotted him again when he came to Main Street and waited for a car to drive very slowly by. It was clear that the driver was trying to see what was happening on the square.

When I was within five feet of him, I said, "Jay." That was all.

He saw me and his eyes went wide. The car passed, and he bolted across the street and down Apple Street. There was no way I could keep up with his young legs, so I didn't even try. I was too stunned by his reaction to go running after him in any case.

I could understand his not wanting to chat with an older Amish woman. Not waiting to speak to me wasn't much of surprise, but why would he run away? More importantly, why would he look frightened while doing it?

Chapter Thirty-Six

"Millie, thank you so much for helping me in the Double Stitch booth today. My stomach was in knots all night thinking about it. I don't want to mess things up again and lose any of the quilts," Iris Young said to me the next day as we put out a small number of Amish quilts for display in the small outdoor booth we had been given at the Harvest Flea Market. They were all Double Stitch had left after the fire. She wrung her thin hands as she spoke. To say that Iris was on edge would be an understatement. If something went wrong with the quilting booth at the flea market this time, I wasn't sure she would ever come to Double Stitch again.

"Iris, the fire wasn't your fault, and I wish you'd stop thinking it was." I patted her hand.

"Ruth thinks it was," she said with wide eyes. "You saw her at the last Double Stitch meeting. She blames me for what happened."

I wrinkled my nose. I would really need to give Ruth a talking-to about being easier on the younger women in the district. It was clear to me that they were all terrified of her. The younger women like Iris also needed to take what

Ruth said with a grain of salt. Ruth was the bishop's wife, not the bishop. Her words were not district rules, no matter how much she thought they should be.

I waved away her comment. "Not really. That's just Ruth being Ruth. You do not have to listen to everything she says. I clearly don't."

The stricken expression on her delicate face told me she didn't believe me. "But you are so independent and brave, Millie. Not all the women in the district are like you. I'm certainly not."

"There is no need for us all to be alike. It wouldn't be very interesting if we were, now would it? Just take a deep breath and remind yourself you're doing a wonderful job. The booth was a great idea."

Iris blinked away tears. "*Danki*, Millie. You have always been so kind, and you've known Ruth longer than any of us."

The quilting booth was in one of the best spots in the temporary open-air market. It was under the large tree on the grounds, so there was plenty of shade. Even on a chilly morning, the shade was welcome because the sun was bright. Too much sunlight could fade the colors in the quilts. Both Iris and I had on heavy jackets over our dresses, and she even wore her bonnet.

"Maybe if you believe she is not that angry at me, it's true." Iris shoved her small hands into the pockets of her jacket and hunched down against the wind.

"It is true." I smiled. "Just try to remember that."

"I do hope the flea market will be inside again before the worst of winter, or it will be difficult to stay out here for a long period of time."

"I hope so too." I gave her one final pat, and my eyes wandered across the field, where Tess and what must have been two of her siblings were unloading a pickup truck full of apples onto two cafeteria-style tables. Just like the quilting circle, the Liebs had a makeshift outdoor setup, since they'd lost their booth in the fire.

I knew not to go talk to her now. She wouldn't want to speak about Ben in front of her family. But I was itching to talk to her. The reason I was at the flea market before it opened was to speak to Tess as soon as possible. I'd hardly been able to sleep the night before, and it wasn't just because of Lois's faint snoring in the room next to mine. She'd spent a second night at my house with my cat, the goats, and me, as our karate-expert protector. Luckily, there was nothing I needed protecting from except my relentless thoughts.

I knew we were getting close to finding out what had happened the night Ben died, and in my heart, I felt Jay knew something about it. Why else would he be scared of me? No one was afraid of me. I was a petite, white-haired, Amish woman who could quilt and had the gift of match-making. There was nothing scary in any of those attributes.

Lois floated back to the Double Stitch booth. I hadn't been sure where she had gone when we got here. "You know, I think this outdoor setup is great. It feels so much more open than when everyone was crammed into the flea market. I know it wouldn't work permanently, but on a nice day like this, it's just so much more pleasant." She put her hands on her hips. "Iris, you look like someone stole your favorite quilting needle. For goodness sake, child, your lower lip is trembling." Lois turned to me. "What happened to her?"

"Ruth," I said, not wanting Iris to get upset again when I had just spent so much time calming her down.

"Ahh, I should have recognized the symptoms. Post Traumatic Ruth Disorder. She gets you every time. I'm sure that Millie already told you, but don't listen to her. She's just an old—"

"She's just the wife of the bishop," I interrupted before Lois could say something that I would regret. Heavens knew she wouldn't regret it.

An *Englisch* man in pressed khaki pants and a dress shirt, complete with a bow tie, came up to our table. He gave the three of us a big toothy grin. "How's it all going, ladies?" he asked in a booming voice. It was one of the times when the voice fit the man, because he was at least six five and round through the middle. "How is everything looking to you?"

"We're fine," I said, unsure who this stranger was. "Are you in the market for a new quilt? They make excellent gifts, especially for the women in your life."

He laughed and put his hand on his stomach. "Oh no, not me. I just came to see how you were getting on. I'm Ford Waller of Waller Properties."

Lois blinked at him. "You're the owner of the flea market?"

He rocked back on his heels. "Sure am. Usually, I would be more upbeat about it, but the fire has been a terrible blow." He said this with a smile.

On closer inspection, I realized that it was the *Englisch* man who had been so angry with Deputy Aiden on the day of the fire. He looked completely different with a smile on his face instead of a mask of anger. It seemed that he had now recovered from the initial shock of the fire. Perhaps that was because his friend the sheriff had made it possible to open the outdoor flea market less than a week after Ben's death.

"The worst thing about the fire was losing one of my staffers. I didn't know Ben well, but from what I was told by my officer manager, he was a reliable worker. He showed up at ten every night for his shift and never once was late. Someone like that is hard to come by, let me tell you. He was the kind of employee that I like to see in my company. I know if things had gone differently, he would have moved up at Waller Properties. My officer manager always seems to know who will work out and who won't. I should really make her the head of HR. She's unstoppable." He laughed as if this was the funniest joke he had heard in a long while.

"Do you mean Flora?" Lois asked.

"Yes, how do—oh, I suppose you know her because she's the one in charge of finding vendors for the flea market." He shook his head. "I should have realized since you have a booth of your own here."

"Right," Lois said, leaving it at that.

"Ben was a friend of mine," I said. "He was more like family actually." My thoughts traveled back to Ben's funeral. I pushed them away.

"I am very sorry," Waller said. "It's a terrible thing that happened. I know Ben wouldn't have meant to knock over that lantern. I'm sure it was an accident. We will build the flea market back better than ever. Perhaps we will even name it after Ben."

I frowned. Waller's last comment was proof to me that he didn't know much about Amish culture. We didn't want monuments built for us or buildings named after us. That went against everything we were taught about humility.

Lois cocked her head, and from her gesture, I knew that a big question or two was coming. "I can see you are very keen to rebuild. Will it be challenging? I would think such a large building would be quite expensive to recreate. Does your insurance cover the cost of the build?"

He laughed. "Goodness no, the insurance doesn't even scratch the surface of what it will cost. If I'm going to rebuild, I want to make the flea market better, with all the newest amenities from self-flushing toilets to Wi-Fi. If people have amenities, they will stay longer, and if they stay longer, they will spend more money. The insurance that I had on that old barn will cover one-sixth of what I want to do, if I'm lucky." He gave a toothy smile. "I had been avoiding making the changes because of cost. Besides, the old barn didn't take much to maintain. I was making money hand over fist with very little overhead. I'll miss that."

"Your profit came from the stall rentals?" Lois asked.

"What you don't understand is that I made twice as much by renting it out as a venue space. The fire really hurt me. Yes, I will get some insurance money for the damages, but the fall season is when I need to make up for the slow times in the year." He looked at the gold watch on his wrist. "I'd best be off to my next booth. It was so nice talking with you ladies." He started to walk away.

He had almost reached the booth across from us, where paintings were for sale, when I ran out of the booth after him. "Mr. Waller, can I ask you another question?"

"Shoot," he said.

"Shoot what?" I asked, confused.

He guffawed. "That's just an expression. How can I

help you? I'm here to help. Help and good service are the missions of Waller Properties."

"Do you know a young man named Jay?" I asked.

A strange look crossed his face.

"I'm only asking because yesterday I stopped by your office to ask how the outdoor flea market worked. As you must know, I don't have a phone in my home, and some-times it's just easier to ask a question face to face."

He nodded. "I believe in doing as much as possible face to face. That's another mission of Waller Properties."

It seemed to me that Waller Properties had many missions.

"A young man named Jay was there, and I thought maybe he worked for you."

"If he was in my office, I know the Jay you're talking about. No, he doesn't work for me. I told him that he had to prove that he could work a full year elsewhere, and do a good job of it, before I hired him."

"Who is he, if I may ask?"

"He's my nephew. Did you need to speak with him about something?" Waller asked.

I stepped back as I processed what I had just learned. "*Nee*, I just wondered. Flora in your office was answering my questions about the flea market when he came in."

His brow cleared. "She would. Flora is a great office manager, and I'm so glad that I hired her. When she came to me looking for a job, I was shocked. I never thought a Kimble would want to work for me after what happened."

"After what happened?" I asked.

"This was their farm. They had a huge horse farm on this very spot, and I bought it in foreclosure. Her father had made some very bad investments in sickly stud horses, and the line got so discredited in breeding circles, the farm went out of business. All of this happened a long time before I came along. At the time, I was looking for more properties to revitalize around the county. Another mission of Waller Properties is to make old structures better and more efficient instead of building new ones. Anyone can throw up a new building, but when you can save one with character, that's a real gift. I saw the farm, which had already been foreclosed on, and went straight to the bank to make an offer that they couldn't refuse."

"Flora was a member of that family?" I asked. I felt as if my heart was beating out of my chest. It was a wonder he couldn't hear it. The sound of the *thump*, *thump*, *thump* beat against my ear drums.

Flora. Flora seemed to be at the heart of everything. Could she be responsible for the fire too? I had to talk to Lois. Now. My thoughts were so muddled on the matter that I needed a sounding board to help me sort it out.

I hurried into the crowd, but before I could find Lois, I came face to face with Flora herself.

"Are you looking for me?" she asked in a cool voice.

I swallowed. "*Nee*, I was looking for my friend Lois." I told myself that Flora wouldn't do anything to me in the middle of the flea market. If she did, there would be far too many witnesses.

"You can look for her later."

I frowned at her. "Then I guess I'll return to my booth."

"Your booth doesn't need you." She paused. "Why don't you walk over to the old burned-down flea market with me? I would like to show you something in the rubble."

"Why would I go anywhere with you?"

"Because I have a gun." She showed me a flash of metal under her coat. I didn't know if it was a gun or not. I couldn't see enough of it to know for sure. "I will shoot someone here at the flea market if you don't come with me right now."

My heart skipped a beat. "Who will you shoot?"

"Doesn't matter. Anyone will work. You are so concerned about people getting killed that you wouldn't want that on your conscience, would you?"

I didn't.

She looped her arm through mine and held it close so that I could feel the hard object, maybe a real gun, that she held in her hand pressed up against my side. "Now, let's go look at the old flea market, shall we?"

This time, I went.

Chapter Thirty-Seven

I wished that I could say that I had the ability to overpower the young woman, knock her down, and steal her gun, but she was forty years younger than me and six inches taller. My mind whirled over how I could get away as she marched me over to the scorched building. Nothing came to mind.

Flora smiled and waved to the people we passed on the way to the building. It was almost as if she was enjoying herself. That was the most terrifying thing.

We went in through the side door of the massive building. The first thing that hit me was the scorched smell. Where we were was dark and smoke damaged. I had a clear view of the middle of the building where the fire had begun. Bright morning sunlight shone on the fire-blackened rubble. There were dusty boot prints all over the ground. I guessed they'd been made by the firemen when trying to stop the blaze, and then by the investigators, trying to discover what exactly had happened.

"Where are you?" Flora asked. She gripped my arm.

I thought it was a strange question since she held me in place.

"Come out," she ordered.

Slowly, a figure came out of the shadows. My mouth fell open when I saw that it was Jay. I had sensed that he was somehow involved with this. My instincts had been right about Flora and Jay, but until right now—when I could be killed—I hadn't been sure.

Jay wrung his hands. "Flora, I can't believe you brought her here. This was such a terrible idea. What do you think we can do with her?"

"We'll do what we must," she snapped.

I didn't like the sound of that in the least.

"But we can't get away with it." Jay's voice was pitched in a high whine.

"She's an overly curious grandmother. No one would be surprised if she just happened to wander into the crime scene and get herself killed in an unfortunate accident," Flora said.

I wasn't a *grossmaami*, but I didn't think this was the time to correct her. She was also wrong that no one would be surprised, because Lois would. She would wonder why I went into the burnt barn without her, and she would be angry about it, too, because she would have wanted to come along. But I wasn't going to mention Lois. I didn't want them dragging her to her death as they were trying to do to me.

"Did you go up into the loft?" Flora asked.

"Not yet," he said in a resigned voice. I didn't like the shift in his tone. I would have been much happier if he'd continued to argue with Flora over what a terrible idea killing me was. I personally thought it was an awful idea.

She glared at him. "Why not?"

"It's unstable. Why should I risk my neck climbing

up there when I didn't know that you were going to go through with grabbing her? I half thought you were joking."

"I never joke," Flora snapped. "And I always do what I say I will. Now get up there and set it up."

Jay bit his lower lip; despite the cold, he was sweating. He wiped his brow and pushed the sleeves up on his sweatshirt, revealing a bright red apple tattoo on his right forearm.

I stared at it. Emily Keim at Swissmen Sweets had told me about the young man with the apple tattoo who had come to see Ben at the Christmas tree farm. She had told me, too, how uncomfortable that man had made her feel. If I had only seen Jay's tattoo earlier, this case might have been solved days ago when Lois and I were at Miller's Lumberyard. However, because of the cool weather, Jay had been wearing a long-sleeved shirt that covered the apple.

"What are you staring at?" Jay asked.

"That just seems like an unusual tattoo."

He glared at the apple and pulled his sleeves back down. "I got it for my grandmother. Her maiden name is Appleton."

I frowned. How could a young man who cared about his grandmother so much that he got a tattoo for her, be willing to kill me, a woman old enough to be his grandmother?

"Jay, I can tell you don't want to do this," I said. "Certainly your grandmother wouldn't want you to do this."

Jay began to sweat even more than before, but he made no move to push up his sleeves again.

"Don't listen to her, and don't be a coward," she snapped at him. "You're just as much in this as I am. And you made it worse by stealing Ben's bike and taking it to your job."

That explained how the bike had ended up at the lumberyard. I realized that it had been a missed opportunity for me. If I had told Deputy Aiden about the bicycle, would the police have found Jay's connection to the murder sooner, keeping me from winding up in this position now?

"I wasn't thinking when I took the bike."

"That's the problem. You never think," Flora snapped.

"I just wanted to make some money. I didn't want anyone to die," Jay said.

"You think I did?" she asked. "That wasn't part of the plan."

"How was I supposed to know that girl would freak out so much and start the fire?" he whined.

My head whirled as I tried to piece together their conversation in a way that made sense. At the same time, I scanned the flea market for something I could use to protect myself. There were so many things to grab, but I couldn't reach any of them while Flora held my arm in a vise grip.

"Millie," Flora said. "You will stand under the block and tackle hanging from the loft above, and Jay will drop it onto you." She said this as if it made perfect sense for me to agree to her insane idea.

"Jay, you don't want to do that," I said. "I can see it on your face."

Jay shook his head. "It's your fault you're here. You should have heeded my warning."

I felt cold. "You threw the rock at my buggy."

He scowled. "And it didn't do any good. You kept asking questions."

"You wanted to warn me to protect me," I said. "You just wanted to make money. That's all. Did you talk to your Uncle Ford about needing money?"

His blue eyes went wide. "How did you know that he's my uncle?"

"Ford just told me. He said he wanted you to prove you could work hard elsewhere before working for him."

Jay balled his hands into fists. "He's selfish. I am his only nephew, and he doesn't have any children. He should be supporting me. He should have at least given me a job, but he refused. He deserved to lose everything we stole from the flea market."

As soon as he said that, the clues clicked into place in my head. "You two! You've been stealing from the flea market. Jay, you did it because you're angry at your uncle." Another thought hit me. "And you, Flora, because this was your family farm."

"Why shouldn't I have money from this place?" Flora asked. "This is my family's land, and Waller stole it from us."

"He didn't steal it," I said. "He bought it from the bank."

"We were going to get it back!" she cried. "We just needed a little more time. The bank said we could buy it back. We had almost scrimped and saved enough to do it, and then Waller swooped in and bought it out from under us."

"He might not have known that you were trying to get it back," I said.

"That doesn't matter! It's English men like him that are taking over this county when it should be left to the Amish and the Mennonites." She pushed me into the spot where she had wanted me to stand, so that Jay could drop the tackle on my head.

How did she know I wasn't going to move? I might not be as agile as I once had been, but I knew enough to jump out of the way if someone was trying to kill me. Jay made his way up the ladder. Flora put me in the spot and held the gun on me. She really did have a gun, and I could see it clearly now as she released my arm and stood across from me.

It was the gun. The gun was what she was going to use to keep me in place. So I would be crushed or shot. Neither of those was a *gut* option. I made up my mind to jump out of the way when the time came. At least I could try to save myself. Kip always told me never to give up. Even when he was dying from cancer, he made me promise him that I would go on and live a good and full life. I meant to keep that promise.

Jay was halfway up the ladder when a giant rope fell from the loft, but not onto me. It hit Flora. She fell to the sooty floor, and the gun went skittering away. Jay jumped off the ladder and went after the gun. I did, too, but he was younger and faster and scooped it up.

Flora lay on the floor, her nose bleeding from where she had been hit with the large rope.

Behind me a small figure scurried down the ladder. It was Tess Lieb.

Flora struggled to her feet.

"What are you doing here?" Jay asked.

"Tess, I told you to stay out of this at the orchard. All you had to do was be quiet."

Tess shivered. "I can't be quiet any longer."

"Shoot them both," Flora said disgust.

He stared at the gun in his hand.

"Do it!"

"Don't!" Tess cried. "You're not a killer."

"I know that! The only killer in this room is you. You're the one who killed Ben. You started the fire," Jay accused.

Tess took a breath. "I know." She looked at me. "Millie, I'm so sorry. I went to the flea market that night to ask Ben to run away with me and get married. My *daed* was determined to send me to Wyoming. I had a lantern with me. But Jay was in the flea market stealing things. I didn't expect anyone but Ben to be there. Before I could find Ben, Jay jumped out and scared me. I threw the lantern at him to protect myself and the flea market went up." Tears rolled down her face. "I was so scared, I ran back home. I didn't know that Ben was sleeping in the flea market until the next morning when I heard he was dead."

"He was sleeping there because someone drugged him," I said. "Was that you, Flora?" It was a guess, but I thought it was a *gut* one.

"Yes, I made those brownies. I knew that Waller would never let me give Ben the night off so that we could take more goods from the flea market. They were just supposed to knock him out." Flora glared at Tess. "You started the fire, so you killed him. Jay, shoot them and let's be done with this."

Jay stared at the gun.

"Oh, for goodness sake, I'll do it," Flora said and marched over to Jay, grabbing the gun from his hand. As she moved, I noticed that a loop of the rope was still caught around her leg. The other end of it was just a foot from me. I jumped for it and pulled tight. She fell forward onto the floor again, but the gun was still in her hand.

She rolled over onto her back and aimed the gun at Tess. Tess made no attempt to move.

"Police!" Deputy Aiden shouted as he ran into the barn from the burnt opening in the building. He was followed by Deputy Little and two firemen. They rushed forward, and Deputy Aiden made short work of taking the gun from Flora and arresting both Flora and Jay.

I held out my open arms to Tess. She ran into them like a child in need of comfort. "It's over," I said.

"I came here to pray, to ask forgiveness for what I had done. Not just forgiveness for Ben's death, but for not loving him the way he deserved. I was selfish and only wanted to marry him to escape my own problems. Because of that, he's dead."

She fell into my arms in tears.

"Shh," I whispered and hugged her close.

Epilogue

"The new flea market building will be up and running by January," Deputy Aiden said to me a week later. "Ford Waller is determined to make it even better than it was before." He sipped apple cider as we stood in the outdoor flea market a week later.

"What about Tess?" I asked. That was what I really wanted to know. Despite what had happened, I felt sorry for the girl.

He frowned. "She's not going to be charged with murder. She didn't know that Ben was passed out in the building. The county has decided to charge Flora with involuntary manslaughter for giving someone a drug without their knowledge, as well as theft, conspiracy, and attempted murder. Jay will be charged with half of those as well. In Tess's case, I was able to convince the judge that the fire really was an act of self-defense on her part."

"Where will she go from here?"

"Not back home, I'm afraid. Her family has kicked her out. I set her up with an English family that can help her until she gets on her feet. They go to my mother's church."

I smiled at the young deputy. "That was kind of you."

"I feel sorry for her."

"I do too," I whispered.

"Oh, there's Bailey," Deputy Aiden said. "I promised I would meet her here. She wanted to shop for props for her television show." He frowned. "I see that she has Jethro with her. My mother must have dropped him off again." He shook his head. "Take care, Millie, and you and Lois stay out of trouble—if not for your sakes, for mine." He hurried over to Bailey and Jethro, and Bailey greeted him with a beautiful smile.

Lois walked up to me, holding another cup of apple cider. "Want me to get you a cup? The Lieb Orchard booth is giving it away for free."

I shook my head. "I don't think I can even smell apples for a little while without feeling sick," I said.

She nodded. "Besides, it's mid-October now. Apples are old news. It's all about the pumpkins now. Is there anything more cheerful than a pumpkin?"

I put on a smile, but I know it didn't reach my eyes.

"What's with the sad face?" Lois asked. "You look like Phillip and Peter when you tell them they can't nibble on the clothes hanging on the line."

"I was just thinking about how quickly everything goes back to normal. The flea market is as busy as it ever was and soon the building will be rebuilt. People will forget about Ben and what happened here."

"That's true," Lois said matter-of-factly. "We can't forget what happened to Ben, but we can move forward. Moving forward is how I've gotten through life. I don't look back."

"That's something I admire in you, Lois."

"*Danki.*" She winked at me when she used the Amish

word. "But I'm going to learn something from all this and remember to look back. If I don't, how can I create a better future?"

Wise words, indeed. Almost like one of my Amish proverbs.

"Tess was so worried about what would happen if she left Holmes County," Lois went on, "that she couldn't budge. She didn't know what to do. She didn't know if she wanted to go to Wyoming or if she wanted to leave the Amish or if she was going to marry Ben. She couldn't decide, and because of that, she got stuck. Being stuck can lead to disaster. You can't assume life will stay the same. In fact, you have to assume that it won't. Make a choice and move forward."

I considered what Lois had said and wondered if I was stuck in my own way. I was afraid of even having a friendship with Uriah because I feared it would somehow change my status as Kip's wife. Kip had been gone twenty years, and still I saw myself as his wife first. I refused to change my identity. I claimed it was out of loyalty, but was it actually out of fear?

"I could learn a thing or two from you, Lois," I said.

"That's good because I learn from you every day, Millie, and it's more than your pithy proverbs."

I laughed. "The proverbs aren't that bad."

She gave me a look, and then her gaze wandered over my shoulder. "Ohmigosh, the furniture vendor is back, and he has a teal coffee table. I have to have it!" And off she went.

I followed behind Lois as she made a beeline for the furniture vendor. I would learn to move forward too.

Please read on for a sneak peek at Amanda Flower's
next Amish Candy Shop Mystery,

Lemon Drop Dead.

Chapter One

The door of Swissmen Sweets swung inward, causing the large display window to rattle in its frame. I stood alone in the front room of the shop and jumped at the sudden movement. It was late afternoon, and the shop would close soon. I looked forward to locking the front door for the night. My boyfriend, Aiden Brody, had promised me a date night that evening. They were hard to come by for us. We both had crazy work schedules. He was second in command at the sheriff's department, and I was constantly juggling Swissmen Sweets, the Amish candy shop I ran with my grandmother in Harvest, Ohio, with my cable television show, *Bailey's Amish Sweets,* filmed in New York City. It was rare that neither one of us had an obligation. Sadly, I had a feeling my night off was about to be a thing of the past when I saw who stood in the shop doorway.

Aiden's mother, Juliet Brook, stood on the other side of the domed-glass counter, beaming from ear to ear. From past experience, I took the giant smile as a bad sign.

On this mild May evening, she wore a green-and-blue, polka-dotted blouse over black trousers and black-and-white high heels. Polka dots were her signature, from her clothes to the black-and-white, polka-dotted potbellied pig under her arm. Jethro stared at me in bewilderment as if to ask how he'd got there and what on earth was happening. Granted, the little bacon bundle had the same expression on his pudgy face ninety percent of the time. Until recently, Juliet had toted Jethro, who was roughly the size of a toaster, just about everywhere she went.

In the last several months since she had married Reverend Brook, the pastor of the large white church on the other side of the village square from Swissmen Sweets, she had been carrying Jethro around a lot less often. At least when it came to church functions at which she had to appear in her capacity as the pastor's wife. Those times when she needed to concentrate on her church duties and spend less time making sure Jethro wasn't knocking over the church alter, she dropped Jethro off at her favorite pig sitter . . . *me*. Now, I had not asked for nor wanted the title of go-to pig sitter for Jethro, or for any other pig, but Juliet had got it in her head that I was the person for the job, ever since I had saved the little pig from an untimely death a couple of years back. Ever since that event, she believed the little oinker and I had a special bond. I wasn't nearly as convinced. So, when she stormed into Swissmen Sweets late that afternoon, I had every reason to believe that Jethro was being pawned off on me again.

"Bailey! Bailey! Is it true? Is it true?" Juliet cried in a breathless voice.

I placed the stack of receipts I was checking against my accounts on the counter. "Is what true, Juliet?"

"Emily!" she cried.

"What about Emily?"

"Oh, for goodness sake, Bailey, you know what I mean. Emily is having a baby! A baby! Can you believe it? It's a miracle. I love babies so much." She gave me a quick glance. "You know I have great dreams of being a grandmother. Can you imagine me as a grandma? I would be the very best." She held Jethro up above the counter so that I had a better view of his face. "Think of how well I treat Jethro."

I wasn't sure how I felt about Juliet comparing a future grandchild to her comfort pig.

She lowered the pig when he began grunting. "Jethro is a good comfort to me as I wait for that happy day, if it ever comes at all." She stared at me from under her lashes.

It took all my willpower not to grunt back in frustration. Over the last several years, Juliet had made it no secret that she would love to see her only child, Aiden, settled down with a wife and family. Since I was Aiden's girlfriend, I was certain she saw me as part of the holdup. The thing was, Aiden and I weren't married, and we had only been officially dating for a year and a half. I thought our relationship was progressing at a natural pace. Juliet begged to differ, and despite the lack of proposal or ring, Juliet considered us engaged. She had great hopes for a summer wedding this year, but, seeing as it was May and we weren't engaged, those hopes would go unfulfilled.

The truth was that both Aiden and I wanted to get married, and we had been talking about it privately with more and more frequency, but our schedules made it difficult. I just didn't know how I would plan a wedding with all of my other responsibilities at Swissmen Sweets and *Bailey's Amish Sweets*. The show had me flying to New York to do promo or film every three months. And *my* calendar wasn't the only problem. Aiden worked long hours as a sheriff's deputy. As the second in command to a grumpy and disengaged sheriff, much of the workload required to keep the department running smoothly fell on his broad shoulders.

A little part of me . . . okay, a giant part, wanted to elope, but I knew Juliet would never forgive us if we did that. Aiden was her only son and her golden boy. She wanted to be there for the wedding. I was pretty sure she wanted Jethro to walk me down the aisle too.

"Yes, I know Emily's expecting," I said. "The baby is due next month. It's not a secret. Everyone at Swissmen Sweets is so happy for her."

Emily Keim was one of my shop assistants. She was a young Amish wife who'd married a Christmas tree farmer, Daniel Keim, a year ago. The young couple was expecting their first child in July. Actually, it would be Daniel's first child, but not Emily's. I was certain that Juliet knew nothing about Emily's history as an unwed mother, and I planned to keep it that way.

"I can't believe that I am just hearing about the baby. I know I have been very caught up in the church. You would not believe everything I have to do as the pastor's wife, and I am determined to be the very best and make Reverend Brook proud."

I smiled. There was something endearing and old fashioned to me about the fact that Juliet still called her husband Reverend Brook even though they were married. "No one would doubt for a second that you aren't the perfect pastor's wife."

She blushed, and then asked in a breathless voice, "What are you going to do about Emily's baby?"

"What am *I* going to do about it?" I asked. As far as I knew there was nothing I could or should do about Emily's baby.

"Aren't you going to have a baby shower? She needs a baby shower! You have to host a baby shower."

I held up my hand to stop her. I thought if she said "baby shower" one more time, my head might explode.

Juliet didn't take the hint. "You're the perfect person to put it on. You're so organized and do such a good job planning events. Why, we can't think of a better person."

I wrinkled my brow. Juliet was putting the compliments on a little thick, and for her, that was saying something. "*We*?" I asked.

"Well, the village of course, but mostly Margot and me. We were discussing it this afternoon when we were tending the church garden. Springtime does mean flowers, don't you know."

I did know.

She set Jethro on the floor. As soon as she did, the shop's orange cat, Nutmeg, crawled out from under the candy shelves next to the café tables. It was his favorite place to hide when he needed a little alone time. The pig and cat touched noses and then started to walk around the front room like the old friends they were.

"So, are you going to do it?" Juliet asked.

"Juliet, I'm pretty sure the Amish don't have baby showers. At least not in the way you're imagining. I would have to ask my grandmother to be sure. Emily and the Keim family would not want to do anything or have any party that was against Amish customs."

"How could a baby shower be against Amish customs?"

It was a fair question, but what I had learned since

moving to Ohio's Amish Country was that not all the Plain People's rules made sense. At least they didn't make sense to my New Yorker mind.

"This is the twenty-first century." Juliet waved her arms. "Even the Amish have changed with the times. Goodness, do you know how many Amish have cell phones nowadays or know how to use a computer? Surely, Bishop Yoder would be open to her having a baby shower. I mean, it only seems right to me. There is no harm in it."

"The Amish who are allowed to use those pieces of technology are able to do so because it pertains to their work. It would be very difficult for them to continue their business without access to a cell phone or a computer in some cases. That's just what it takes to run a business these days. We can't make the claim that a baby shower is work related."

She put her hands on her hips. "We have to do something for Emily. Goodness knows, her sister won't do anything."

I winced at this comment, mostly because it was all too true. Emily and her older sister, Esther, hadn't spoken since Emily got married and stopped working at the family's pretzel shop. The especially awkward part of it was they saw each other every day. Emily worked part-time for me at the candy shop, which just happened to be next door to Esh Family Pretzels, where Esther spent every waking moment of her day.

Jethro put his snout to the floor and followed the scent until he found my large white rabbit, Puff, sleeping curled up in the corner of the front room. He snuffled the rabbit, and Nutmeg swatted him away. Puff yawned and scooted over, making room for the small pig, which wasn't much bigger than the rabbit. It seemed to me that I would have to put Puff on a diet. Who knew a bunny could get so big just eating vegetables?

"Honestly, Juliet, I do like your idea. Emily and her new baby should be celebrated, but it's really up to Emily whether she would like such a party. I don't want to do anything that might embarrass her in front of her Amish district."

"It could be a surprise."

I wrinkled my nose. I knew from experience that Emily wasn't one for surprises. "Let me ask her, and then we can take it from there."

"Ask her now!" She clasped her hands in front of her chest. There was nothing that Juliet loved more than a party. I knew she had hoped to celebrate a wedding this year. Maybe this baby shower would fill that void.

"She's already gone home for the day. I promise to ask her at the first opportunity tomorrow."

"Well, we can go to the Christmas tree farm and ask."

"Let's not be too hasty. If you and I roll up to the farm, she will think something is wrong. Give me one day, and I promise to get you an answer."

She pressed her lips together as if she wasn't keen on this idea.

"You have my word."

"It seems to me that I have no other choice," she said. Her Carolina drawl was more pronounced than usual, demonstrating her disappointment. "You'll need to ask her quickly because Margot has already reserved the square for the shower this Saturday. We thought two in the afternoon would be the perfect time."

"She's already reserved the square?"

"She had to. You know how busy the square can be this time of year." She clapped her hands. "Jethro, it's time to go."

The pig lifted his head but didn't move from the spot where he was cuddled up with the cat and rabbit. My best friend, Cass Calbera, who was the head chocolatier at JP Chocolates in New York, insisted that the three animals needed their own social media platform because they made an odd trio. I hoped that she never mentioned the idea to Juliet, because Juliet would be all over it.

Juliet marched over to the pig and scooped him up. She walked to the door and said, "Don't delay about asking Emily, Bailey. She needs a shower." With that, she went out the door.

After Juliet and Jethro had gone out the door, I closed it and locked it behind them. I looked down at the cat and rabbit still snuggled together in the corner of the room. "Dollars to donuts we are hosting another party."

Nutmeg meowed as if to say, "You sure are!"